A Witch's Quandary

by

Tena Stetler

This is a work of fiction. Names, characters, places, and incidents are either the product of the author's imagination or are used fictitiously, and any resemblance to actual persons living or dead, business establishments, events, or locales, is entirely coincidental.

A Witch's Quandary

Cover Art by *Kristian Norris*

The Wild Rose Press, Inc.
PO Box 708
Adams Basin, NY 14410-0708
Visit us at www.thewildrosepress.com

Publishing History
First Edition, 2021
Trade Paperback ISBN 978-1-5092-3692-3
Digital ISBN 978-1-5092-3693-0

Published in the United States of America

"This is an outrage! It's my firm." Bram bellowed slamming his fist down on the table. Sparks flew in all directions creating a red-hot spider web of power crackling across the tabletop. Everyone at the table scrambled back or stood. Dillon caught the malevolent spark in his father's eye a split second after Gale. She had already brought her hands together. The room sizzled as she conjured a ball of fire and with a few words sent the witchfire and spell at him.

"What have you done?" Bram screeched as the fire and spell hit him center mass. "Witchfire too? Bitch." He slid to the floor.

Iris ran to his side, tears spilling down her cheeks, she wiped his sweat-soaked brow with a napkin. "You just couldn't stop, could you? What did you do? Make a deal with the devil? We should have put a stop to it. To you."

Bram slowly shook his head and murmured, "It's my firm." He raised his gaze and glared at Gale pointing a bony finger at her. "You'll pay for this." Then turned his attention to Dillon. "I told you nothing good would come from aligning yourself with this witch. Her blood is not pure. Diluted by the Fae power of her…"

Dillon stood at Gale's back his hands steady and supportive on her shoulders as she said nothing. Eventually, she turned her emerald green eyes to him and held his gaze. "I couldn't let him divide the family with that dark magic."

Praise for Tena Stetler

"Charm Me Again - The author's writing is so descriptive that the reader feels like they are actually there during the conflicts. The reader is drawn into this story from the first page and stays engrossed until the last word!"

~ Stephanie - InD'tale Magazine

"Hidden Gypsy Magic - From the moment I stepped into the pages of Hidden Gypsy Magic, I fell into a beautiful, magical world. When the story was finished, I wanted to touch my kindle and disappear into the world Tena Stetler created."

~ Mary Morgan, Author

"I was completely captivated & swept off my feet!! Absolutely one of the top books I've read all year."

~ Ally- Reviewer

"I'm always impressed when any author can create such a bond between her characters & the readers. Tena Stetler has an immense talent for that and more."

~ N.N. Light

Dedication

I am forever grateful to my readers for whom I write the stories.
A special heartfelt thanks to my husband, Bruce, whose support is unwavering.
My editor Lill Farrell rocks! She makes my books shine.
The staff and authors at The Wild Rose Press are the best support an author can have.

Chapter 1

Her World Spun on Its Axis, Crashed, and Burned

After dodging the sidewalk puddles from recent rains, Synn, Bridget, and Colleen stood in the bright sunshine outside the locked wooden door to Pixie Magic, Gale's apothecary. Shades were drawn and the "Closed" sign hung in the window of the door. The usual sparkling crystals hanging in her windows were dull and lifeless. No rainbows bounced around in the showroom. This was a stark contrast to the usually bright, friendly storefront. "What do you suppose is going on with Gale?" Synn mused aloud. "Her store has been closed for nearly a week."

"Don't know, but I ran into Erin and Tiarnan walking the jagged cliffs this morning when the sun was only a golden hue on the horizon." Cori's voice sounded from behind the group. "They wouldn't tell me what was going on with her. Only that she'd tell us in her own time."

Bridget spun around. "Hi there, Cori. Didn't hear you walk up. What ya doing here? Shouldn't you be entertaining somewhere?" Bridget teased. "Like Shaughnessy's tonight?"

"I'll be there. Don't worry. Not my fault, I missed last week because your boyo failed to tell me he'd scheduled me to perform with the band Wednesday night for Tim's birthday," Cori said testily. She blew out a breath and smiled. "Sorry, didn't mean to take it out on you. Quinn is on my shit list. Anyway, needing a refill on my lotion is what brought me round. Me hands are near to cracking." She held up her hands for the others to examine. "Me other lotion doesn't match the rose scent that Gale fixed up for me." Her cheeks flushed bright red. "Amos doesn't like the scent either."

"Who's Amos?" Synn cocked her head in question and glanced at Cori.

"Her sweetheart." Colleen giggled.

"Oh, do tell. Didn't know you'd narrowed your playing field to one guy." Synn snickered. "Did he pop the all-important question?"

Cori fisted her hands on her hips. "Not yet. But aye, he's the one." She raised her hands to her warming cheeks shyly. "I haven't even told Gale yet because…" She waved impatiently at the closed store.

****

Inside the shop, Gale watched and listened to the exchange of her friends, hoping they'd just leave. She wasn't ready to face them. This morning, her mirror had revealed dark circles under her normally bright green eyes and skin puffy from tears. *How can I explain? I'm still not sure I made the right decision. But my livelihood depends on my opening the shop. I've got to face everyone some time. Might as well…*

"I think she's in there." Cori cupped her hands around her face, pressed her nose to the glass, and tried to peer in the crack between the shade and the window where sunlight streamed in and spread across the polished but dusty hardwood floor. A shadow loomed over the end of the sunny stream.

She stepped back out of the stream of sunlight—too late.

Bridget knocked on the window. "Hey Gale, we can see you. Whatever it is, your secret is safe with us." She rapped on the window harder this time.

Bells tinkled, after a *creak* and a *groan*, the door opened a crack. She unlocked the chain that allowed only a three-inch opening. "Been ill. Don't feel like company."

Bridget barreled through, knocking her aside, and shoved the door open wide. The other women cautiously followed in their friend's wake. Never one for mincing words, her friend narrowed her eyes and stared. "What the hell is up with you?" Bridget paused in the center of the dismal showroom and glanced around, then returned her penetrating gaze to Gale.

Synn remained stuck in place, appalled at Bridget's lack of decorum. "Gale, we were worried about you."

"We've been friends for years. Never a secret between us. I've never known you to even have the sniffles. Now out with it." Bridget paced hands on hips, eyes narrowed sizing up her friend. "Heard Dillon went back to Scotland last week. Is that what this is all about?"

Gale blew out a breath and flipped her long ginger braid over her shoulder. *I should have known better than to keep this from my friends.* "Anyone want tea besides me?"

"I wish I had time," Cori began. "But I really need the rose lotion you fixed up for me. I'm out, and Amos tossed my alternate lotion. Said it stunk."

In spite of herself, she giggled. "Men can be so…pig-headed, stubborn, and unappreciative." She shuffled behind the counter, slid open a mirrored case, and took out a large bottle of creamy pink lotion. Reaching for a smaller bottle in the lower cupboard, she poured a quarter of the contents from the larger into the smaller decorative bottle. "There, that should hold you. I keep a supply of your lotion on hand. It's popular." She screwed the cap back on the big bottle and returned it to the case. "Here you go." Handing the smaller bottle to Cori, she smiled. "Sorry to cause a problem."

Cori handed her payment and took the bottle. "No problem. I was worried when you were closed for so long." She took the top off the bottle and sniffed. "Perfect." Spilling lotion into her hand, she offered the others a dab, then rubbed it into her own hands. "Gotta go. Thank you so much." She nudged Bridget with her elbow, whispering, "I'll call tonight to get the scoop."

"I'm standing right here, Cori." She fisted a hand on her hip. "Dillon left me. Okay. That's the scoop."

"What?" the women cried in unison.

"Well, you can never trust a Scotsman." Bridget flounced across the floor to wrap an arm around her.

"It's not him. It's his family. They issued an ultimatum. He buckled and returned."

Bridget took her by the shoulders and gave her a little shake. "Even worse. A man that won't stand on his own two feet. Believe me, you're better off without him."

Despite her determination to put on a brave front, a big tear trickled down her cheek. She viciously wiped it away with the back of her hand. "He said we'd figure something out. But I haven't heard a word since he left four weeks ago. So…" She waved her hand toward the corner of her showroom. A straw broom with a black handle of embedded glittering gems slid neatly out onto the floor and began sweeping with wide strokes.

Synn narrowed her eyes and continued to stare suspiciously at her friend. "Is that the way of it?"

"Oh, okay. He requested me to go with him. But I can't leave my store, my friends, uproot my life here, for what? Have his rich family look down their nose at me?" She shook her head vehemently. "He implied if I didn't go with him, it was over between us."

"Figured it was something like that." Synn patted her arm. "You sure that was what he meant? Our emotions can be misleading at times of turmoil. Don't close that door, yet."

"Whose side are you on?" She glared at Synn.

"Yours of course, but…" Synn held her tongue.

"Good riddance, I say." Bridget released her and touched one of the dull crystals. "What's wrong with these?"

The condition of the crystals had gone unnoticed until Bridget brought them to her attention. She studied them swaying gently in the windows and from the ceiling of the shop. For the moment, she ignored the question. "I knew you wouldn't understand. It's exactly why I dreaded opening the shop so everyone in town would tell me I told you so. Irish and Scottish, like oil and water, shouldn't mix. But it wasn't that way with us. It was…"

Out of the corner of her eye, she glanced at a sparkling royal blue cloth spread across the glass top showcase and snapped her fingers. The cloth swiped the top of the case, bounced from crystal to crystal, then settled on the shelf behind the register. Still, the crystals seemed dull.

Momentarily, Synn watched the antics of the broom and the cloth, then glared at Bridget. Her gaze softened as she turned her attention to Gale. "We do understand. It's just that we were so worried. Bridge forgot herself. Right?" The demon's voice held a warning tone.

Bridget nodded vehemently.

Slamming her hand down of the glass top case, she narrowed her eyes. "Now you pity me. I won't have it." She scrubbed her hand over her face and straightened. "Did the rest of you girls need something or just come here to harass me?"

The broom swept up to Gale, nudged her to the side, finished the spot where she stood, and returned to the corner. "Thank you, broom," she said absently.

"I need one of those at my house." Bridget glanced at the broom in admiration.

"Don't I know it. Can you imagine how easy cleaning up the pub would be?" Synn giggled. "Does that come in a mop version?"

"No. Well, I guess it could. I just don't have one." She tried a weak smile. "I've had it since childhood. Kinda a joke among our family. You know traditional witches, pointy hats, striped stockings, and brooms." She shrugged. "We're about as far from what most consider traditional witches as they come."

"It's not just a spell then?" Synn still eyed the broom. "Aye, not many can claim the King of Faeries as their uncle."

"Ladies…We're trying to have a conversation, and it's not about the bleeding broom." Colleen crossed her arms across her chest. "Now back to Dillon. Do Erin and Tiarnan know?" her friend asked, concern

6

wrinkling her brow.

She nodded. "Erin was helpful. But her advice was patience and to wait it out. Erin like Synn questioned my interpretation of the conversation. Do you know how hard that is? Especially when there's no communication. It's like I never existed." Her blood heated, coursing through her veins all the way to the tips of her ears. "His family."

Snatching the blue cloth mid-swipe, she began polishing the handprint she'd left on the glass top, then moved to the rounded edges of the showcases with vigor. The crystals in the window brightened at her glance, then sparkled when she blew lightly in the air. Tiny bells tinkled as air shimmered with magic. "That's better." She brushed her hands together and returned the cloth to the shelf.

Bridget snapped her fingers. "I know exactly what you need. A girl's night in. Synn and I have to work the weekend. But Monday we'll party."

"You don't have to do this. I'm fine," she insisted.

"We do have to. No wiggling out of it." Bridget searched her friend's face. "You're not all right. We'll bring the drink and you bring snacks. It's a date." Bridget wiggled her finger in front of her face in warning. "If you don't show, we'll hunt you down. Got it?"

She laughed. "Got it." The despair weighing heavily on her shoulders lifted a little.

"Even better, Saturday night stop by the pub, the first pint is on us. Have a bite to eat, enjoy a bit of company. Quinn's band is performing. Cori will be playing the fiddle. Always brings in a crowd from near and far. A dance with a hottie…The weekend brings them out and is exactly what you need." Synn giggled and fanned herself.

"Since when are you an expert on hotties?" Gale sent a challenging stare in Synn's direction.

"Oh, please." Bridge gave an exaggerated eye roll. "Look who in bloody hell she's married too."

All the women giggled, making Synn's face blush. Even Gale joined in. "Point well taken." She hesitated to survey the store. "Maybe I do need a change of scenery. I'll see you Saturday night. One condition. No setting me up. Understood? Or—I'll leave immediately."

"You've got it," the women chorused.

When Bridget held her arms behind her back, you could never trust she didn't have her fingers crossed intending to do exactly what she promised not to. So she added, "I mean it, Bridget."

"Okay, okay." Bridge raised her arms in a gesture of surrender. "You don't play fair—you know that?"

"Yep. Known you since we were both in nappies. Always a plotter you were. Even before you could toddle." She hugged her friend.

Chapter 2

Back in Scotland Personal Dynamics are Strained and the Family Firm is in Chaos

Dillon stepped off the plane into a pea soup fog with drizzle reflecting his mood. *Why couldn't she simply give it a try here? But oh no, her world is in Ireland. She couldn't abandon her friends, business, and family. So what if her uncle is the King of Faries/Fae over there?* Now that the fog of anger lifted, the reasons she listed made sense. *Perhaps I should have suggested that she visit while I sorted out the situation at the law firm. Kind of a support thing.* He waved his hand savagely in the air. *What's done is done. I'm moving on.*

His family's law firm was one of the oldest and most trusted, or had been, in Glasgow. With all the economic upheaval in recent years, his family's firm had remained rock solid. Or so he thought until the phone call from his grandfather. *Why should I be forced to uproot my practice to apply to go on the Roll of Solicitors in Ireland? Though I have more than the required education and experience. Never mind, I don't get along with my brothers and father. And let's face it, I'm not all that excited about practicing law in the first place. At least not the kind of law you spend every waking hour working.*

Yet, when his father threatened to disinherit him if he went through with the marriage to Gale, he came running back with his tail between his legs. Well, that wasn't quite true, he still had a few tricks up his sleeves. He'd tried to discuss the situation with her. Convince her to move to Scotland for a while until things settled down. His parents would get to know her, even like her, if given a chance. Provided she'd keep her opinions to herself and powers hidden. What bewildered him was the fact his father couldn't abide a witch more powerful than he. *What in bloody hell does that matter?* Gale's family's power and reputation, not to mention her stubbornness, had sunk their chances at happiness.

He grabbed his baggage and steered it toward the doors of the Glasgow airport, shoving the whole sordid affair to the corner of his mind where he'd deal with it later.

A limo with the firm's logo on the vehicle waited at the curb for him. The chauffeur rushed around to open the door. "Welcome home, sir."

"Thank you—I think. Hi ya, Ian. How have you been?" He shoved the suitcase in the boot and closed the lid.

"Fine. And yourself?" Ian stood for a second behind the car, then sprinted to the open door.

"Terrible. But I'm here as ordered." He slapped the lid and walked to the door Ian held for him.

Ian tipped his hat back a bit. "Where's your lass?"

"In Ireland. And she's not mine anymore." *Those words hurt more to say than I thought they would.* His posture crumpled as he slid into the limo. *What a damn fool.* He'd been questioning his motives since leaving

Ireland. *Am I here because Grandfather requested? Or for the money and prestige being a partner at the family law firm offered by his father.* To his surprise, after mulling it over all this time, he came to the conclusion it wasn't the firm, but his grandfather's mysterious request. He hadn't come right out and said something was wrong at the firm, but in his own way implied it, requesting help. Never could he turn his back on his grandfather after the support he'd shown him during his father's demands of Dillon as a young man.

One regret was how he'd handled the situation with Gale. His Scottish temper had gotten the best of him when she refused to accompany him. An ultimatum would not set well with an independent Irish lass, such as Gale, and he knew it.

"Sorry, sir." Ian closed the door softly. Once inside, the chauffeur turned around to face him. "To the firm or home?"

He sighed. "Wherever I'm required to be."

"Yes, sir. The firm it is.. Your father is waiting." The driver hesitated for a moment. "Your brothers and sister too."

"Great. An ambush." He glanced at his phone hoping to see Gale's name pop up. It didn't. *And she calls me stubborn.* His stomach did a flip, and nausea ensued as Ian pulled up in front of the prestigious law firm with its tall glass doors etched with the scales of justice and long, vertical silver handles. He opened the vehicle door himself and stepped on the sidewalk. "Might as well get this over with. Then I can go to my hotel."

"Sir? There's a big celebration and dinner at the family estate tonight. Your presence is required.

Actually, it's in your honor. Will you need me anymore this afternoon? Since you'll be riding with Mr. Dunlop."

"They have it all planned. Don't they? No. Stick around. I am feeling ill from travel."

"Sir? Can I get you anything?"

"New family members?"

The chauffeur chuckled. "Not sure that's an option. Where do you want your bags?"

"Right where they are for now. Not staying at the family estate. I have reservations at Blythswood Square for a few nights. Until…"

Ian shook his head. "Your father will not be happy."

"Gee, now there's a news flash. Don't tell him. Wish me luck." He stalked toward the building, grasped the silver handles, and felt the magic confirm his signature. Even that routine procedure raised his ire. He shoved through the glass doors of Dunlop Law Firm and crossed the huge, polished floor of the reception area, his footsteps echoing. An island of plush gray carpeting surrounded the lobby seating. Recent publications fanned out across glass-topped coffee tables.

The cushy seating was new. Comfy chairs had replaced the stiff high-backed wooden chairs. A coffee and tea bar occupied the far corner of the room. More than likely stronger spirits were hidden in the cabinets below. Or maybe still only in the partners' offices. The area was deserted. Thank the Goddess for small favors.

A wide circular staircase wound its way to the sprawling second, third, and fourth floors. He opted for the easy way. Crossing the lobby, he punched the up arrow elevator button and waited. "What the hell am I doing?" A strong urge to bolt rushed through him. *No. I'll finish this once and for all. Be it today or a week, or year from today, I'll walk away free to do as I please. Without family interference.* Until then, he'd play nice, or at least try. *Would Gale wait for me?*

The shiny stainless steel elevator doors slid open with only a small hiss on the partners' second floor. He stepped out to find his father, two brothers, and sister lounging in the waiting room. "Well, good evening."

"Same to you." His father strode across the floor hand extended. "Good to see you. How was your trip?"

His brothers glanced up at him, then stood, smiles pasted on their faces. Same ol' same ol'. They'd been required to remain as back up.

His sister's smile was genuine. "So you finally buckled under the pressure of the family dynasty. I'd hoped better from you."

He spread his arms wide, palms up in surrender. "It is what it is until it isn't. Great to see you, Patrice."

She laughed. "Now that's cryptic. And the little brother I know. Can't wait to find out what it means." She advanced toward him arms open and engulfed him in a hug. "Good to see you too. Sorry, it's under these circumstances," she whispered so no one else could hear.

He returned the hug and grasped her by the shoulders. "How's it all going?"

"Oh, you know." She shot a knowing glance over her shoulder. "Difficult, long hours, no appreciation."

"What did you expect? You're an attorney." He chuckled, turned to his older brother, Aiden, who extended his hand in greeting.

He clasped the hand and grasped his brother's shoulder. "So how's the family?"

"Todd and Amy are at that difficult age. Lana is frustrated at the hours I keep. Can't say as I blame her. But…"

Taking a step away, Dillon grinned wickedly. "Yep, demands of partnership in a large firm. You could always go out on your own," he offered.

Aiden shot a quick glance at their father. "Right. We all know how that would go."

Dillon shrugged. "Control. It's all about control."

"You should know?" his brother snipped.

"We're fine as well. Thank you for asking," his father interrupted sulkily.

Narrowing his eyes, he surveyed his father and siblings. "To what do I owe such a welcoming party?"

Examining her well-manicured nails painted a deep purple, Patrice flashed a sardonic smile, then jerked her head toward her father. "Figured it would take all four of us to convince you to attend the celebration in your honor tonight. Or drag you kicking and screaming."

"That's enough," his father roared. "Dillon has returned to the fold and will be attending the celebration willingly."

"Unfortunately, Father, you're wrong about that. I have your car waiting outside to take me to my hotel. I'm not feeling up to a party after my long journey." He stopped to finger the glass or maybe it was a crystal slab with all the firm's lawyers listed. His name was newly inscribed at the bottom of the partners' list. "Partner, huh? How did everyone who has been here for years feel about that?"

"Doesn't matter. It's my firm. You're my son."

"As usual, you're wrong. A firm should run like a well-oiled machine. Everyone doing their part knowing their value. Throw in a few disgruntled employees because the younger son of the managing partner is awarded a partnership and you have everything out of sync. Not good. Tomorrow we'll talk about my position and length of time I'm forced to remain."

"If this is about your lass, it was a bad match. She was way below your station. So best you came to your senses and ended it. There will be plenty of lovely lasses to occupy your time at the party tonight."

He raised an eyebrow. "I guess they'll be disappointed. I'll be at my hotel until I report to work tomorrow." Returning to the elevator, he punched the down arrow. "Nice to see you. Enjoy the party." He eyed his father. "You'll make my apologies." The door to the elevator slid open. He stepped inside and hit the close door button while his father sputtered curses. Patrice slipped in the door just before it closed.

"This is not the return of the prodigal son?" His sister smirked at him, then her eyes turned dark and disapproving. "Did you break her heart? Gale was such a nice witch. Powerful too. She'd done this family good."

"No. It wasn't that way. I asked her to come with me. She refused."

"Good for her. Bad for you." She held his gaze for a couple of beats. "I've a feeling this isn't finished."

"Nope, not by a long shot. But I'm here to perform my required duties, until…Well, I'm not at liberty to discuss…"

His sister clapped her hands in delight. "An old-fashioned mutiny. What fun. You and—" She hesitated

15

a beat glancing at him quizzically. "Grandmother or Grandfather unleash the Dunlop wrath?"

"I've no idea what you are talking about. I stated my purpose." The chime sounded and the elevator door slid open. "This is my floor. A car awaits. "

"Tell Ian I said hi." She wiggled her fingers in a small wave, then leaned out the doors. "Huh, I thought maybe they'd materialize here in the lobby and cut you off at the door. Or at least a shower of fireworks on your way out." She sighed. "Disappointing. Lunch tomorrow?"

"You got it. Provided you aren't grounded for not bringing me back."

She scrunched up her face. "Oh dear, was that my assignment?" Examining her nails again, she buffed them against her aqua silk blouse. "So sorry to fail." She giggled as the doors closed. "I'll buy you a few more minutes to get clear. Hope you know what you're doing. Father is going to be furious."

He sprinted across the lobby and shoved the heavy glass doors open to find Ian lounging against the car. The driver opened the door, waited for him to enter then strode to the driver's side, and slid inside.

"Where to sir?"

"Blythswood Square." He pulled out his phone and scrolled through the numbers.

"Sir, if you don't mind, may I suggest a bite to eat before you retire? The food at Blythswood isn't…well it's expensive and not…"

Absently, he paused for a minute and looked at Ian. "Okay, where do you suggest?"

"Little pub around the corner from here, great food, and good music. You look like you could use a pint or two. Maybe the friendly company of the female persuasion. If you don't mind my saying."

He paused to look up and glance in the rearview mirror. "That bad?" He shook his head vehemently. "No women. Not now. Not ever."

"Don't you think that's a bit—" At the stormy expression reflected on his face, the driver paused. "Shutting up. Sir."

His gaze returned to his phone. "The pub will be fine. I'll have a bite and a pint, then I can walk to my room. You'll be back in the morning to pick me up for work? Or I can rent a vehicle."

"Yes, sir. I'm tasked with driving you wherever you want to go. Provided I still have a job tomorrow."

Shoving his phone into his pocket, he gave his full attention to Ian. "What do you mean?"

"Your father is a force to be reckoned with on a good day. After not bringing you to the celebration, he will be furious."

"If I don't want to go, it's no reflection on you." He tilted his head and peered at Ian, who shrugged.

"Fine. We'll stop at the pub, have a bite, a couple of pints, and I make an appearance at the damn party. Wouldn't want to cost you your job. But I won't be staying long, and that will be on my father, not you."

"Whatever you say, sir. But if you're going to the party, food will be much better at the celebration."

"Ian, cut out the sir crap. We've known each other since I was a kid. No one's around, drop the formality."

"Yes, sir...uh, Dillon."

His eyebrows shot up and eyes narrowed. "Better. Now let's get something to eat. I can't take my family on an empty stomach." He leaned back in the seat, closed the smoked glass partition between them, and took out his phone again. This time he scrolled to a number and touched the green icon. After only a couple of rings, a male voice answered.

"Dillon, what in bloody hell are you doing? Bridge said you and Gale broke up. You went back to Scotland. Are you crazy?" A loud crash of cymbals sounded from Quinn's end of the phone. "Sorry about that, we're setting up in Shaughnessy's for a gig. Cori will be on the fiddle." He paused for a beat. "But you don't care about that. What can I do for you?"

"I need your help with something. But you can't say a word to anyone. Including Bridget."

"Got ya. Count on me. What you need?"

Chapter 3

A Wish and A Prayer Doesn't Right an Upside Down World.

Gale stood in her flat above Pixie Magic staring in the mirror. Still dressed in her broomstick patchwork skirt and brightly colored, embroidered white blouse from work, she tucked a strand of ginger hair back in her braid. A tear slid down her cheek as she opened the dresser drawer. A black velvet box was nestled among her fine lingerie. She carefully picked up the box and opened it. Sparkling in the overhead light was the three-carat marquise diamond surrounded by emeralds engagement ring he'd given her. She wiped the tear away with the back of her hand. Oh, how happy she'd been eight months ago when Dillon asked her to be his wife. They knew obstacles stood in their way, mainly his family. But he'd assured her, he was prepared to deal with them. She snapped the lid shut, replaced the ring box, and closed the drawer.

Tonight would be the first time she'd been in Shaughnessy's without Dillon or her ring. There would be questions she wasn't prepared to answer. How had she let Bridget and the girls talk her into this? Even her Aunt Erin and Uncle Tiarnan, King of the Faeries, claimed a night out would do her good. *What'd they know?*

She conceded that Erin and Tiarnan knew a little about forbidden love between families and the wrath of an angry father. Erin had spent years never able to leave their Sidhe during the day because of the curse her father cast upon her. The spell had been broken by none other than a vampire and a witch a couple of years ago. She blew out a breath and wove a lavender ribbon in her braid to match her skirt. Checked her makeup, then she changed into comfortable shoes. Kicking up her heels in a step dance or two might take her mind off— *Who am I kidding?*

Picking her phone up off the bed, she scrolled to Bridget's number, then paused. Bridget would only send one of the other girls to get her, and they wouldn't take no for an answer. Then she'd be at their mercy with no ride of her own when she wanted to go home. *Suck it up.* Reaching for the strap of her purse, she stomped to the kitchen, raked her keys off the counter, and let the door bang shut behind her.

****

Lively music, delicious aromas of freshly baked bread, and Mulligan stew wafted out into the night as she tugged open the heavy wooden door. Hearty laughs and voices raised in song, some off-key, welcomed her. A knot tightened in Gale's stomach. *This is the first time I've been to Shaughnessy's without Dillon since we announced our engagement.*

Ready to bolt, she turned and ran into the broad chest of Quinn, Bridget's fiancé. "Shit." Wildly she glanced around. Nowhere to run. Bridget was closing in fast from the pub's main floor, and Quinn had her blocked in the doorway. Shoulders slumped, she trudged into the establishment.

"Thought you'd try to run if you made it this far." Bridget's voice rang with smugness. "Happy you ventured out. I was about to send reinforcements."

"Get the lass a pint." Synn grinned, sidling up to the bar her hand outstretched. Gavin returned the grin, giving her a wink, and slid a stout pint across the bar.

She snatched the pint offered, took a couple of sips, and set her mug at the end of the bar. "Well, as long as I'm here, how about a lively tune, Quinn?" She glanced around the room. "Who's up for a dance?" Her reputation as step dance champion three years running made her dance partners scarce.

After there were no takers, Quinn hopped on stage and grabbed the mic. "Aww come on, lads, 'fraid of being danced under the table by Gale?"

"She's on the market again," Gavin shouted from behind the bar. An uncomfortable silence prevailed for a beat, then wolf whistles and yells erupted.

Quinn frowned at Gavin. Synn slapped her hand on the bar, jumped up, reached over, and grabbed him by the front of the shirt. "That's not for you to announce." Synn's feet dangled on the other side of the bar as she tried to regain the balance of her upper body.

Gavin clasp his hand over hers and pried her fingers loose. "Sorry." He turned and mouthed to Gale as he released and lowered Synn to the floor.

"A lot of bloody hell good it does now, boyo." Synn sent him an "eat shit and die" look before stalking to her friend's side.

Her face warmed from her neck to the tip of her ears. Glancing at her ringless left hand, she jumped off the barstool, nearly landing on Synn. Before she could sprint to the door, Gavin vaulted over the bar, caught her hand, and whirled her onto the dance floor. "I really am sorry. Just trying to liven the place up a bit. Get you a few dance partners."

"I know. But dance partners 'tis not what I need right now." She tried to shake him loose, but he tightened his grip.

"Let's dance." A mischievous grin spread across his face and sparkled in his eyes. "Or not too sure of your abilities?"

"In your dreams, boyo." She gave him a friendly shove.

"That's the lass I know." He started the step dance.

Quinn led his band in a lively jig while she met Gavin step for step. Mary and Tim, Gavin's parents, and former owners of the bar, clapped in time from behind the bar. Synn leaned back, elbows on the bar, and clapped too. After two quick tunes, Cori bounced on stage with her fiddle and shoved Quinn off the stage onto the dance floor. He replaced Gavin and step danced a third and fourth song with her.

At the end of the fourth, she escaped, gasping for air to her fresh pint provided by Mary at the end of the bar. "Whew, it's been too long for that kind of back-to-back dance." She took a long swig of her pint and plopped it down on the bar. The frothy liquid sloshed in the icy mug, threatening to spill over the edge. She fanned herself with a napkin.

A tall muscular man with the brightest blue eyes sauntered over to where she sat. "Where's the Scotsman?"

"In Scotland on business." She offered nonchalantly glancing around for one of her friends. *Not totally a lie.*

"Not a permanent situation?" The man offered a friendly smile, putting a hand on her shoulder.

She narrowed her eyes and shrugged his hand off her shoulder. "It remains to be decided." *Now that was a bold lie. Never a good liar.*

"How about I buy you a drink? We can grab a table over by the cozy fire and have a wee talk?" He touched the small of her back.

Electricity zinged up her body. *Warlock.* She'd deliberately disguised her magic signature before entering the establishment. Not everyone in town knew her secret, and she planned on keeping it that way.

Sure she'd never seen him before, his advances unnerved her. "Thanks for the offer, but I'm going to stay right here with my friends." She winked at Gavin and waved at Synn across the room where her friend was serving drinks. Bridget sailed across the floor taking orders and serving food but paused to stare at them.

The man deliberately glanced at and lingered on the naked finger of her left hand. "Don't be that way, sweetheart. I mean no harm, just a friendly drink to raise your spirits." He touched her back again lightly.

She glared at him. "What makes you think my spirits need raising? I'm just fine. Thank you for your interest." Sliding off her chair, she made a beeline for the ladies' room. Once inside, she leaned her back against the ancient wooden door. *What are you going to do now, hide out all night?*

With a gentle push, Bridget entered the ladies' room. "Is there a problem?"

"I don't think so. That guy just made me feel uncomfortable." She leaned over the sink and splashed cold water on her face.

Bridget waved her hand dismissively. "You've been out of circulation for a while. It's probably first night jitters. He's cute."

"It was more than that." She wrapped her arms around herself to keep from shivering. To her surprise, the glint of silver gauntlets, cool on her arms, started their ascent up her forearms.

Synn rushed in the door, wiping her hands on her apron to disguise her silver gauntlets that decided to make an appearance. She stopped and surveyed the women. "Gale, when was the last time you ate?"

She blinked, trying to remember when was the last time she'd eaten, shoving her arms in her skirts. "Not sure. Maybe a muffin this morning?" She narrowed her eyes at Synn. "Why are your magic guardian gauntlets making an appearance?"

"What…They're not." Synn shoved her arms behind her back, then slowly raised them in front of her. "See."

"Synn, I know what I saw, and your gauntlets were disappearing as you came in here." Gale shook her finger at her friend then raised her own arms "Something is not right."

Her friend's eyes glittered in surprise. "Don't know. I was serving table ten when that yummy guy walked in—cruised over to you. Next thing I knew, you ran in here, followed by Bridget, and my gauntlets started up my arms."

Wide-eyed, Bridget's gaze shifted from Synn to Gale and back. "Oh NO. Last time—"

"Calm down." Synn rested her hand on Bridget's arm. "It was just a malfunction. It happens. Feeds off my emotions."

"And apparently, mine. We need to talk." Gale blew out a breath. "Remember the first time you told me about the gauntlets appearing followed by the sword? You were shocked to discover that born a demon, you were descended from the ancient guardian Fae warriors. It had been a battle to learn to control your emotions thusly the weapons."

"How could I forget. A sword hanging over my bed in front of god and everyone. You got a sword too?"

"No, not in my linage according to Erin. The gauntlets are mine, and I could use a little help controlling them. Attached to my emotions, correct?"

"Yeah. The more the surprise emotion, the more they'll come out to protect. Take a deep breath, shove the scared, anger, and uncontrolled emotions away. Even surprise. You'll be fine. Takes time and practice. You've got this." Synn took her friends hands in hers and gave a little shake. "Sisters in the ancient Fae guardian guild. Who could have predicted?"

A loud knock on the door sounded. "Hey Bridge, table three is demanding your presence. Now." Tim's irritated voice came through the door.

"Coming." Bridget checked her makeup in the mirror and shot a stern look in Gale's direction then Synn's. "This conversation isn't over. I may be a mortal, but…" she whispered tersely and whipped out the door.

Gale narrowed her eyes at Synn. "What really happened?"

"Don't know. It occurred exactly as I told you. That guy who was putting the moves on you had magic.

Think he's trouble?" Synn shoved her hands in her apron pockets. "Or it could have been our protective instincts feeding off each other brought about the reaction. Who knows? Now that there's two of us with this particular ability, we'll need to pay more attention to each other." Synn eyed her suspiciously. "When did you discover you had the ability?"

"Erin alluded to it years ago, but when it didn't manifest, figured it skipped me. Then tonight…bam." Gale wiped her sweaty hands on her skirt. "I hope he's not trouble. Maybe a disgruntled warlock that didn't get his way caused the reaction. Should have worn jeans." She took a paper towel from the dispenser, ran cold water over it, and put it at the back of her neck. The beginnings of a headache threatened.

"What you're wearing had nothing to do with his intentions. I felt it." Synn crossed her arms over her chest and tapped her tiny foot.

"Thus the protective mode of your gauntlets. Lucky your sword didn't make an appearance." She shook her head while still holding the cold wet towel to her neck.

"But it wasn't protecting me…It was you. Is there something you're not telling me?" Synn stared at her.

"Nope, it's all out in the open now. You better get back out there before Gavin pounds down the door." She tried to give Synn a little shove toward the door.

Synn stood her ground, arms still crossed, eying her friend speculatively. "Nope. Unless you're coming out with me."

Throwing the paper towel in the trash, she yanked open the door and peered up and down the hallway. "Are you happy now?"

"Aye." Synn followed her friend out, down the hallway, and into the main pub area. Gavin curled his finger at her in a come hither gesture.

Glancing in all directions, Gale cautiously moved through the crowd in front of the stage to the corner of the bar where her warm half-finished pint sat. *No sign of Mr. Good-Looking Warlock.* As she approached, Tim took the glass and replaced it with a frosty mug. The beer foamed to the top but didn't spill over until she picked it up and tried carefully to take a gulp. The dark amber liquid ran down the glass and dripped off the bottom.

Gavin swooped in and grabbed a towel, wiped the mug, then the bar. "He left right after Synn raced into the ladies' room. I assume that's who you were scanning the crowd for. What's going on?"

"Nothing. Girl stuff. I imagine Synn will tell you all about it tonight." Her shoulders slumped, and she rested her head in her hands. The day had caught up with her, and she was ready to go home. But...worry niggled at her mind. *Was he waiting outside for me?*

A light touch on her shoulder made her jump. She whirled around to find her cousin, Cori, backing out of her way with her fiddle case in hand.

"Hey, any chance you could give me a ride home? My set is done for tonight, and I'm beat." Cori leaned on the bar and tilted her head toward Gale. "Appears your little dance demonstration wore you out."

"Aye. I can give you a lift home." She gathered up her bag and waved goodnight to her friends pointing at Cori.

Bridget met her at the door. "Monday night. Don't forget. It's a girls' night in. Hey Cori, you're invited

27

too, if you don't have plans."

"Sounds like fun." Cori gave her a thumbs up. "Gotta check my schedule. I'll let you know."

When she jerked the heavy door open, it protested with a loud *groan*. "This door has to be male. It's always complaining." She laughed.

Cori giggled. "Never thought of it that way. But you could be right."

Outside the mist was cool and the shadows foreboding. She glanced up and down the deserted street the music and conversation inside the pub a mere hum in the night.

Once inside the vehicle, she locked the doors and started the engine.

"So what gives with the guy dogging you tonight? Gavin's stupid comment didn't help. But the vibes Mr. Tall-Dark-Dangerous was giving off in addition to his magic signature spells trouble with a capital T." Cori huffed out a breath.

"Aye. Never saw him before in my life. So let's drop it. I'm beat. Got a pounding headache. No sign of him when we left. Thank the Goddess."

Cori settled in her seat and watched out the window. "Got a picture of him with my phone. Going to circulate it around the local pubs and see if anyone knows him. Just to be on the safe side. No one at Shaughnessy's had seen him before either."

"Probably a tourist passing through town. It's the season." She stopped the car in front of Cori's cottage. "Have a good night. Get some rest."

"Aye. You do the same. Put up strong protection spells around your shop and flat," Cori warned.

"Always have those wards up. Along with

disguising my magic signature. Not taking any chances. May call Tristian if the guy makes another appearance. What do you think?"

"Not a bad idea. But if it turns out to be nothing, Tristian will be pissed," Cori warned, climbing out of the vehicle. "He is the Demon Overlord's right hand man and enforcer. He could come down like hellfire if he sees fit before he sorts it all out. Bruce, the Demon Overlord, would never allow that these days."

"He doesn't react like that anymore. He has teams to do that for him. On the flip side, gives Hannah a reason to come home for a visit." Gale shrugged as the door closed and turned the vehicle toward home. Her heart beat a tattoo in her chest as she parked behind the Pixie Magic, cut the engine, and sat for a moment checking her protection spells. "Nothing." She cast a wide discovery spell over the area. *Nothing again.*

She released a breath she hadn't been aware she was holding and got out of the car. On her way up the steps to her flat, a thick mist crawled along the ground. Quickly she yanked her keys out of her bag, waved them in front of the door, and tripped the motion detector on the porch light. Golden light pooled on the ground highlighting the mist while it took the shape of a man in a multicolor sweater, jeans, and boots. "Tiarnan." Relief flooded through her as she breathed a sigh of relief. "You gave me quite a fright."

"How's my favorite niece this fine evening? Your aunt thought she detected a bit of a magical eccentricity tonight. Was she right?"

"Aye, my gauntlets made an appearance in the bar. No big deal. Better now. What are you doing here?"

"Congratulations, she'll be thrilled. Been waiting

for years. But your trepidation was palpable at our Sidhe. Erin wanted me to check on you. So I disguised my signature and—" He spread his arms wide. "Here I am. Tell me what's troubling you, lass?"

She explained the situation at the pub, Synn, the strange magic wielder, her feelings of foreboding, and that of Cori. "Synn's gauntlets tried to make an appearance too. According to Synn, the gauntlets were feeding off each other. Should I contact Tristian?"

"Your cousin's description of Tristian is not wrong. He can be a disagreeable sort." He paused for a moment. "Better since marriage and management. Still the best at his job. Let me inquire around a bit before we bother him. Tonight all seems calm. Your protection spells didn't trip. I'll walk you up the stairs and into your flat to make sure."

"I'm fine. No need to bother."

"No need perhaps. If I don't, I'll never hear the end of it from Erin. So in with you." Tiarnan made shooing motions with his hands.

Inside her flat, nothing was amiss. She said good night to Tiarnan then closed and locked the door. With her back leaned against the door, she gave her arms a quick rub, a slight smile curved her lips, then her gaze swept the flat. *Empty, lonely, too quiet.* Snapping her fingers at the fireplace, she smiled as flames raced up the logs ready for her return. She checked her phone in hopes of a message from Dillon, but to her dismay there were none. *Pathetic.*

With a tap, the screen darkened and she promised herself never to hold out hope again. *It was my choice. Maybe I should have gone with him. Second guessing myself is only making me more miserable. His family hates me. If I only could figure out why?* She banished thoughts of him to the back of her mind, wiggled out of her clothes, and stepped into the shower.

Warm water cascading over her tense muscles felt so good she almost moaned. After turning off the water, she slipped into a comfy flannel gown and slippers, wrapped a towel around her wet hair, and padded to the living room where the fire cheerfully crackled and popped in the hearth. She microwaved a bowl of potato soup, added crackers, and paused at the refrigerator.

What the hell. Inside the fridge, she took out a bottle of wine, turned and grabbed a glass from the cupboard, then padded into the living room, settling into her lounge chair in front of the fire. The aroma of the soup made her mouth water as she poured the large glass of wine and watched the amber liquid wink in the firelight.

Chapter 4

Chaos in the Family Law Firm—Investigation Under Way

It had been over a month since the disastrous celebration party. At least one good thing came out of it, Ian was still employed and at Dillon's beck and call.

Quinn phoned to recount the fiasco at the pub. "Was it possible your father had anything to do with the suitor Gale chased off?"

He thought for a moment. While the ruse was something his father would have concocted, thus far he'd found no evidence his father had anything to do with it. "No, I don't think so. But you never know. I'll investigate. Thanks for letting me know." He disconnected the call.

Hesitating only a few seconds. He touched in Patrice's number for a video call.

"What is it now, little brother?" she answered in a cheerful voice as her face come into focus.

He repeated the phone conversation with Quinn. "Any chance Father would do something like that?"

"Doubt it." She paused, a finger tapping on her scarlet painted lips. "But I wouldn't put it past him. I've done a little snooping for reasons of my own and didn't run across anything indicating he was involved in something like that. But he has files I can't access, so I can't rule that out."

"Thanks. See you in the morning." He disconnected the call and relaxed against the high-back leather chair. *Missing Gale, I am.*

Still, he didn't like someone making moves on his woman. Well, she wasn't exactly his woman, but... Thank goodness the man had not made another appearance, according to Quinn, and things were quiet in Ballycotton. He'd last spoke to Gale the night he left and she refused to come with him. She was correct in her decision. He could see that now. His parents had no intention of accepting her into the family.

Their attitude had nothing to do with her being Irish, but everything to do with her powerful magic family. The secret even Gale didn't know, or did she, had been unearthed by his grandmother. By sharing it with his parents, she'd intended to make his family more receptive to Gale. It had the opposite effect. A decision his maternal grandmother, Lily, had regretted and been extremely apologetic.

She vowed to discover why his parents, specifically her daughter, Dillon's mother, had gone along with Bram's hell-bent desire to destroy Gale's relationship with him. His father had always been envious of others with stronger magical powers, which baffled him since his mother's rare displays of magic appeared to far exceed his father's ability.

He rubbed his eyes and ran his fingers through his hair. Maybe a week later, his grandmother on his father's side discovered the same secret, only she'd come to only him. *Why did these people have to meddle in his personal affairs?* On his next opportunity to visit his grandparents alone, he'd discuss his recent observations. Until then, he'd play nice with the people at the law firm.

Unfortunately, as he'd predicted, several senior partners snubbed him. The working environment was toxic, at least for him. Patrice claimed it was his imagination, but he was positive it wasn't. A knock on his door ended his contemplations for today. "Come in." He pushed up from his chair.

His brother, Royce, stuck his head in the door. "Got a minute?"

Taking his seat again, motioning toward the chair in front of his desk for Royce. "Sure. What's up?"

Royce stood for a couple of beats, then eased into the chair, slapped a file on the desk between them, and slid it toward Dillon. "I need research done on my case that goes to trial next week." He waved his hand in dismissal. "Before you say anything, I am aware I should have looked into this sooner. But the evidence is clear cut. Magic was used in a public square where hundreds of mortals had gathered in celebration of St. Patrick's day and witnessed the client's display."

Dillon held up his hand palm toward Royce. "Stop right there. Since when does this firm take on magical cases? One half of the distinguished solicitors in this firm are mortal, not to mention the support staff. Isn't Father well respected in the mortal courts? It appears the firm is doing very well without magical cases. We are not going to start that now, not ever."

"Well, about that…Too late. It's one of the reasons Father insisted on bringing you on board at any cost." Royce stared at the floor for a beat, then brought his gaze up to Dillon's. "He started taking these cases about eighteen months ago. It was about the time Father got crosswise with a warlock on the council. Not privy to what happened. There were whispers in the community about an incident, but when Patrice went digging, Father threatened to have her censured. She backed off but has been a thorn in his side since."

"Why is it that Patrice is the only one that stands up to Father around here? I understand that Mother doesn't even practice here anymore. How is that possible? They continued the family legacy and enhanced the firm's integrity together."

Royce shoved to his feet. "I can't answer your questions. But I did confront Father over this, and that's why I am working on these cases. No one else knows about them. I still don't know why we're doing it. But after our last confrontation, where he asked how much my family depends on my income, I do as I'm told and go home to my family. Clarice doesn't work. She stays home with our five kiddos. Our plan from the beginning. Didn't figure on my job being threatened."

"Wow. This place is a bloody mess. Unfortunately, after what you've told me, I don't see it getting any better because I'm here. I'll challenge his ass at every turn, given the chance. I don't need this job."

"But you do need the license, especially if you go back to Ireland." His brother reminded him.

After a couple of moments of contemplation, he nodded. "True. But I'm not afraid to get to the bottom of what happened approximately eighteen months ago to cause such chaos in this firm and our family. I owe it to Grandfather. I've nothing to lose."

"Don't be so sure. His influence is far-reaching. Never doubt it." Royce shoved his hands in his pockets and rocked back on his heels. "So will you do my research, or not? I'd ask Patrice, but she's extremely slow at it."

"Probably because she doesn't want to do it. She's smarter than both of us in the legal research area." He flipped the file in front of him open and perused the pages. "O'Sullivan. Huh? Did this man have a good reason for what he did? Never had any run-ins with the magical law before from what I can see. Where are the witnesses' statements? Hell, man, where is his statement?"

"I haven't had time—" His brother's face turned beet red.

"Looks to me like you have a lot of work to do. Research is the least of your problems from what I can tell." Closing the file, he tapped the keys of his computer, then stared at the screen. After a few minutes, he lifted his gaze over the computer to his brother. "According to the newspaper account, there was some type of magical attack on the square. The article doesn't go into detail."

"Of course not. It took place in front of mortals. Your friend from college wrote it and knew better." He tapped his fingers on the desk nervously. "Didn't she come from a magical family, but had no powers of her own?"

"Ah, I see it's Cork who wrote it." At his brother's baffled expression, he rephrased. "Ella Mallory. We called her Cork in college because you could never shut her up. Always told her to put a damn cork in it." He smiled at the recollection. *A long time ago.* By the glimmer of hope in his brother's eye, he figured Royce remembered. "No way she'd let anyone dictate what she wanted to write—back in the day. Must be… "

His brother snapped his fingers. "She's the one who was sweet on you for most of your college years. You two were a hot item for a little while. What…your last year?"

"Longer than that. It was off and on again until I met Gale. I knew when I first laid eyes on her, she was the one. But I broke it off with Cork first. It was an amicable break-up, mostly. Hell, we knew it would never work. As stubborn as we both were, we just couldn't let it go. Until—Gale."

Royce returned to his seat and shifted impatiently in the chair. "So now what? You going to help me out?"

He pointed his finger at his brother. "You best stick your nose in the research books. Not to mention get those witness statements and our client's statement. I'm going to talk with Cork." He shoved up from his chair, picked up the file, and opened the door. "You going to sit in my office all day? Out with you." *Royce isn't the legal scholar that Patrice is, but this type of shoddy work isn't like him either. Something isn't right.*

His brother trudged out of the office. Dillon locked the door and tested the protection spell. *The last thing I need is Father nosing around my office.* His father had never been able to break the protection spells he cast. It was another sticking point between him and his father. He certainly hoped that was still the case. Pausing for a few seconds outside the door, he unlocked it, strode back into his office, and collected his briefcase. Stuffing his laptop with a few more files he left. Once again, he locked the door feeling better at leaving nothing behind.

Taking his cell out of his pocket, he touched in Ian's number. "Hey, you close?"

"Aye, 'round the corner at the coffee shop with some blokes. What do ya need?"

"You in front of the office in five. We're going to the Daily Record office."

"What for?" After a moment of silence then a loud crash, Ian said, "I'll be there."

****

Dillon walked in the Daily Record. Not much had changed since his last visit a few years ago. Maybe a few updates, such as computers, welcome desk, but the dingy cubicles remained the same as he walked by the empty reception desk. Years ago there'd been a bull-dog of a woman guarding the reporters. To get by her you needed a great scoop, important business, or an apple fritter—not necessarily in that order.

Since he had none of those, he was relieved she was no longer the gatekeeper, at least at this time. Smiling at the recollection, he continued down the row of reporters' desks listening for a voice he recognized or a crop of fiery red hair piled atop her head with a pen or pencil stuck through it. At least that was how he remembered her.

Suddenly a declaration of "As I live and breathe," echoed through the room over the noise of ringing phones and animated conversations. A mass of fiery red hair bounced above all the cubicles. "It can't be Dillon Dunlop." The tiny pixie-like woman barreled down the aisle headed directly for him.

She'd always had more energy than should be allowed in one person. And a voice that needed no microphone. "Hi there, Cork." He braced himself for sudden impact. A couple of feet from him, she screeched to a stop, her tennies squeaking in protest. He put his hand out, and she engulfed him in a hug. "How'd you know it was me?"

"It's been years since someone called me that. Same old seafaring aftershave." She sniffed and smiled wide. "So what brings the great Dillon Dunlop to my humble workstation?"

"You never were one for small talk." He laughed as the years between them melted away. *Same ol' Cork.*

"Nope. Heard you're engaged to an Irish lass. Never would have thought. Bet Da was none too happy about that." She tilted her head up at him.

"You'd be exactly right." *Don't need to go into the current status of my love life.* "Anyway, my brother has a case going to trial next week, and we have some discrepancies I'd like to clear up."

"Still cleaning up after Royce, huh? Didn't do his homework and now you have to haul his arse out of the fire." She laughed. "Same old Dillon. When you gonna grow a set?"

Ignoring the verbal jab to his manhood, he shook his head. "Something like that." He glanced around the room, which had grown suspiciously quiet.

"Thought you were going to make a life in Ireland. Leaving that family of yours behind. What ya doing back here?" She narrowed her eyes at him. "Not working out as you planned?"

"How about I take you to lunch? Way too many ears in here."

She snickered. "Some things never change." Standing on tiptoe, she met several curious glances. "No scoop here. Stick your noses back in your own stories." She whirled around and slipped her hand through the crook of his arm heading for the door.

"Lunch it is. Your lass won't mind you dining with an old flame?"

"Nope."

Again she abruptly stopped, her well-worn tennis shoes squeaking a protest. "Gotta run back to my desk, grab my bag, and phone. Don't want to miss anything." She pivoted and sprinted to her desk, returning quickly. "Let's go."

"Ladies choice." Holding the door open for her, he motioned for Ian. The sleek gray limo pulled in front of the building.

"Oh, I love going in style, but the diner is only a couple of blocks and I'd rather walk. Sitting all day at a computer isn't healthy." She leaned over and waved at Ian in the passenger window. "Not today, handsome. We'll walk." She paused a minute more. "Nice ride."

"Since when do you stay put anywhere long enough to worry about sitting all day's effects on your health?" He squinted into the sun, removed his sunglasses from his coat pocket, and slipped them on. Though his legs were much longer than hers, he had to double-time his steps to keep up.

"I only have an hour before I have a meeting with a source on a juicy new exposé I'm working on." She slowed at the corner to wait for traffic.

"The O'Sullivan incident. What really happened? I read the newspaper account, but—there's more."

"Oh, so that's what you're here for. Pump me for information.' She lowered her voice and glanced around. Not a soul in sight. "Not a popular topic. I wanted to run with the true story, but someone higher up, much higher up shut it down...Hard. You know me, don't take shit from no one, but when it came down to that story or my job…Well, I'm still here. Get the point?" She crossed the street and slowed at a little diner on the corner. Yanked the door open, waved to a waitress, and pointed to the corner booth. With a nod from the waitress, she made a beeline for the high-backed booth.

He followed her and slid in on the opposite side of the booth. Leaning over, keeping his voice quiet, he continued. "I do, but my brother has Mr. O'Sullivan as a client. Trial is next week as I said, and he was all prepared to let his client take the fall. Didn't even look into the matter. No witness statements. No statement from the client. Who does that?" The diner was nearly deserted. It was too early for the lunch crowd and too late for breakfast. Making it the perfect place for their clandestine meeting.

She chewed on her bottom lip while glancing around. In hushed tones she began, "I was on scene. The witnesses disappeared. Sam, uh, Mr. O'Sullivan, was spouting all this stuff about being attacked. Claimed he had no choice but to defend himself. During the incident, the wind was blowing so hard you could barely stay upright. The scene was so chaotic. I gave him my card and told him I'd be in touch. By the time I contacted him, not twenty-four hours later, he had nothing to say. At the time, he claimed to be attacked by a magic wielder. As if."

She sniffed. "By who or what? I couldn't tell you. He was screaming weather mage and other unintelligible words. Bottom line, something invisible picked him up and slammed him against the ground. Hard. Got pictures of him in mid-air. Naturally, he retaliated. At about the same time, the wind died completely, and no sign of—anything. I can't tell you anymore. Nor did you hear this from me. I will deny it. Need my job. Understand?" Lines creased across her forehead as her eyes narrowed while she studied him.

He scrubbed his hand over his face. "How the hell are we supposed to defend this man? You know the penalties for using magic in front of mortals. He could be spellbound for the rest of his life or worse."

She shrugged. "Be creative. Get your girlfriend to help. Hear her family is very powerful." She waggled a finger in front of his face. "But I can't be involved, or a fate worse than death could befall me. Why does this shit always happen around you? I said to myself when all this went down—" She poked her finger in his chest. "Bet ol' Dillon will make an appearance. And here you are." She spread her arms wide.

"She isn't…Never mind. This is why Father never became involved in uh… these types of cases. What the hell happened around here?"

"Scuttlebutt? Your creator got crosswise with a powerful individual. Paid the price." She picked up the menu and waved the blonde pony-tailed waitress over. "I'll have a burger, chips, and vanilla shake. I'm kinda in a hurry, Pam."

The waitress scribbled notes on a pad, then looked expectantly at him.

"I'll have the same. Except I'll have a pint. Unless you have something stronger."

"No, sir." Pam jerked her chin toward the building across the street. "Pub over there has whiskey and the like when it opens in a few hours."

"Never mind. Make it a chocolate shake, I've got to return to work anyway. Best be sober. Last thing I need is—" He shifted his gaze from the waitress to Cork. "Well, you know."

"If I was you, I'd get back on the plane to where you come from and forget you ever heard of O'Sul… him. You never belonged in a big stuffy firm even with your talents." She eyed him over the menu a couple of minutes, then held up a hand. "No, I still don't want to know."

"Not that easy."

Pam returned with the shakes. "Food be up shortly." Then she hurried off to another table.

"Never is." Cork paused for a couple of beats. Put the menu back in its place. "Remember when we said no one would ever tell us what to do? Adulting sucks."

"You got that right. At the moment, I appreciate your info. Any chance I could get a copy of those pictures? I'll make sure the source is anonymous."

"Pushy bastard, aren't ya." She snickered. "Some things never change. Won't do you any good without a legal source."

Carrying a large tray, the waitress stopped at their table, doled out the food, and dashed away.

"I gotta have something. Can't let him take the fall when he had no choice." He took a large bite and chewed. "This is great."

"Told you. Besides, Pam minds her own business. Good place for meetings."

"Figured." He took another bite and wiped his mouth with a napkin.

She took a drink of her shake. "Your honor is going to get you into trouble and probably me too. Yeah, I'll get 'em to ya."

He started to hand her his business card, then

yanked it back and wrote Gale's e-mail address on the back. Send them to my attention at this address."

"Can't do that, electronic trail. They'll be at her business within the next twenty-four hours." she winked at him. "I got connections. Certain things leave no trail. I have a couple of trusted friends like you."

"Of course." By the time he'd finished his meal, she was slurping down the last of her shake and grabbing her bag.

He waved to the waitress, pointed to the table, and left enough money for food and tip.

"Gotta go. See ya around." She kissed him on the cheek, shoved the strap on her shoulder, and with a wave to Pam started out the door.

He pushed up from the table and bumped into a man shoving his camera into a waist pack and hurrying toward the door.

"Wait," Dillon called, sprinting after him.

The man shoved Cork out of the way and disappeared out the door.

"What the Hell?" Without hesitation, Cork gave chase.

By the time Dillon got to the door, Cork was standing outside on the sidewalk looking up and down the street. She raised her arms in an exasperated motion, then dropped them to her sides. "He simply disappeared."

"This doesn't bode well. Think he heard anything?"

"No. He didn't register on my radar until I stood up." She groaned. "And kissed you. Now there's a recent connection between us to be splashed over the front pages of the gossip rags. Not good for me."

"Shit."

Chapter 5

Girls' Night In Interrupted.

After sweeping the floor, dusting all the glass cases, and scrubbing the muddy footprints from the tiles, Gale flipped the sign to closed. *How did I get talked into this especially after the pub fiasco?* Covering the glass showcases with a soft lint-free cloth, she switched off the light. *Could have used magic to clean the shop, but the freshly washed scent wasn't the same.* She sniffed and smiled.

The sliver of moon cast wavering shadows across the building as she closed and locked the door. The fresh rain-washed breeze felt good against her heated skin. As soon as she unlocked the car, a warning sparked, then a large hand touched her shoulder. She swallowed a scream and swung around, her hands fisted in front of her the beginning of a gauntlet glinted across the back of her hand, she sucked in a breath, and remembered Synn's warning.

He held up a hand as if to fend off a blow. "Good evening, Ms. Booher. How are you this fine evening?"

"Fine, busy." She kept her keys between her fingers and the ignition key accessible. "We're closed for the evening. Open at nine tomorrow morning."

"Thanks for that information, but it's you I wanted to see. How about I buy you a drink at your local pub?"

He smiled at her, but it didn't reflect in his narrowed eyes.

"Sorry. I've plans this evening. My friends are waiting. If I'm late, they'll come looking for me." *Now, where did that come from?* She tried to keep the fear out of her voice as she peered into the face of the same strange man that had approached her at the pub on Saturday night.

"Didn't mean to scare you. Thought we could have a couple of drinks and get to know each other. Nothing wrong with that, is there?" He gently brushed his knuckles over her cheek.

"No, there's not. But I'm…uh…engaged." She felt the flush to her face, she never was a good liar. The all-important naked finger of her left hand shown as she pushed his hand aside. *Why didn't I use the other hand?*

He caught her hand and turned it so quickly pain radiated through her wrist. "I didn't see a ring."

"Let go. You're hurting me. I, uh, took it off at home to wash my hands and forgot to put it back on. I was running late this morning," she stammered. *He knows, Goddess, he knows.*

"Sorry." He paused, his gaze slowly sliding down her body. "You sure about that?" A smirk played at the corners of his mouth.

"Of course, I'm sure. Besides, it's none of your business. Now if you'll move out of my way, I have to leave." When he didn't move, sparks arced from her palm as she shoved him aside and reached for the car door.

Yelping, he stared at his hand as it sizzled.

At the same time, her phone chimed. "See? My friends are calling to see where I am." The phone chimed again, she yanked it out of her bag and put it to her ear. "I'm on my way."

"What?" a confused male voice on the other end answered.

She ended the call just before a loud blood-curdling screech came from the trees overhead. *Oh, no. Not now, Masked. I'm fine, no need to…*

Her message was too late. A larger than normal barn owl silently swooped down from the trees, the bird's long legs, sharp, powerful talons extended aiming for the stranger's head.

"Holy mother of God." The man ducked covering his face with his hands and cowering before he screamed as the bird caught his ear and the jaunty cap in one talon before soaring high into the trees, hooting raucously. Covering his ear with his hand, blood streamed from between his fingers and he stumbled backward. "Damn bloody bird bit me."

"Well, to be precise, she only cut your ear with her talon and stole your hat. Don't think she'll be returning the cap. And it could have been much worse. Now leave." She pointed to the road while her other hand grasped the door handle.

"What are you, some kind of witch?" He swore again. "You haven't seen the last of me. I'll be back."

"Thanks for the warning. But please, don't bother." She yanked open the vehicle door, jumped in, slammed it shut, and locked it. Shakily she inserted the key in the ignition, took a couple of deep breaths, and turned the key. The engine roared to life. When she stepped on the accelerator, tires spun and gravel spewed in all directions. A quick glance in her rearview mirror and she slumped in her seat. There was no sign of the man.

Still not believing it, she twisted and turned to survey all areas of sight. *I didn't imagine this...did I? Of course not. Magic is not what I need right now.*

A few minutes later, Bridget's house came into view, and relief flooded through her. She slowed the car in front of the house and stopped. Before climbing out of the car, she checked her hair and makeup in the rearview mirror, then took a deep breath trying to settle herself. A few wayward strands of ginger hair had escaped her braid, and she tucked them behind her ears.

Hands still shaking, she slid out of the car, then leaned against the cool metal as she waited for her hands to still. A soft hoot came from the trees beside the house. Masked was perched in the large oak tree. *Didn't trust I'd be all right. Huh, guardian owl?* She snickered, noting the owl still held the man's hat in her beak shredding it to pieces. Quinn sauntered out as she made her way up the sidewalk.

His gaze flitted over her face and brow furrowed when he touched her arm. "Hey, you all right? You're white as a sheet." Pivoting on his heel, he yelled. "Bridge, Gale's here. You owe me nine euro." He grinned sheepishly as color rose in his cheeks. "Little wager."

"What, that I wouldn't show?" She fisted her hands at her waist and glared at him.

"Something like that." He studied her face again. "You look positively…"

"A fright." Bridget flew out the door and finished his sentence. "What happened?"

"Nothing." She lied and walked into the house behind her friend.

Bridget took her by the shoulders, spun her around,

and shook her gently. "Tell me what happened. Or I'll call Quinn back in here to stand guard on our girl's night in."

She blew out a breath and told her friend what happened. "The bugger just won't take no for an answer."

"Wish I'd been there to see that. You praise Masked?"

"Of course not. Owl's supposed to listen to me. Be my protector." The words were no sooner out of her mouth than she regretted them. Bridget would take the bird's side.

"Exactly what she was doing."

Quinn returned to the house and leaned one shoulder on the doorframe. "Need me to stick around? Cost you a couple of pints."

Bridget elbowed Quinn gently out of the way, then stepped out onto the porch looking up and down the street. "Did he follow you?"

"No. Funny thing, a split second later, I looked in my rearview and he'd disappeared without a trace. No mode of transportation. Nothing. Even Masked returned to the tree." Following Bridget out onto the porch, she glanced around then up into the treetops. She shook her finger heavenward. "You stay put. No more shenanigans, Masked. You hear me?"

From an overhead tree, the bird dropped what was left of the hat. Pieces of cloth fluttered to the ground. With a screech, the owl circled the house, then landed in the treetops behind the house.

"Apparently, she doesn't trust you to be safe." Bridget craned her neck in an effort to catch sight of the bird.

She shrugged. "Guess it won't hurt to have her standing guard. Anyway, Saturday night at the pub, I picked up a faint magic signature from the man. But tonight, he had to be disguising it. Didn't even sense him when I left the shop. You know I'm careful when I leave the shop alone." She glanced at her friend for confirmation. "Masked didn't screech until he advanced on me."

Bridget nodded in agreement. "Don't think he'll be back tonight?" Her friend's forehead creased in concern.

She shook her head. "Doubt it. Masked cut his ear pretty good with her talon."

Bridget glanced at Quinn. "No, you go on. We'll be all right. Cori, Synn, and Colleen will be here shortly. Maybe Kate will stop by too."

"Okay. I'm headed over to Gavin's. We may stop back by later to check on you. Call if you need us." He leaned over, brushed his lips over hers, and lingered a beat or two. "Sure you don't want me to stay?" He eyed Gale and frowned.

"Aye." Bridget returned his kiss, waited for Gale, then closed the door, and locked it securing the deadbolt. "What the effing is that guy's deal?"

"I've no idea. Wish I knew. Mind if I put up a protection spell for tonight?"

"No. Go right ahead." Bridget pulled the curtain aside and peeked out the window. "Synn and Colleen are here. I think that's Cori's car behind them."

Synn bounced out of the vehicle, a box covered with a blanket in her hands and a mischievous grin on her face. She sprinted up to the door. Colleen followed with covered dishes of food.

"Oh, I forgot the snacks in the car. Brought lemon bars, tins of peanut butter biscuits, and bags of crisps." She flung open the door, greeted the women, and dashed to the car. After the others made their way inside, she cast the protection spell. Once again, she glanced up and down the street seeing or feeling nothing amiss. Before going inside, she sent Masked a mental message to stay alert. A soft hoot was her only reply.

She eyed the covered box in the middle of the floor. The women gathered around the box talking in hushed tones, then turned to peer at her.

"What are you guys up to?" She moved closer and heard a whimper, then a whine, a yip, and a series of barks. "What have you done, Synn?"

"Nothing. Well, something. Someone had to do something. I couldn't stand thinking of you all alone in your lonely, quiet flat. Saturday night you were so lost. Your despair nearly crushed me. Gavin and I put our heads together, and we came up with this solution." She beamed, pointing at the box.

"Don't just stand there. Pick up the blanket and have a look." Bridget inched closer and picked up one corner of the blanket. "Awww…"

She closed her eyes and blew out a breath. *I don't need this right now.* But she couldn't have been more wrong. Leaning over, she picked up the other corner of the blanket and peeked inside. A little black fur ball rushed to the corner, wet nose twitching, and put her paws on the top of the box. The puppy wiggled from head to toe, backed up, whined, barked then charged the end of the box. With one paw over the edge, the pup promptly started chewing on the corner of the box.

"She's teething. You might want to get her a few more chewies. Her crate, bowls, food, leash, brush, shampoo, rinse, a few chewies, and potty pads are in Colleen's car." Synn started toward the door. "I'll go get them."

"What in the world made you think I needed or even wanted a puppy? Do you know how much work they are?" Before she picked up the pup, she knew it was a mistake, but she picked up the furball anyway. It nuzzled against her neck, then spread puppy kisses all over her face with its little black tongue. She giggled and hugged the fuzzy creature to her.

Synn stood with her hands on her hips. "Of course I know how much work a puppy is. And at the worst time of my life. They are also more company than you can imagine. My pup, Storm, well she's a dog now, saved me more ways than I can ever count."

"You are the one that rescued her in that blinding rainstorm in front of the pub if memory serves correctly," Gale shot back.

"We rescued each other," Synn conceded. "Just like this wee lass will rescue you."

"I don't need rescuing." She swore as the puppy chewed on the button to her jacket, breaking it in half. Quickly, she reached into the pup's mouth and extracted the two-button pieces before the furball could swallow them.

"See, you're a natural. Crisis averted." Synn smiled smugly.

"Whose idea was this?" She glanced at the other women as they tried to look innocent and failed miserably.

"Fate had a hand in this too. You see, Gavin has a

supplier in Wales whose wife raises chow chows and runs a rescue for the breed. Raised right and socialized, they make the best guardians and companions. She would be perfect to help you at the shop. The customers would love her, and she'd never know a stranger. Anyway, this lass was the last and the smallest pup in the litter that came in last week.

"The owner died suddenly, leaving the mother and seven puppies. They were turned over to the rescue. Gavin's supplier asked if he knew of anyone looking for a puppy. We thought of you right away even before…well, I sensed something was wrong the first day you didn't open your shop. Wanted to give you space. But when Bridget here got worried after a week, an intervention was necessary."

The other women cooing and petting the pup bobbed their heads in agreement.

"The supplier dropped the order and the pup yesterday. Perfect timing. You were so melancholy Saturday night. Nearly broke my heart. I almost brought her to you last night…" Her cheeks pinked. "Gavin had other ideas."

"Besides, the rest of us wanted to see her too." Colleen rubbed the pup's ear, and its little chocolate brown eyes started to droop.

"You might want to take her outside and see if she has to pee before she takes a nap." Synn pointed to the ball of fur. "Let me go grab her leash. Not leash trained yet. That'll be up to you. She'll just roll over and chew on it, but that way you have her under control. Bridget's backyard isn't fenced or puppy-proof." Synn raced to Colleen's vehicle and was back quick as a wink handing the leash to Gale.

"I have no say in this matter?" She took the leash and clipped it to the pup's harness.

"Nope. Let me rephrase that. The wee lass needs a name. And that's up to you." Synn grinned, tugging her toward the back door.

She opened the door and walked outside, leaving Synn standing in the doorway. "Well, pup, it looks like it's you and me against the world." The crescent moon hung in the sky amid the twinkling stars. A whoosh of wings broke the silent night. The owl soared in front of her landing in a nearby tree and hooted. "Masked, appears we have a new family member. What shall we name her?"

She lowered the furball to the ground. Masked made another pass taking a closer look, banked left, then returned to the tree. True to Synn's words, the puppy promptly rolled over on her back, feet flailing in the air as she bit down on the leash, shook her head, and chewed. She sighed and grabbed the leash out of her mouth. "You've a lot to learn, little one." She could have sworn she heard Synn snicker. When she turned to confront her friend, Synn was engaged in a conversation with Colleen in the kitchen with the door open.

Finally, the pup did her business, raced around her tangling the leash around her legs, and chewed on her pant legs before they returned to the house. She picked up the furball, detangled the leash, and placed the sleepy puppy in the box. The women's noisy chatter while setting out the snacks and picking out movies to watch didn't seem to bother the pup as she drifted off to sleep. They emptied a bottle of wine before the first movie started.

A knock on the door was barely audible. However, she sensed Katie's arrival. "Hey, Bridget, Katie's at the door. Want me to get it?"

"Sure." Wrinkling her nose, Bridget stared at the door for a minute, then tossed the deadbolt key to her.

"Welcome, come on in. Were you in on the puppy ambush too?"

Katie scrunched up her nose and rolled her eyes. "They went through with it?"

"Aye, they sure did."

"Well, I suggested they check with you first, but was overruled unanimously." Katie scooted into the room and peeked at the pup. "She sure is a cutie and so tiny. Won't stay that way long. Look at those paws."

An hour later, after consuming a few glasses of wine and junk food, Gale wove her way to the front door between movies. "I need some air. Be right back."

Bridget jumped in front of her, threw her hands across the door in a grandiose display. "Not by yourself, lass." Her friend hiccupped twice, then proceeded to tell the others what had occurred before Gale arrived. "No one leaves the house alone," Bridget declared.

Colleen got to her feet, swayed, then plopped back onto the sofa as Cori and Katie watched wide-eyed, sitting cross-legged on the floor. Synn padded toward the front door.

"That's wise since you don't know who or what this person is," Synn agreed. "I'll walk outside with you. Need a little air myself."

"Okay?" Gale eyed her friend, who still barred the door.

"That works." Bridget moved aside and opened the

door, allowing her and Synn to step out onto the porch.

Once they were outside, Synn closed the door and broached the delicate subject. "Is this an unwanted suitor or something more dangerous?"

"Unwanted suitor, I'd wager. No reason to believe otherwise. Dillon's family got what they wanted. He's back with them practicing at the family firm. I'm out of the picture. End of story."

"But is it?" Synn searched her friend's face solemnly. "I'd wager not. Not by the hurt heart of yours. Did you make the right choice? No regrets?"

Quiet for several beats, she blinked back tears. "No choice." She whirled on Synn and pointed a finger at her chest. "Would you willingly go where you're not wanted and endure his hateful family?" Her voice turned soft. "Sorry." Stepping off the porch, she walked around the side of the house glancing up in the trees. A soft "hoot" answered her actions.

"Understood. More than you know. But wouldn't he have stood up for you? After all, he asked you to marry him."

"Then we'd be two miserable people instead of just me. They'll never let him—Oh, never mind." She wiped her face with the back of her hand. "Saw Mary and Tim at the pub. Are they back from traveling for a bit?"

Synn followed her around the back of the house. "You're changing the subject. And we're not through. But, yes, business has picked up with the new menu Gavin created. We've not had time to hire more help and with tourist season coming…" Synn threw up her hands in frustration.

"Mary and Tim are between trips and graciously

volunteered to help out. Screen the applicants. That kind of thing." A brief smile curved her lips. "They are wonderful people. Hannah and Brandy along with their husbands will be visiting in the next couple of months. Tim and Mary are looking forward to seeing them."

"You are very lucky to have married into the Shaughnessy family," she said gloomily. "After what you've been through, you deserve it. I'm so happy for you."

"Don't I know it. Thank you." Synn grinned. "Didn't think I was going to let you off that easy. How do you know he isn't miserable in Scotland without you? Rumor had it he didn't get along with his family, to begin with."

"I don't. However, he decided to return. By the way, who have you been talking to? Seems you are the recipient of a lot of rumors recently."

Totally ignoring the question, Synn continued, "And yours not to go with him. Just say'n my gut says you're wrong." Synn's mouth formed a thin line. "Not what you want to hear. I'm no good at diplomacy, especially where my friends are concerned. I care too much to not say what's on my mind. I've made enough mistakes in my life to be an expert."

"Okay. I'll give you that...but his family is powerful and unrelenting."

Synn skidded to a stop on the path in front of her. "You are one of the most powerful and tenacious individuals I know. Now with the membership in the FAE guardian guild, why cave in matters of the heart? What did you tell me when we were confronting the evil magic running through my blood? To believe in me, conquer and control the magic. I did. Now you have to do the same thing, only the evil magic is his family, uh, parents, maybe just his father? Siblings?"

"Not sure on that front. I'll give it some thought. Don't want to contact him only to have him tell me there is someone else." She turned the corner and walked toward the front of the house.

"Again. Better to know and move on than carry that huge torch for nothing. On the flip side, what if he wants to be with you as much as you do with him?"

She winced. "It'd be a shame."

"Exactly my point." Synn straightened. "You know what you have to do. Now let's go back inside and try to get the other girls sobered up before their men come to get them." She snapped her fingers. "If you need someone to watch your pup while you go to Scotland, I'd be happy to. Since I sprung her on you without warning. Besides, Storm would love the company."

"Thanks for the offer. Who says I'm going to Scotland? I'll let you know." She paused for a moment. "I believe we're all spending the night."

"Not me, I've work tomorrow. Remember what I said about being short-handed. Bridget has the day off. Gavin will be by to pick me up after the guys finish their poker game."

She laughed. "You still say his name dreamily. That's so cute."

Synn waved her hand in dismissal. "Oh, I do not. It's your imagination."

"Nope. This time I'm right." She hip bumped Synn as they walked up the steps to the porch.

"Maybe." Synn grinned and pushed the door open.

Inside, Cori had already put the coffee pot on and was arranging mugs on a silver tray. Synn poured the coffee into the mugs and handed the empty pot to her. Cori pointed to the additional glass pot on the warmer. "We got more if needed. Gale, bring those delicious peanut butter biscuits in the tin out with you."

She picked up the tin and started across the room when out of thin air, a picture materialized and floated to the floor face up. She sucked in a breath. The tin crashed to the floor when she picked up the picture.

"What's this? Where'd it come from?" Bridget leaned over her shoulder. "Oh, no."

"There's got to be an explanation." Synn reached for the picture.

She turned her gaze on the rest of the group, then pinned Synn. "I guess I have my answer." Unable to stand the pitying glances from her friends, she sprinted for the door, tears rolling down her face. When she yanked open the door, she ran headlong into the broad muscular chest of Dillon. For a moment, she was mesmerized by those wild blue eyes and mane of reddish-brown hair framing his gorgeous face. A face that had to have been sculpted by angels. Then reality slapped her upside the head.

Chapter 6

An Unexpected Surprise and Eating Humble Pie— Not a Good Experience

"Oof." He caught her in his arms. She twisted out of his hold and slapped him across the face leaving angry red marks and welts. She ran toward her car.

"Don't let her get in that car as upset as she is," Bridget called huffing and puffing behind Synn. Cori, Colleen, and Kate emerged onto the front yard.

"You got some explaining to do, boyo." Synn smashed the picture against his chest as she hurried after Gale. Suddenly, the demon disappeared and reappeared between Gale and the vehicle, blocking her entrance. "You're not driving in your condition. Come back into the house. We'll sort this out. Afterward, either one of us will drive you, or you'll stay here."

The silent wings of a ghostly shadow emerged from the treetops. A loud screech sounded, and the shadow dove for Synn.

Gale put her hand up, and the bird halted mid-air. "She's not a danger. Back off."

In a warning tone, Synn said, "Call your bird off. I don't want to hurt her, but I won't allow her to attack us."

"Leave me alone. I'm fine to drive." Sparks flew from her fingertips, but Gale glanced up and gave the owl a silent command to stand down. The bird hovered for a couple of beats, screeched in frustration, then circled to land on the front peak of the house watchful of the humans flooding into the yard.

"Aye, right. Tears are streaming down your face so hard you can't even see where you're going. Nope, not letting you go anywhere. Now either turn around and walk into the house, or I'll port you." She shrugged. "Your choice." Synn lounged against the driver's side of the door examining her aqua nail polish.

Gale stared defiantly at Synn. A ball of magic power formed in Gale's hand, and she bounced it from one hand to the other. When it became apparent Synn wouldn't back down, Gale had no desire to hurt her friend. Shoulders slumped, she turned, extinguished the crackling ball of energy, and trudged toward the house. *The gauntlets didn't even attempt to make an appearance. Smart magic.*

Staring at the picture shoved at his chest, he shook his head. "It's not what it looks like."

"Gee, isn't that just like a man. Explain how it appears to you. Because to us, it looks like you are being kissed by a beautiful woman and enjoying it." Synn spat out, pausing to point out this afternoon's date stamp on the picture before accompanying Gale into the house.

He ran his fingers through his hair and followed the others, pausing just inside the doorframe. Now he was positive someone had followed him to Cork's office then the diner. That person had deliberately snapped pictures, forwarding the most incriminating to his fiancée, uh, ex-fiancée.

This has my father's handiwork written all over it.

Father didn't believe it was over between us. Or if he did, he wanted to nail the coffin shut. He couldn't let it end like this. She was worth fighting for. He was going to have to come clean about everything.

If there was anyone he could trust, it was Gale. But he couldn't do it here in front of all these people. Too big a risk, should something get out. What about the pictures Cork was to send to Gale? Were they safe at Pixie Magic? Before he could reach out to Gale—

A loud pop sounded. Gavin appeared in front of Dillon. "What the bloody hell is going on here? I felt shockwaves all the way to me house." Gavin paused to survey the room, then glanced outside. "Quinn and Amos are on their way. Had to interrupt the poker game as there 'twas a problem at the pub."

The owl flapped her wings and let out several screeches in succession. Finally, she circled the house and landed on the porch railing clicking her beak angrily.

Gavin glanced at the picture Dillon held. "Good God, man, what have you done?" Gavin tore the picture from his friend and stared at it. "Who's the woman?"

"An old friend from college. Nothing more. She's a reporter. I met her for lunch to find out what she knew about a case involving magic that my brother and I are working on. This picture was taken completely out of context." He took the picture back and glanced at Gale. "We need to sort this out alone. Now."

"A bit bold of you after that." With her well-manicured fingernail painted in purple with silver sparkles, Gale pointed at the offending picture and glared at him drilling the point of the fingernail in his chest. "You made your position quite clear when you left. Now a few weeks later, you're here making demands. Take your picture and yourself back to Scotland. Don't darken my door again." She whirled around and marched into the kitchen.

The women closed ranks around the entrance to the room. Dillon shoved the restraining hand of Gavin away and made his way to the women. "You're not doing Gale any favors by keeping her from me. This is between us and none of your business."

"You break her heart. We come to her aid. You show up to do more damage. We won't allow it. The way I see it, she doesn't want to talk to you. So leave, while your manhood is still intact." Synn raised an arm, gauntlets shimmered up one arm and a sword floated in the air above her.

Gavin sprinted over to his wife, wrapped an arm around her waist, and pulled her to him, whispering in her ear. Dropping her arm behind her back, the sword disappeared with a quiet pop, and Synn sent Dillon a scathing look. "You hurt her again—" She left the threat up in the air as Gavin tapped her lips with his finger.

"I'm going to take Synn home now. I suggest the rest of you do the same."

Bridget stiffened. "Excuse me. This is my home."

"I wasn't finished," Gavin said in a calm tone. "I believe Dillon and Gale are headed to Gale's flat for a conversation."

"Not bloody likely." Gale called from the kitchen.

"Come on, ladies, let him through to at least plead his case." A strong breeze swept through the room. When Gavin turned, Quinn and Amos strode into the room. The screen door banged shut behind them.

"Party over already?" Quinn quipped.

"Yeah." Gavin pointed a thumb over his shoulder. "Dillon is back. There seems to be a misunderstanding between him and Gale. Not something we should be involved in."

Quinn cleared his throat and shifted uncomfortably from foot to foot. "Saw Tiarnan and Erin walking the cliffs. Appeared they might be headed in this direction."

Oh shit! I don't need their interference in this mess. Panicked, Dillon gently removed Bridget from in front of the entrance to the kitchen and scooched through. Pausing to face the women, he held up one finger. "Give me a minute. If she won't come willingly with me after that, I'll leave. Fair enough?"

Quinn sidled up beside Bridget. After whispering something, he tugged her farther from the kitchen.

Cori the only one left in the entrance stepped away toward Amos. "I hate to abandon this sisterhood, but it's late and I've an early morning tomorrow." She glowered at Dillon. "You do any more harm to my cousin—Tiarnan and Erin are not the only ones you'll be dealing with. In case you're wondering, you're no match for us. Keep that in mind, boyo." She spun on her heels and slipped a hand through Amos' bent elbow guiding him toward the front door.

"Gale, we need to talk. There are things we need to discuss."

"I agree, starting with that." She pointed at the picture in his hand.

He glanced over his shoulder at the front door. "Don't take this wrong, but I don't need Tiarnan's interference in this mess. Can we please finish this conversation in your flat?"

"Why should I leave with you only to allow you to trap me in my own home?"

"I wouldn't do that. I didn't insist you go to Scotland with me after telling me no. I won't do that now. But there's more going on than I first thought. I don't want to be there, but I can't leave until the situation is corrected. Now please."

"Who's she?" Gale pointed at the picture. "What's she mean to you? If your answer satisfies me, I'll leave with you. Otherwise, you'll leave."

His shoulders slumped, and he gave one final glance at the door. "Remember I told you about Cork, the girl I met at university? She's a reporter now. A damn good one."

"The girl you had a serious relationship with?"

"Aye, and the one I broke up with because we both agreed we weren't meant to be together. This picture is her and I in a public diner. She was kissing me goodbye after our clandestine meeting." He blew out a frustrated breath. "There is nothing between us but friendship. She witnessed an incident involving our client—one she wasn't allowed to report the true facts on. I contacted her because I needed to know what she saw. My brother has to try the case next week. Our firm represents…That's all I can say in this public venue."

Her brows knitted together, and her face tightened. "Why should I believe you?"

"Because I've never lied to you. I warned you about my family before I asked you to marry me."

"But I didn't expect you to go running off to Scotland at their beck and call." Rocking back on her heels, she pretended to study the floor. "You're right. You never lied to me. I told you in the beginning if you ever lied to me, we'd be over." She reached out her hand, he clasped it then she turned to her friend. "Bridget, we're going somewhere to talk. Thanks for everything."

They stepped out the back door right into the path of Tiarnan and Erin. Before Tiarnan could spout a word, Gale held up a hand. "Hold that thought." She rushed into the house and picked up the box with the sleeping puppy. As she swept through the rooms, Synn added a small bag of kibble and bowl to the box before her friend flew out the back door. "I've…we've got something to discuss. I'll get back to you. Promise." With that Gale, the box, and Dillon disappeared.

Reappearing in her flat above her shop, she took a step back, shifted the box, and released his hand, then stared at pictures scattered face down on the floor. "What the hell. These weren't here when I left. It may be in your best interest to start talking." She gave him a withering glance as she carefully set the box on the floor and picked up the pictures. The puppy stretched and yawned, then rolled over its little eyes closed.

If looks could kill, I'd be dead on the spot. He cleared his throat and drew in a deep breath. "Where'd you get a puppy?"

"The girls thought I needed companionship. Synn took it upon herself to get a puppy. Said we belonged together. It's a long story." She took two steps away from the sleeping pup and shuffled the pictures.

"Those are the pictures I started to tell you about but felt the matter best be discussed in private. Those pictures could get Cork in a heap of trouble. She could lose her job and her reputation tarnished among other things."

Slowly, she stared at first one picture, then the others. "What in the hell happened?"

"That's what I'm trying to figure out." He leaned over her shoulder and glanced at the pictures.

"What is that?" She pointed to a blurry object in one of the pictures.

"A dark mage that didn't want his or her picture taken, I'd guess."

Her hand shot to her mouth. "But look at all those...are those mortals in what appears to be a park? This took place in a public area?"

He nodded, then pointed to the picture where a man was sprawled on the ground. "He's our client."

Flipping to the next picture, she gasped. Blood spattered and pooled over the ground, a pile of ash smoking, and horror-stricken expressions frozen on the faces of the witnesses. "Oh, Goddess...The mage didn't survive? Someone's going to pay for that."

"Not sure. No evidence of a mage in the case file. The charge is using magic in front of mortals. His claim was self-defense, but there are no witnesses that will come forward, including Co—my friend to corroborate our client's version. These were sent to me anonymously, and the person will swear she never saw them if confronted."

He took the pictures from Gale. "Which I would never do. I trust you completely, so I had the photos sent to you. At the time, there was no connection between you and Cork. Now...we are going to have to be creative, deceptive, and careful. Only our most trusted friends can know the truth."

A baffled expression crossed her face. "The truth about what?"

He looked down at her naked left hand for the first time and noticed she wasn't wearing his ring—her engagement ring. Things were worse than he'd hoped. His thoughts concerning the case derailed. "You have to know my feelings never changed about you."

She stiffened, then fisted her hands at her sides. "Really?" She paced around the room. "I'm afraid I don't understand. Several weeks ago, you indicated if I refused to go to Scotland with you, it was over between us. Made it pretty clear our engagement is off. You don't treat someone you love like that. So no I don't have to understand that."

Staring at the floor, he began, "I wasn't thinking straight. I'd just received an ultimatum from Father threatening to destroy my life as I knew it. All I'd worked for most of my life at his behest, if I didn't return to Scotland, immediately." He made an exploding motion with his hands. "Not ninety minutes later, I received a call from my grandparents—my father's parents."

He hesitated for a couple of beats. "Guess we'll have to deal with that information later. I should have explained…No. At that time nothing made any sense. I couldn't explain it to you when I didn't understand myself. But I guess I couldn't have mucked it up much worse." He raised his gaze to hers hoping to see a tiny spark of warmth. There was none. Confusion mixed with a tiny fleck of fury is what he saw in those beautiful green eyes if he was lucky.

"You're not making any sense at the present. It's best if we just walk away now." She sniffed, drew in a breath, and let it out slowly.

Something she did often when coming to a difficult

decision. This conversation wasn't going well. Not how he'd intended. Fearing his father would find out he had no intention of letting her go kept him from telling her everything. *But has the firm bugged her home to make sure? Am I being watched even now? At least there was no evidence anyone followed our magic trail when we left Bridget's home. I never figured to be followed to Cork's place either, until it happened.* His head ached with the possibilities and his heart ached at her cold expression. *I've got to make this right.*

"That's anger talking." His brow crinkled as a memory popped up. "What was going on when I called? Your voice sounded strange, and you didn't make any sense. Which is why I ported right over here. Only to discover once I got here I had no idea where you were."

She waved her hand in dismissal. "A strange situation that has nothing to do with…" She stopped mid-sentence. Her mouth opened and closed without a sound.

He crossed to her, risked taking her in his arms, and held her tight for a moment. Then gripping her by the shoulders, he held her away from him. "Tell me what happened. What's wrong?"

She began slowly. "Who knew you were coming?"

"No one. I didn't myself until I heard your voice and got this awful feeling in the pit of my stomach. I was afraid something terrible had just happened and I was too late to stop it. When I couldn't locate you, I went straight to the pub. Quinn had just arrived for an emergency of some kind and said you were at a girls' night in at Bridget's place. He was none too happy with me either."

"Which is how you found me. Even though I had disguised my magic signature? Well, that clears up that little detail."

"Why did you disguise your magic signature? You had no idea I was trying to contact you. Did you?"

The puppy whined and scratched at the box. "I've got to let her out. We don't do puddles around here." She picked up the pup.

"Does she have a name?" He leaned over and rubbed the pup's ear.

"Not yet." She took the puppy outside.

Chapter 7

Still Waters Run Deep As Do Treacherous Family Ties

After returning from letting the pup out to do her business and run around a bit, she poured a little kibble in a bowl and set it in the box. Then she scavenged a cereal bowl for water. As the puppy gobbled up the food, she turned her attention back to Dillon.

"Why would I expect you to contact me?" She bristled and moved around the room nervously. *How much to tell him? Was he or his family behind my unwanted suitor?* Hurt colored her decision-making. The Dillon she knew would never do such a thing. But his family? This man standing before her was her Dillon, she could feel it, but she couldn't clear the hurt or desire to make him hurt as she had. "Want some tea or coffee?" she blurted, walking toward the kitchen. *I need something to do with my hands.*

He blinked at her. "I could use tea. Unless you have something stronger."

"Not a good idea under the circumstances. We both need a clear head to talk this situation through. Don't you think?"

"I suppose." He glanced longingly at the bottle of vintage whiskey on a kitchen shelf.

As she put the kettle on and got down the tin of tea, her Aunt Erin's voice flowed through her mind. *Put aside the childish feelings. They only serve to distance you from your true love. He's asking for your help. To deny him would be the worst mistake of your life. We're here if you need us.* The voice faded away and left her feeling irritable and vulnerable at the same time.

"Gale—Gale." He waved a hand in front of her face. "You all right?" His forehead wrinkled in concern as he pinched the bridge of his nose with thumb and forefinger.

She startled. "I'm fine, just thinking." A few minutes later, the kettle whistled and she prepared the tea, handing him a mug, and taking one for herself. Glancing around the room, she spied a tin of peanut butter biscuits she'd made this morning and snatched them. Motioning him into the living room with her mug, she handed him the tin, then snapped her fingers toward the hearth where a cozy fire rose up and now crackled.

She settled onto the couch, took a sip of her tea, then patted the cushion beside her. "For this to work, you have to tell me exactly what is going on. What you suspect and what you plan to do about it. Most importantly, you have to tell me where we stand as a couple."

Setting the tin of biscuits on the little wooden table in front of the couch, he eased down beside her and wrapped an arm around her shoulders. Taking a long draw of his tea, he set the mug down and gazed at her. "My feelings for you are as strong today as the day I asked you to marry me."

"Then why the ultimatum? Either I go with you to

Scotland or we're through? I took that to mean the engagement was off. It ripped my heart in two. You don't just come back from something like that on a whim. Was I wrong?" Setting her mug on the table beside his, she twisted her hands in her lap waiting for his response, unsure if this was the right way to attack the situation. The altercation with the stranger remained very much on her mind.

Sheepishly, he glanced at her before releasing a heavy sigh. "It was anger and frustration talking as I said before. Hurting you was never my intention. You gotta believe me. Now it's more complicated. My father and family believe the engagement is off. I want them to continue to believe that for the time being. Because it plays to my agenda. A ruthless situation that works to my father's strengths. For now." He paused for a moment, rubbing his chin.

She raised a brow. "I don't think I like this new Dillon."

"My sister may have her doubts. Anyway, my father is hiding something or he's done something that negatively affects the law firm. When Great-Grandfather, Owen, established the firm, he had mortal solicitors as well as members of his family of witches that worked there in varying capacities. To be in compliance with the magic council, he had to choose which individuals he'd represent.

"Because of the strictly enforced covenant against using magic in front of mortals, he couldn't do both without getting into trouble. He had no desire to limit his practice to magical creatures. Well respected in the mortal community, he built his practice with them. For over one hundred years, our firm has never taken on a magical case. Until now. The entanglement of accidentally having a non-magical solicitor run across the magic case or cases would be catastrophic."

Straightening, she leaned forward intrigued by the situation. "Okay, so why now?" She reached for her mug and took a sip.

"That's the million-dollar question. My guess. No one in our family has the balls to stand up to Father and challenge his decision, except maybe my sister."

Snorting a laugh, she choked spitting tea all over in front of her. "Your sister?" She set the mug on the table.

Chuckling he picked up a napkin, wiped her mouth, and dabbed at her shirt. "She's the only one that would—besides me. I intend to do exactly that when I return after I give these pictures to my brother and decide how to proceed in this case. I can't let an innocent man be punished."

"How can you defend him and not be caught representing magical and mortal? Clearly against the rules." Gale tapped her fingers on the tabletop.

"I'm still working on that. The other thing that bothers me, if there's one case, there could be more that no one but Father knows about. Then we're back to why."

She held her hand up. "Stop. One problem at a time. First, for the ruse and time being, we are not engaged?"

There was a loud knock on the door to the shop. He jumped. "Are you expecting anyone?" When he glanced at her, one eyebrow winged up.

"No." She padded downstairs and was surprised to see Gavin standing at the door a folded crate and bags in his hands. She opened the door and stared at him.

"Synn said you'd need the puppy's things before tomorrow. You left your keys on the counter at Bridget's place, so we brought your car back too. Figured you might need it tomorrow." He looked at his watch before setting the crate and bags on the floor. "Today."

"Thank you."

"No problem. Gotta go, Synn is waiting in our lorry." He hugged her and closed the door behind him.

For a couple of minutes, she peered at all the stuff wondering where she would put it all in her tiny flat. *Time to clean out the closets.* She screwed up her face at the thought. Dillon appeared behind her and she squealed. "Don't do that."

"What? Did I hear Gavin's voice?"

She slapped at him. "Aye, Gavin was here." She pointed to the crate and pile of bags. "He brought the pup's stuff and my car back."

"Oh." He guided her up the stairs. "Where were we before Gavin so rudely interrupted us? Ah…yes. Our engagement should be back on. If you'll have me after I've mucked things up so bad." He leaned into her and brushed his lips over hers at the top of the stairs. "But the ruse will remain. If you can handle it? Safer for both of us until we can sort it all out."

She took his hand and tugged him into the flat. Before she could admonish him for creating this mess, her traitorous body wrapped her arms around his neck, deepening the kiss, parting her lips, allowing his tongue to explore and dance with hers. Desire zinged through her as they tumbled on to the couch. *Physical attraction had always been our strong suit. Sex is not on the table, not until...*

But her body continued to open to him, allowing his feather-light caresses along the side of her breast, as he nibbled at her jaw, then his tongue slid between the cleavage presented by her stretchy V-neck shirt. When he lifted her into his lap, his hard ridge beneath her reminded her what he had to offer and how badly she wanted him. As if reading her mind, he pulled her shirt over her head and opened the clasp of her bra.

Somewhere in the back of her mind, a little voice was screaming for her to make him stop. But her body overruled the voice as he shifted her across his lap. Cupping her breasts, he lowered his warm mouth over each, his tongue circling first one nipple, then the other, until both were hard little berries. She arched toward him panting and her chest heaving. Sucking in a breath she attempted to sit up. "Wait. I'm not thinking clearly. We can't do this now."

"Why not?"

"You left me," she howled, though half-heartedly. Her words should have given her more determination, but they didn't. She wanted this, him, right or wrong. It was wrong and she knew it but no longer cared.

He caressed her cheek with his hand. "I wasn't thinking straight when I left. I've missed you. I never should have left," he said in a rough whisper, easing her down into his lap again. His hand slid to her waistband and fingers flipped open the button of her jeans. Moisture gathered between her legs as his fingers continued to caress, tease their way to her center, pushing her panties aside. Her legs willingly spread, giving him access. He thrust one long finger inside, then another, curling into the sweet spot and she moaned.

She arched against him. "Dillon. Don't stop." A second later, she crashed over the cliff of ecstasy. He continued his ministrations until the tremors stopped and she was sprawled across his lap spent. She gazed up at him. Slowly the corners of his mouth turned up in a wicked smile. Again, her brain called foul, but her body relaxed in the glow of satisfaction. *What have I done? This is not the way to straighten out this mess. It's only making it worse.*

"Does it make up a little for what I've put you through?" he murmured, leaning over, and breathing a kiss at the pulsing hollow of her throat.

Mortified, she sat up, grabbed her shirt from the back of the couch, and attempted to slide out of his lap. "No, no, no. This never should have happened." Keeping her voice low, hoping not to disturb the pup, she struggled into her shirt and straightened it, glaring at him.

He raised an eyebrow. His wild blue Scottish eyes pleaded with her. "Not even a little bit?"

She blew out a breath. He was too close. She tried again to move away, but his arm snaked around holding her in his lap and against his hard ridge nestled at her backside. His warm body felt so good, and he smelled fantastic. He was wearing her favorite aftershave. Not that she didn't enjoy his normal musky, citrus spice scent. "No."

Her body still hummed with excitement and desire. *Damn him. Oh Goddess, I want more.* Their relationship had always been physical. Never being able to get enough of each other, which apparently hadn't changed. But there was more, much more. At least she'd thought there was. *What a damn mess*. At last, he released her, and she crawled out of his lap, let her gaze follow the hard ridge in his jeans and felt no remorse for leaving in him that condition. At least not at the moment. "So where to do we go from here?" Distancing herself from him, she settled at the far end of the couch.

"The bedroom?" he teased.

"Think again, boyo."

"I'm not sure. The fear in your voice when you answered the phone had me porting without thinking about the end result." He sighed. "On one side, our engagement shall remain in flux to anyone but us, until such time as it befits us to change that status. Be much easier on both of us. On the other, flaunting it in his face might be the only way to catch him off his game and find out what is going on. If that becomes necessary."

"What about your grandparents? Their phone call was equally upsetting to you. What's going on there?"

He shook his head and toed the edge of the rug at his feet. "One problem at a time." When he glanced at the watch on his wrist, he let out a low whistle. "I'd better be getting back."

"Oh no, you don't. Leave here now, and you'll not darken my door again." Hands fisted at her hips, she shoved to her feet and planted herself between him and the door. "We settle this thing between us tonight."

He slumped back against the couch, his eyes closed, he pinched the bridge of his nose. "Can you handle the scorn of my father and my family?"

"Why should I?" She frowned at him. "Can't you control their behavior toward me? You're a grown man.

Made your choices. Either stay here and let the rest of them handle whatever is going on—or…"

"That's the problem, if I want to make my home here and practice law in Ireland, there is a process to complete. Among other documents that have to be submitted, I need two character references from other solicitors. One must be from a solicitor in my family's firm that has five years standing.

"If my father has tainted the firm, this will reflect badly on me and my request for admission to the Roll of Solicitors in Ireland, and I may be denied. If he chooses to trash my reputation, again admission may be denied. The family firm is the only place I've practiced. Grandfather may be willing and able to assist me in the Roll of Solicitors. He's always stood for me against the scourge of my father." He threw up his hands. "Now you see my dilemma. The reason I left. I had to be in my father's good graces to make a life for myself here. Yet, life without you…"

"Why didn't you tell me? We could have worked it out together." She paused for a moment moistened her dry lips. "It's me. I'm the problem as far as your family is concerned."

"Aye. But once I get to the bottom of what's going on at the firm, you'll be the least of their or my problems. If my investigation finds wrongdoing on the part of Father, which I suspect, I'll end up ruining the firm's reputation, thusly any chance to work in Ireland."

After considering the circumstances he laid out before her, she sighed. "Tough call. What can I do to help?"

He straightened. His jaw set in a hard line, his chin

jutted out as the warmth in his eyes cooled. "For starters, you can tell me what in bloody hell is going on here. A man bothering you at the bar, then comes to your home? Did he appear at Bridget's too? Is that what was going on when I called?"

Time to spill it all and see where the pieces land. "I don't know who he is. He knows an awful lot about me. He was disguising his magic signature. I'm sure of it. At the pub, I figured he had too much to drink and was looking to get laid. But when he appeared at my house, I got worried. I should have paid more attention. At least Masked took care of that for me. Now with the info, you've given me about your family—could they have sent him? If they did, why? What did they have to gain? You were gone. I wasn't wearing your ring."

"Not something most men would notice, unless…he was looking for it. Sent to look for it." He slapped his hand on the table. "Confirmation."

She paused and tapped her finger to her lips. "Funny thing, he mentioned I wore no ring when I told him I was engaged. Just to get him off my back. Looking back, maybe he was sent to verify your story?" She shrugged. "Maybe I'm way off base. Or maybe I blew your gambit."

Dillon's face flushed. The muscle in his tight jaw twitched as the vein in his temple pulsed. "Sounds like something my father would do. We need to find out for sure. If so, there is only one way to play this."

She arched an eyebrow. "How?" Their luck ran out. The puppy yipped and scratched at the box. *After I take her out again, gotta get her into the crate.*

Chapter 8

Return to Scotland a Little Wiser

Reluctantly leaving Gale's flat, he ported to Scotland and arrived before dawn, stalking the halls of the family firm. Finding no one there, he made his way into his father's office, rifled through his desk, checked behind the books hiding the safe. He found the old safe had been replaced with a new state-of-the-art safe. Magic wards were in place where there were none previously. He had no trouble breaking the magic. This was a mortal firm. Why the magic now? His grandfather and father had always said the antique safe added to the charm of the old building. Clearly, something had changed.

Maybe it happened with the rest of the upgrades he'd noticed when arriving. He needed the combination. Nothing else unusual stood out, so he returned to his office, his footsteps echoing on the hardwood hallway floors. The carpeting in the offices drowned out the conversations of the client and solicitor. He pushed open the door to his office and back-pedaled a few steps. "What are you doing here?"

"I could ask you the same thing."

"It's my office." Swallowing the lump in his throat, he willed his heartbeat to return to normal. He whipped the pictures out of his briefcase and tossed them at his brother. "Not sure how you're going to introduce these into court. But your client is innocent. It was self-defense."

Royce sifted through the pictures, made a groaning sound, paused, and loosened his tie, then stared at his brother opened-mouthed. "Where'd you get these?"

"Anonymous source." He eased into his high back leather chair.

"Like hell." His brother reached over the desk and grabbed Dillon by his colorful tie, yanked him out of the chair. "Now I'm going to ask you one more—"

"Boys, boys, what is going on in here?" Patrice stood in the doorway in her wrinkle-free white linen suit, a Cheshire cat's grin curved her lips. "Fighting already this morning?" Sashaying across the floor, she leaned over and peered at the photos spread across the desk.

She made a clicking sound with her tongue. With one long hot-pink painted fingernail, she moved the pictures around. "Looks like your case just got a lot more interesting. Trial starts tomorrow?"

"No shit. Do you even know what you're looking at?" Royce snatched up the pictures and shoved them into the case file.

"Afraid so." She took a folded newspaper out of her purse and slapped it down on the desk. The paper flopped open. "Father gets a look at this, and he's going to be furious."

On the front page of the gossip paper was the picture of Cork kissing him. The caption read Prodigal Scot Returns. "Reconnected with your old flame, huh?" His sister pulled out lipstick, brushed it over her lips, and glanced at him. "Your lass isn't going to like it."

"Already dealt with." He slowly walked around his desk, closed the office door, and turned to face his siblings. His voice deadly calm. "What do you two know about Father having me followed?"

Royce's face turned bright red all the way to the tips of his ears. "He wanted to make sure you were telling the truth about ending your relationship with the Irish woman."

Patrice stared at her manicure. "Didn't think he'd really go through with it. Told him not to, it'd piss you off. But…" She pointed at the picture. "Guess he didn't listen. Backfired on him, I'd say."

In a flurry of activity, Royce took the pictures out of his brief case and set flame to them. "No proof."

"Sorry to burst your bubble, bro, but the pictures have been sent to the Council, anonymously of course, with the case number on them. I kept a copy. Let me tell you how this shit is going to go down. I'm going to take the case to trial claiming I'm doing it for a friend."

Royce's face turned from scarlet to eggplant as he puffed out his cheeks.

"I'll use the pictures. No mention of this case will be made to anyone in this firm, especially Father. I want him to come to me. Understood? When I'm finished, the case will disappear. When another one appears, I want to know. What I've said doesn't leave this room. Understood?"

Both nodded their heads. Royce headed to the door first, yanked it open, and stomped out without a word. Ashes of the burned pictures followed him, then fluttered to the floor.

When Patrice went to leave, he called her back. "We need to talk."

"Kinda figured you'd say that. What can I do for you, baby brother?" She smiled up at him.

"Stop calling me that for one." He motioned to the chair in front of his desk, closed the door again, then took a seat. "What do you know about Father sending someone to Ireland to spy on Gale?"

She sat, crossed her left leg over her right, and bounced her left leg while she examined her perfectly manicured nails. "Well, I was passing by Father's door, it was open a crack, which is unusual these days, and overheard him bellowing, how long have you been in Ireland? Then he paused for a moment and began again. 'She's one little witch. Track her down.' This conversation was with someone on the phone. Probably could have heard him even if the door was closed. Then he concluded with 'Seduce her. You do know how to do that?' Afterward, he slammed the phone down and cursed.

"Could have been for a case?" He cocked an eyebrow.

"Not bloody likely. Like you, he's not on the Roll of Solicitors in Ireland."

"Why didn't you tell me this when I arrived?" Eyes narrowed, he tented his fingers on the desk in front of him.

"Figured you were pissed enough. Didn't want you spoiling Mother's little celebration for you. She's an innocent in all this, you know."

"No, I don't know. She's as guilty as he is for allowing him to do this. Grandfather... Never mind."

"What. What about Grandfather? Have you talked to him?" She stopped fidgeting and stared at him. "She couldn't stop him, and you know it. He wants you home

85

and without the witch." She bit her lip. "What's the deal with Gale? What did she ever do to the Dunlops?"

"She's more power in her little finger than the whole damn Dunlop family. Father doesn't like it." Pride swelled inside him at the thought of his witch. "If Father knew the secret Grandmother unearthed, he'd blow a gasket."

"What secret?" His sister's eyes flew open wide.

"Not at liberty to discuss it. At first I wasn't sure Gale knew, but—pretty sure she is aware."

Patrice snorted. "So the relationship isn't over. What kind of game are you playing? He'll ruin you if he finds out."

"Not if I...Is there anything else I should know?" He pushed up from his chair and stood at the window watching the storm clouds gather. *They were in for a blow tonight.*

"Depends. Are you going to let me in on your plans?"

"Not yet. I need you to go about your business as usual." He pointed at her. "You're a terrible liar."

"Only personally. Professionally I can skirt the truth with the best of them." She buffed her nails on her blouse.

A slight smile tugged at the corner of his mouth. "Aye, bet you can. Want to second chair the trial with me?"

She picked up her purse off the floor and pawed through it. "What about Royce? He'll be furious."

"Already is. He can't pull this off. I have no intention of giving up my source for these pictures regardless of any threats the council makes."

"What do you have on—" She waved her hand in

dismissal, then stared intently at him. "—I don't want to know, do I?"

"Probably not. At least not now."

"Sure. I'll assist you with the trial. But I've got a caseload of my own this week to juggle."

"Schedule them with Royce. Then come back here and we'll get to work. I'm betting the trial will take less than a day."

****

Two days later, Dillon and Patrice strode out of the Council of Magic office with their client. All charges were dismissed.

Dillon shook hands with his client. "Get out of here and lie low. Disappear for a while. Take a vacation. Someone on that council is dirty. They're going to be gunning for you now."

"My family and I are leaving the country this afternoon. Booked a flight under my wife's sister's name, like you suggested. No magic trail. What about you?"

"We've got it handled." He smiled. *Nothing could be further from the truth.*

Patrice grinned at him. "Shall we return to the firm and watch the fireworks?"

"Nope. Make him chase us down. I'm going back to the hotel." He climbed into the back seat. "Can we drop you off somewhere?"

"No. Boyfriend lives around the corner. I'll spend the weekend with him."

"You sure? No use subjecting someone else to Father's ire." He winked at her.

"Jeff can hold his own. Father doesn't like him either. Which is probably one of the reasons we've been together so long. Four years this summer." She snickered and closed the vehicle door. Waving to Ian, she traversed the street against the light.

That's a record. Didn't even know she was with someone. "Drop me at the hotel, Ian, then disappear until Monday morning." He raised the divider, took out his phone, and tapped in Gale's number. She answered on the first ring.

"Hullo, handsome." Gale's cheerful lilting voice raised his mood exponentially.

He relaxed against the back of the seat. "Have you heard from our contact?"

"Aye. You're not going to like it. Only rumblings of a deal. Probably discuss it face to face. The contact has gone on a planned holiday and assignment."

"Good. Did you talk to Erin?"

"Aye. She's happy to help."

He rubbed his hands together. "Fantastic. I'll see you soon." Ending the call, he closed his eyes and leaned his head back against the cool, leather seat. Raindrops pattered on the roof of the vehicle. His brolly rolled across the seat and onto the floor. He picked it up as the vehicle slowed to a stop. Ian hopped out, unfurled his brolly, and opened the door.

When his chauffeur offered the umbrella, he shook his head. "Have my own. But thanks. See you Monday." He pushed the lever, and the navy blue brolly popped open. Sprinting into the hotel, he paused to wave at Ian as the car pulled away from the curb.

****

Gale flipped the closed sign around in the window and locked the store. "Come on, Trouble, let's take a walk." She didn't feel like going home and glanced at the sky. The gray clouds and drizzle of the day had given away to a clear sky and pleasant evening. Besides, Cori was playing at the pub tonight. *It would be fun to hear and watch her play and dance. The woman was talented. If Dillon showed tonight, he'd have to find her.* She scribbled a short note and left it on the kitchen table.

Her cell phone played a merry tune. "Hullo."

"Hey, Gale, why don't you and the pup come by the pub? Storm is in her play yard out behind the establishment. I'm sure she'd like some company. A night out wouldn't hurt you either." The cheerful sounds of the pub nearly drowned out Synn's voice.

"Funny you called. I was thinking the same thing, only I was going to leave Trouble in her crate."

"You named that sweet pup—Trouble. Shame on you." Synn snickered.

"She earned it fair and square. That dog is into everything. All my wooden chair legs in the flat have been altered with puppy teeth. She likes those better than her chewies. I keep her crated in the shop when I can't watch her. Heaven only knows what she'd get into there. Great idea. Get Gale a puppy."

"Aww, you know you love the little creature."

She glanced down at the pup that now walked almost properly on a leash and sighed. "I do. She's a great companion when she isn't tearing, chewing, and generally causing chaos." Stopping, she reached down and scratched Trouble behind the ears and under her chin.

"Great. See you soon." Synn ended the call.

A night out with toe-tapping music, friends, and a pint or two sounded wonderful. Besides playing with

Storm, Trouble would be all worn out and might sleep through the night. *A win-win in my book*. All this cloak and dagger business had her on edge. Knowing only part of the situation bothered her. If the truth be known, Gale was a bit jealous of Dillon's and Cork's relationship and the trust they had in each other. But she had to believe Dillon knew what he was doing. She'd tried to wheedle a bit of information out of Cork, but the woman was as tight-lipped as Dillon.

Cork assured her the less she knew the better. The sky was a fiery blaze of orange, yellow, magenta against a dusky sky as she shrugged into her jacket. When had it gotten so late? Hurrying along the deserted sidewalks, she pulled her jacket closer around her. When the pub came into view, she relaxed a bit and slowed her pace. "We're almost there," she crooned to the pup.

The bright lights appeared out the establishment's windows and pooled in puddles of yellow on the street. The heavy wooden door *creaked* open. Laughter, voices, and music spilled out into the night as someone exited the pub. Increasing her steps to cross the alley beside the pub, an arm snaked out and caught her around the waist. She squealed, felt the sliver gauntlets slide up her forearms as she whirled around and came face to face with the stranger who'd been stalking her.

Trouble growled and barked, then yipped as the man kicked the pup with his foot. The pup went end over end. Screaming, she stomped the heel of her shoe into his foot, slammed the heel of her hand up hard against his nose. Blood spurted all over her new blouse and streamed down his face. She cursed. He bellowed releasing his hold.

She twisted to shove an elbow into his solar plexus, knocking the air out of him. To her chagrin, magic took over and sparks shot from her palm as she shoved hard against his chest. He howled and grabbed at his smoldering shirt. She used the opportunity to kick him hard between the legs. He cursed, pushing her as he crumpled forward. She stepped out of range and shoved her foot against his arse. He sprawled face first onto the ground.

Panicked she scanned the area for mortals, then located Trouble cowering at the side of the building. She scooped up the shivering pup and ran for the entrance of the pub. Suddenly, she stopped short to make sure the gauntlets had disappeared. Luckily, no sword hung in the air as it had with Synn. That particular piece of DNA didn't seem to be part of her birthright. Just recently she had learned that her lineage also included the ancient guardians as Synn's had.

A revelation that both thrilled and worried her since she previously witnessed Synn's learning curve to control the Fae magic. Coupled with her witch powers and her temper, the Fae magic could be uncontrollable under the right conditions. She could only hope those conditions didn't occur until she had a chance to confer with Tristian.

Since the supposed breakup with Dillon, her ordinary world had spiraled out of control. Further contemplation came to an abrupt halt as the pub door swung open, she sidestepped the two burly men rushing out.

"You okay, lass?"

Brushing her hair from her face, she recognized Finn, husband to Sara who frequented Pixie Magic.

"Aye." She pointed to the man curled in a fetal position cursing in the entrance of the alley as he attempted to get to his feet and limp off. "He jumped out of the alley and grabbed me. He kicked my pup." Trouble buried her face against Gale's chest, and she rubbed her reassuringly.

The other guy thundered down the street after the stalker. But again the man appeared to disappear into thin air.

Finn asked, "Do you know him?"

"No. He's been stalking me. Showed up at the pub a while back, then at my house. But he's not been around recently. Until tonight."

Finn held the door open for her. Once inside, she started across the floor only to have Bridget catch her hand. "Hey, you're bleeding. What happened?"

She glanced down at her hand, blood was smeared on the palm of her hand and dripping down her wrist and filled Synn in. "Not me blood."

Synn ducked under the pass-through and took the pup. "I'll take her out to play with Storm so she'll forget the whole incident."

"No. I want to check her over first."

Synn held the wriggling pup up in the light so she could run her hands over the furry body and check her face, paws, and body. "See she's fine. You on the other hand—" Synn slid a glance to Bridget.

Assured Trouble was unhurt, Gale allowed her friend to tug her down the hall into the ladies' room and run cold water over her hand, turn it over, and rinse the backside. Once satisfied she was telling the truth, Bridget stared at her and asked again, "What in bloody hell happened?"

She managed a wane smile. "You should see the other guy."

Bridget frowned and planted her hands on her hips. "Quit avoiding the question. Spit it out."

Leaning against the wall, she glanced in the mirror and understood why everyone was so concerned. Her new blouse was torn, the hem of her skirt was ripped where she'd caught her shoe in it when she'd stomped on his foot. She sighed. "Remember the guy that's been popping up here and there asking for a date? He jumped out of the alley and grabbed me around the waist. He scared me and kicked Trouble. I used a few self-defense moves we learned in the class last year. Came in real handy." She frowned. "Then the magic tried to help out. I curtailed it before any mortals were privy to the tiny display. Your bouncers took off after someone. I assume they did their job. Or magic is the way of it which would stymie them at every turn."

"Hadn't considered that. Still, we need to call the police or Tristian? Is he magic folk?" Bridget tilted her head to the side.

"Aye. But don't call anyone. I'll get a hold of Dillon." As soon as his name was out of her mouth she regretted it. Bridget was like a dog with a bone, her friend wouldn't let this go. After spending most of the last week or so dodging Bridget's questions, now she just blurted out his name.

"So you two are back together. I knew it," Bridget said smugly.

Trying to stem the onslaught of questions, she whispered, "Not necessarily, you've got to keep this between us. Can't even tell Quinn. Otherwise, there could be dire consequences." She took hold of

Bridget's arm and squeezed. "Promise me."

"Aye. Now let go. You're cutting off the circulation." Bridget twisted her arm.

She released her friend and finished washing the blood off her hands. Not much she could do about the torn clothing now that everyone had seen. She'd fix it later a home with magic. "Sorry. I mean it. When it's all over, I'll explain everything. But I can't right now."

"Promise. I'm worried about you."

"I promise. Could use a pint." She strode out the bathroom door and through the crowd toward the bar.

Bridget hurried ahead of her. "It's on the house."

Her friend pulled a pint and set it down in front of her. She took a long draw from the glass. "Mmmm…that hits the spot." She licked the froth from her upper lip and glanced up at Bridget wondering at the wide grin on her face. She turned around in her seat. Dillon held the door to the pub open as he sauntered inside.

Her heart thundered in her chest as her stomach did flips. Relief flooded through her at the same time anxiety knotted her stomach. Unsure as to what had brought him here, when their planned meeting wasn't until next week, she waited for his approach, staring down at her naked hand holding her pint. *Are we continuing the ruse or…*

He came up behind her and turned her to face him. "What the hell happened to you?"

"Altercation with a stalker. I should charge him for the replacement of my blouse and skirt." She fingered the tear in her blouse and glanced down at her skirt glad she'd gotten cleaned up before Dillon appeared. "I handled it."

"So that's what I felt. But you shouldn't have to handle it. I should have been here."

"Don't be ridiculous. I was just outside the pub. Finn and his friend came to my rescue and chased the guy down. Don't know what happened afterward. I came inside."

"All right. I'll drop it, but…"

She put her finger softly against his lips. "Don't spoil the night. I'm fine. You're here now. Let's enjoy ourselves. Please."

He wrapped his arms around her waist and nuzzled into her neck with a lingering kiss. "I missed you."

"Me too. What happened to keeping the secret?" she hissed.

"Change of plans. I'll be spending the weekend in Ireland." He raised a hand signaling Gavin. "A pint please." He slapped euros onto the bar. "Keep 'em coming. We're celebrating."

Gavin grinned. "It's about time you came to your senses, boyo." He pulled a pint and slid it down the bar. The mug slowed to a stop in front of Dillon. The dark liquid sloshed from side to side as foam dripped from the rim of the glass to the bar.

Chapter 9

Relaxing in Ireland a Calm Before the Storm Hits

She watched him take a long draw of his pint. He stood and held his hand out to her. "Dance with me?"

Her heart all aflutter and butterflies danced in her belly like when he first asked her out. She took his hand. He whirled her out onto the dance floor. At some kind of signal from Dillon, Quinn grinned at Cori who started an old-fashioned Irish jig. Dancing across the floor as her cousin played, Dillon challenged her to a step dance competition.

She answered his steps and added more difficult ones. He matched her step for step at first. She nodded then winked at Cori who increased the beat. By the end of the third song, Dillon raised his hands in surrender.

"You win. Danced me under the table you did." He snatched her hand and cut through the crowd to the bar. Grabbed his pint and downed it. Wiping his mouth with the back of his hand, he blew out a breath. "You may be able to outdance me, but you can't outdrink me."

She narrowed her eyes and a sly smile curved the corners of her lips. "Wanta bet?"

He grinned. "So is it a wager, then?"

Gavin slid another pint down the bar to Dillon. He grabbed the icy handle and took another long swig.

Still a bit winded, she took a couple of sips from

her stout and eyed him. "What's gotten into you?"

"The surprise and fear I felt from you earlier tonight had me tied in knots. Been one hell of a day and I couldn't get here soon enough." He took another chug of his beer. "Where's your pup? Leave her home alone in her crate?"

"No, she's out back playing with Storm. FYI, I can handle myself." She took a long swig of her beer and wiped a bit of foam off the tip of his nose. "What about your family?"

He downed the rest of his beer and looked to Gavin for another. "Sis and I decided to disappear for the weekend. Father is going to be furious. Don't know where Royce is hiding out and don't care. Ma is probably playing the peacemaker. Aiden has been on holiday since I got back. He's in for a surprise next week."

Gavin's eyebrow winged up in question, but he slid another stout down the bar. The mug came to stop in front of him without a slosh. He picked it up and guzzled half.

"What did you do?" she asked hesitantly. "Wait." She caught his hand, led him down the hall to the office, and closed the door behind him. "Less likely to be overheard in here."

Backing her against the wall, he took her in his arms and kissed her deeply. His hand caressed her body with feather-light touches that sent desire and lust careening through her nether regions. "Dillon, not here. Someone could walk in on us. Rein it in. We'll go back to my flat later."

"Aye, we can. I intend to do exactly that. Won't be near as much fun as the thrill of possibly getting caught." He brushed his lips over hers, taunting, teasing, then tugged her blouse out of her skirt and skimmed his hand over her thin lacy bra. His breathing increased as he trailed kisses down her neck, across to her cleavage teasing his tongue along the soft crease. Against her better judgment, she leaned her head back giving him better access, not caring they could get caught. All she wanted was him. He licked farther down, then lifted his head, caught, and held her dreamy gaze. "See what I mean? Doesn't really matter." His voice was a seductive rumble and she loved it.

Footsteps sounded on the hardwood floor of the hallway. She sighed, wishing they'd locked the door as he pulled away a wicked grin on his face. Quickly, she straightened and tucked her blouse into her skirt, fingering the tear at her shoulder for a moment before the door handle turned.

Katie barged in. "Oh, sorry. Didn't know anyone was in here." The skin crinkled around the woman's eyes as they sparkled knowingly. "Should lock the door if you don't want to be disturbed." Katie snickered, then picked up a tablet from the desk, turned on her heel, and flounced out of the room.

She peered at Dillon, and they burst out laughing. "What are we, horny teenagers?"

"Would appear so." He took her hand and kissed it. "We'll continue this later."

Her legs felt like wet noodles, the rest of her body was screaming for more, but she ignored it all. "The reason we came into the office is so you can tell me what happened without being overheard."

"I liked what we were doing better." Attempting to straighten his tie, he cursed and yanked it off, stuffing it in his coat pocket. He unbuttoned the first three buttons on his shirt. "It's warm in here."

"If you don't stop, I'll lock the door and have me way with you." She giggled and ran a finger down his bare upper chest and unbuttoned the next one.

He caught her hands. "Darling Gale, don't you want to know what happened, or shall we port directly to your bedroom? I'm good either way."

After a couple of beats, she smiled. "Bedroom." She slithered against him, breathing a kiss at the pulsing hollow at his throat. Her breast crushed against his chest as she ground against his arousal. Easing back, she whispered against his lips, "Only kidding, tell me what happened."

"Tease. Gonna cost you." His mouth covered hers hungrily, more demanding, sending spirals of ecstasy through her. Raising his mouth from hers, he gazed into her eyes. "Two can play that game." His hand cupped her breast. "Now what will it be?" Seduction rumbled deep in his throat. "Shall we lock the door?"

She eyed the door, then blew out a breath. *He's right. The danger of getting caught upped the excitement.* "You did that on purpose."

"Of course." He held her against him, his hands fondling her arse. "As you did to me. May I suggest we get the business out of the way, so we can enjoy each other the remainder of the night? I assure you, it will be worth the wait."

"I suppose." Her lower lip stuck out in a pout.

He kissed her lip, drawing it into his mouth, then released it with a little nip and sighed. "I took the case away from Royce. He was prepared to let our client take the fall. I suspect on Father's orders. Patrice and I did a substitution, then appeared for the client. Though he was reluctant at first, we put him on the stand. O'Sullivan didn't want to tell the truth and was willing to take the fall."

He shook his head. "Not sure what's going on. But when I reminded him he could face being spellbound for life or worse, he agreed to tell the truth. When I introduced the pictures, several of the council members' eyes went wide at the same time. You should have been there to see it." He chuckled. "I'd already provided copies to the head of the council and the prosecution. When I entered the photos into evidence to support our client's testimony—" He shrugged. "—wasn't much else to do. Oh, the council insisted I present the person who took the pictures. I refused, citing that person was part of my legal team and was covered by client privilege. They didn't buy it. Threatened me and my license. I didn't give an inch because the pictures told the whole story. They had no one to refute our client's story."

"In other words, you blindsided them." She snickered. "I love it."

He slung his arm around her shoulder, leaned in, and kissed her cheek, then brushed his lips over hers. "Sort of, but I did it by the book." Crossing the floor, he opened the door. "That's it. I need a drink."

"You've probably had enough. How about coffee and a bit of food instead?" She followed him down the hall and back into the pub. "What happens now?"

"We wait. There is something nefarious going on at the firm. Our one-hundred-year-old stellar reputation is going to take a big hit if I can't get to the bottom of it and repair the damage. Royce is no help or is in cahoots with Father. Aiden is an unknown at this moment." Before he could wave at Gavin, two pints slid down the bar to them. He grabbed the first mug and nearly drained it. Turning the glass around in his hand, he traced the frosty handle with his thumb. "Ahhh…that's great. But the lady here seems to think I need some coffee and a bite to eat." He took another drink.

"Aye, wise woman." Gavin took a mug from under the bar and filled it with steaming coffee.

She took the second glass and sipped. "Are you going back tonight?"

He took a drink of the coffee and nibbled at the brown bread Synn set in front of him. "Hell, no. I'm spending the night with my arms wrapped around your naked body. Pleasuring us both. Tomorrow? Maybe the same." He slid a seductive look in her direction. "Unless you object."

"No objections here." She leaned over and breathed a kiss below his ear. He let out a low moan.

Taking another swig of the coffee, he popped the rest of the bread in his mouth. "We need to get out of here." He jerked his chin toward two men sitting at a table behind them. "Paying a bit too much attention to us." He pushed up from the bar, waved Gavin over, and paid the tab.

Gavin glanced from Gale to Dillon and shoved the currency back Dillon. "On the house after what happened to her tonight." His gaze traveled to the rip in her blouse. "Too bad about that."

"Yeah, it was new. Not your fault." She eased up to stand beside Dillon.

"Ya staying around?" Gavin clapped his hand on Dillon's shoulder. "Tristian and Hannah will be here tomorrow night and Sunday. Ma's cooking up a big feast on Sunday."

Tim and Mary wandered over to stand beside Gavin. "We'd love to have you both join us for Sunday dinner." Mary put a hand over Gale's arm. "How about it?"

"I'll be there. Dillon may have to return…"

"Nope. I'm staying all weekend. We'll be glad to come. Thanks for the invitation. I'd like to talk to Tristian anyway."

Mary slapped her hand on the bar. "Tristian is coming to relax. No work complications or discussions."

Dillon raised his hands in surrender and smiled. "Understood."

She covered a wide yawn with her hand. "I think me day has caught up." Then she glanced at Dillon who nodded. "We're going to take off for the cottage. See you on Sunday. Early afternoon all right?"

"Aye. Tristian and Hannah will be arriving late morning." Mary grinned.

"What can we bring?" Gale asked.

"Your homemade lemon bars. Everyone loves 'em. I can't seem to get mine to be the flaky consistency of yours. Even using your recipe." Mary wiped her hands on her apron, then reached around back and untied it.

"It's me grandmother's recipe. Has a bit of Fae magic in it," she whispered.

"I figured it was something like that. Now off with you two. Get some rest." A twinkle sparked in Mary's cornflower blue eyes. "Or whatever you have planned."

Gale's cheeks heated as Dillon's seductive snicker rose. They slipped through the kitchen, waved at Tim as they exited the back door, stopped to pick up a sleeping Trouble, and ported to her flat above Pixie Magic.

Inside, she slipped the still sleeping pup into her crate with food and water and locked the latch with fingers crossed the wee creature would sleep the rest of the night.

He crept up behind her and turned her to face him. With his arms wrapped around her crushing her, he pressed his lips to hers hungrily. "Finally."

"Worth the wait. Remember?" she murmured against his lips returning his kiss with reckless abandon. Blood pounded in her brain as her pulse quickened, her breathing increased to match his, and her knees began to tremble. With a flick of her wrist, they were naked. Clothes neatly folded on a nearby chair.

He raised an eyebrow as a seductive smile curved his full delectable lips. "Two can play that game, lass." A wave of his arm and they were floating above her bed. The sensation was so surreal, she studied the bed from above as he lowered them onto the soft comforter. "Much better, don't you agree?" His hands began an arousing exploration of her soft curves. Caressing the inside of her thigh, he traced a sensuous path between her legs. She moaned as he teased her legs farther apart and stroked her, thrusting a finger, then two inside her. His arousal was hard against her side as he lowered his head, and his tongue explored her nipples that firmed under his touch.

"That's enough. I want you now."

"A bit demanding, aren't you?" He snickered. "Can be arranged. But first…" He slid down her body, spread her legs wider with his broad shoulders, and let his warm breath waft over her intimate parts. His tongue swirled and teased. She writhed beneath him, her fingers tangled in his hair, holding him in place as she moaned. "Oh, Dillon. Please take me—Now."

A seductive smile curved his lips as he continued his ministrations, bringing her to climax before lifting his head and sliding up her body until he was seated against her opening. His gaze locked on hers, he slowly pushed inside until he filled her, then paused. "Is this what you had in mind?"

"Oh, aye." Her breath came in pants as she arched up to meet him, then moved with him. Together they found the tempo that excited their bodies, soaring higher until the peak of ecstasy had her clutching his backside with her fingers and screaming out his name. He followed her over the edge of pleasure with a deep groan.

Stars burst high overhead, leaving colorful streamers slowly fading. Tied to her feeling of ecstasy, her magic never left any doubt. Spent, she lay sprawled across him, her curves molding to the contours of his muscular body. She'd missed the intimacy of their lovemaking. His breath was warm and moist against her face as he leaned in to brush a kiss against her lips, then rolled over to the side. He pulled her against him in a cozy spoon position. His arms wrapped around her as she drifted off to sleep.

Thoughts of what lay ahead of them invaded her dreams. Not enough information to form a conclusion, the details and Scotland spun in her mind until she awoke disoriented and frustrated. Soft snores in the dark reminded her she was not alone. She rolled over to see his peaceful expression, even breathing, and his body in a relaxed state. Far from the condition he'd tried to hide all evening.

Mary will be upset, but I've got to talk to Tristian… we've got to talk to Tristian. Walking blindly into whatever was going on at Dillon's firm was irresponsible and foolhardy. *He can't do this alone.* No matter how hard she tried, the questions kept circling. *Did his father really send someone here to stalk and seduce me? Why?* It was suddenly crystal clear to her that his father didn't believe their relationship was over. *What lengths would he go to ensure that outcome?* Beads of sweat formed at her brow, then trickled down her temple.

Would he dispose of me to force Dillon to do his bidding? She swept a hand across her forehead to wipe away the moisture as her heartbeat increased and fear reared its ugly head. Taking several small breaths, she calmed herself. Masked hooted quietly in the tree outside her window. A whine and a yip sounded from the living room, alerting her to the fact that Trouble was no longer asleep in her crate.

Slipping quietly out of bed, she shrugged into her robe and padded downstairs. "What's a matter, girl? Need to go outside?" she crooned to the puppy while unlocking the latch. Quickly, she clipped the leash on the pup's harness, and they sprinted to the door. Once outside, Trouble immediately did her business, then bowed down on her front paws, her rear end wiggling in the air, and yipped.

"Shhhh…it's the wee hours of the morning. Can't we just go back to bed until the sun comes up?"

The pup cocked its head, wiggled its ears back and forth, then yipped again. Trouble pounced on a toy, left in the yard from the day before, squeaking it continually. She grabbed the toy and tossed it several times until the pup quieted down. "Time for breakfast." She trudged up the stairs to her flat, the puppy scampering along ahead of her. Inside, she washed and rinsed the bowls from the night before and filled them with fresh water and kibble. Bolted the bowls in the crate and tossed a treat inside to tempt the pup to voluntarily enter her crate. Fingers crossed the pup would sleep a few more hours, she padded upstairs and fell into bed.

She must have dozed off, because the next time she opened her eyes, the sun streamed in the bedroom window highlighting the auburn streaks in Dillon's tousled sable hair. His sculptured facial features reminded her of the handsome Highlander rogues that no doubt existed in his family tree. She listened for the pup. When no sound filtered upstairs, she touched Dillon's cheek, and his stunning deep blue eyes rimmed with thick, dark lashes, the envy of any woman, blinked open. His luscious full lips curved up in a devilish smile, easing her trepidation. A talent he'd possessed since she'd first laid eyes on him.

He reached over and gently caressed the little creases between her eyebrows. "What's got you frowning so early this morn, *Mo Ghràidh*"

She loved the Gaelic endearment meaning "my eternal love" as the words rolled off his tongue in Scottish brogue. "Nothing. Rough night." She took his fingers and kissed them before letting him wrap his arms around her again. "I like watching you sleep. You seem so at peace. Rather than carrying the weight of the world on your shoulders as you were when you walked into the pub."

"Not fair. I was worried about you."

"Maybe. But that's not the only reason. I see the trouble in your eyes and feel the turmoil in your heart. Have you so soon forgotten Fae blood pulses through my veins as well as the telltale witch's magic?"

"I'd never make that mistake. Your Aunt Erin taught me the ways of your family. Not looking forward to facing her again under these circumstances." He sighed heavily. "What are the chances I get tangled up with a Fae/Witch married to Tiarnan King of Faeries either?"

"Luck of the draw." She laughed. "Once we explain everything. We need to do that soon. They will understand. It's not like they've never faced family tyranny at its worse. Whose father banishes his only daughter to the Sidhe of her Faerie lover never to allow her to see sunlight or feel it on her face again?"

"True. But at least they knew what they were up against."

"For centuries. And no control over fixing it." She crossed her arms across her chest.

"I see your point. How about we get up, fix a quick breakfast, and take a walk along the cliffs? The pup will like that."

"Make her easier to manage at the shop too." She glanced at the clock on the wall. "It'll have to be a quick walk. I need to open Pixie Magic in a couple of hours."

"Can't you take the day off?" He reached for her, his hand slipping between her legs, fingers teasing, stroking. "I'll make it worth your while." He waggled his eyebrows.

"No. My customers depend on me." Despite her

words, her legs spread, allowing his ministrations. She closed her eyes. Suddenly, she was whisked out of bed in his arms, his fingers still teasing, thrusting, arousing. She squealed, wrapped her arms around his neck, and kissed him softly.

With a wicked gleam in his eyes, he grinned. "Time to shower." His low seductive rumble echoed as he carried her into the bathroom, lowered her feet, and pressed her against the tile wall. She lifted her legs and wrapped them around his waist, allowing his hard length to slip inside. "I've missed you."

"I can tell. I've missed you too."

****

His handsome, sculpted face was framed by a fall of wavy sable hair still damp from the shower. Droplets of water glinted in the sunshine streaming through the curtains on his muscles that rippled as he gingerly picked up the jeans folded in the corner of the bedroom from the night before. *Goddess, he was gorgeous and knew how to use that sexy body to satisfy a woman in every way imaginable.* A shiver of desire shot up her spine. It had always been that way between them.

"Now, you've made me late." She pursed her lips. "I need to do inventory, order supplies, and make up the lotions and things my customers may need while Erin is running the store." Naked, she watched him pick through his clothes with a look of disdain on his face. Her lips twitched. "There are still a few pairs of your jeans and shirts hanging in the closet. I haven't had time to throw them out."

"So you weren't ready to toss me aside just yet." He grinned.

She raised an eyebrow and stared at him. "Not had

time. As far as tossing you out, that's still pending." She slowly wiggled into red lace panties and matching bra before slipping into a brightly colored broomstick skirt and pastel pink blouse with flowers embroidered around the neck. Light blue sandals completed her outfit. She twirled around in front of the full-length mirror loving the way the skirt moved. Glancing at her reflection, she caught his predatory gaze locked on her from the doorway of the closet, a look of male appreciation glittered in his eyes.

Her heart warmed. Actions meant a whole lot more to her than words. His expression said it all. Desire continued to simmer deep inside her. She glanced at the clock and sighed, braiding her hair, then flipping it over her shoulder. "Like what you see, boyo?

"I liked what you had on before. You know if you didn't have panties on, we could…"

She tossed her hairbrush at him. "Make me later than I am already."

He dodged the brush and smirked. "But it'd be worth it. I guarantee satisfaction." Waggling his eyebrows, he took a step out of the closet, wobbled on one leg tugging on a pair of black jeans, then pulled on a gray and red striped polo. As his head popped out of the shirt, he smirked. "I left several of my favorites here." He paused at her withering glance. "Can I help you in the shop?"

"Sure. You can do the inventory while I mix up the lotions and potions." She turned and peered at him thoughtfully. "What if word gets back to your father you spent the weekend with me?" Padding into the kitchen, she filled the coffee pot with water, poured it into the coffee maker, and set the glass pot on the warmer. The water on the bottom of the pot hissed and popped while she got out the filter and measured the freshly ground coffee beans, inhaling the delicious aroma.

She switched the coffee maker and warmer on before popping blueberry bagels into the toaster, getting down glasses, and filling them with orange juice. Returning to the cupboard, she grabbed travel mugs and set them beside the coffee maker.

He followed her into the kitchen, his boots clicking on her hardwood floor. "I've been mulling that over and deciding how to go at this problem. On one hand, it'd be easier to obtain information at the firm if we continue the ruse. On the other, by having you appear, engagement ring on and by my side, Father may get angry enough to make a misstep I can capitalize on." Picking up the coffee pot, he poured the steaming, rich liquid into mugs and breathed deeply. "Mmmm, that smells delicious." He handed her a mug.

She chewed on her bottom lip before speaking slowly. "In a way, he already has. Do you think he gave the case to your brother knowing Royce would enlist your help?" The bagels popped up. She set the mug down and slathered blueberry cream cheese on the toasted sides, then put them on a plate. Sipping her orange juice, she stared at him over the rim of the glass and considered the situation.

"No, I don't think that was the plan at all. My brother is or at least was Father's yes man. The fact that Royce didn't do his due diligence on the case and had to enlist my help was his screw up. Typical Royce behavior. Father will be furious." He took a bagel from the plate and bit into it. "Which is part of the reason

Patrice and I made ourselves scarce this weekend."

"So he's going to be gunning for you come Monday." She frowned, bit into her bagel, chewed, then finished off the orange juice. When she picked up the steaming mug, she held it warming her hands for a moment.

"Father and Royce both, most likely." He washed the bite down with a swig of coffee and took another. Waving the bagel around in the air, he continued, "Father is a methodical thinker. The only way you can get ahead of him is to catch him off balance. His temper has always been a weakness."

After finishing breakfast, she put the dishes in the sink, ran water over them, and added a squirt of dish soap. He transferred the coffee to the travel mugs topping them off, put the lids on, and jerked his chin toward the back door. "Shall we?"

"Wait, I have to get Trouble out of her crate and leashed up." She sprinted to the pup's crate where she was whining to get out. "I know, little one. But you can't be in the kitchen when we're eating. Not a good way to train you according to Synn." After a couple of tries, she finally got the leash clipped on Trouble's harness and the dog raced to the back door. She slipped on her favorite lavender cable-knit sweater. The weather was warm, but the wind off the ocean would be brisk.

Sunshine warmed her face as they strolled up the path to the cliffs. The breeze heavy with brine tugged a few strands of hair out of her braid, and she tucked them behind her ears. At the overlook they paused, fingers laced together, enjoying the view. They watched Trouble pounce on the flowers and sniff at the path

111

until a look of horror spread over Dillon's face.

Her gaze darted around the landscape. "What's wrong?"

Chapter 10

Encounters of the Royal Kind—Mixing Business with Pleasure Can be A Potent Combination

Gale followed his gaze. A smile curved the corners of her mouth. Erin and Tiarnan stood arm in arm a few yards down the trail. She raised her hand high in an enthusiastic wave. Erin returned the gesture, and the couple began to walk toward her, Dillon, and the pup.

Dillon groaned. "I'd hoped to put this off for a bit longer." He pasted a smile on his face and followed her quick step up the trail.

"Better to get it over with than to stew on it. You've got enough irons in the fire to burn down an entire forest. Besides, they'll understand. Once you explain."

"Provided King Tiarnan doesn't curse me into oblivion before I can explain," Dillon muttered.

With a wicked smile, she said, "'Tis a chance you'll have to take." She walked into Erin's arms enveloped into a hug.

Erin peered down at the wriggling pup sniffing her sandals. "Who have we here?"

Gale rolled her eyes. "Trouble. Synn and the girls decided that I was lonely at the flat and needed a companion and protector." She pointed to the happy ball of fluff tugging at the leash to get to Tiarnan.

Erin laughed. "May be a while before the wee little creature is any good at protecting. But as a companion, I agree." She bent down and rubbed the pup under the chin. Trouble tried to chew on her fingers, but Erin was too quick. "I've heard about puppy teeth."

"Oh, she tried being a protector the other night, but…"

"Do tell." Erin raised an eyebrow.

"That's a tale for another day." Gale jerked her chin toward Dillon and Tiarnan.

"Probably for the best," Erin agreed.

Tiarnan raised an eyebrow, his stare icy as he met Dillon's gaze. "What have you to say for yourself, young man." Tiarnan offered his hand.

Relieved to have a chance to put things right, he shook the hand offered. "I'm not making excuses, sir. A family situation caused me to act irrationally. Instead of confiding in Gale, I gave her an ultimatum without explanation. At least that was my first mistake, and it tumbled downhill at a high rate of speed from there." His shoulders slumped as he stared at the ground.

"I hear tell Bram Dunlop's unfortunate actions have led to him participating in shady deals that could cost your family the firm. 'Tis a shame as hard as your ancestors worked to build its stellar reputation." Tiarnan's brows knitted together as his eyes narrowed. "Not sure our Gale should be mixed up in the situation dropped at her feet."

"That makes two of us." *Should I ask Tiarnan what he's heard? Probably not the path I need to travel right now.* "I'm at a loss as to how to proceed without incurring my father's wrath or destroying the family firm. Not sure who I can trust. Well, that's not entirely true, my sister has always had my back. My mother appears to have left the firm, and any other siblings can't be trusted at this time." He paused a couple of beats. "I shouldn't be burdening you with my problems."

Tiarnan nodded, his lips pressed tight together. Rocking back on his heels, he glanced from Gale to Erin with warmth in his eyes and sighed heavily switching his gaze to Dillon. "'Tis quite a tangle you've got. I'm not burdened by it. You're the one to straighten it all out or go down in flames." The King of Faeries shrugged. "My interest is that my niece not be hurt by you, your actions, or your family. Should that happen, there will be hell to pay." He tented his fingers and continued his icy stare while his facial expression was unreadable.

That was the worst part for Dillon. From an early age, he'd learned to read people, their body language, their facial expressions, and it made him an extremely good solicitor. His grandfather taught him never to lean on magic for his profession. His father had adhered to the same principals—until recently.

"If you involve Gale, how do you intend to protect her?" Tiarnan tapped his tented fingers together impatiently.

"I'm afraid she's already involved. Her assistance led to the acquittal of my client and the release of an innocent. Believe me, I had no other choice." He wiped his sweaty hands on his jeans. *This inquisition is worse than Father's scrutiny when I returned home and the trial I took from Royce.*

A sly grin spread across Tiarnan's features. His eyes glittered as Erin placed a hand on his arm. "That's because it matters. Gale matters. It's a good thing, lad."

"H…how'd… You aren't supposed to be able to… My mind is shielded." Dillon stammered.

A knowing look passed from Gale to Tiarnan. "Well, boyo, you're almost family. You'll soon learn that things in the Faerie world are not always as perceived. Gale will be able to hold her own against your family's powers easily. But your protection is expected should you need and accept her assistance in this endeavor."

Tiarnan shook his head slowly. "I've already given my permission for you to wed my Gale. I'll not take that back, but…" He pointed his finger in Dillon's face. "Have a care with her, or you'll answer to me. And they'll never find the body." The resonance of his voice echoed off the cliff faces and faded into the crashing waves of the ocean below.

Neat trick. Wish I could do that. Might come in handy. He abruptly stopped mid-thought. "Shit."

Tiarnan roared with laughter as he wrapped his arm around Erin. "A Fae talent for which there is no shield. We'll finish our walk, then Erin will join you two at the shop." They turned and began to stroll up the path the way they'd come. Tiarnan whistling a haunting tune. He paused and turned. "You might do well to consult Tristian if dark magic is suspected." The Faerie King continued whistling, and soon Erin's melodic voice accompanied him in the Irish ballad.

Gale glanced at her watch as she picked her way down the path. "Gee, I didn't realize we spent so much time with them. We have a full day at the store before I can leave for any length of time." She turned to him. "Have you figured out about us? Engaged or not?

Remaining here or Scotland?"

"Oh we're official, but I'd like to keep my family guessing for a little while. It should work to our advantage." *I hope.*

She snickered. "If you don't want me reading your mind, you need to stop thinking so loudly."

He frowned and stared at her. "Have you always been able to read my mind? You should have told me."

"Ability, yes. Did I use it? No. Out of respect for our relationship, I let your shield stand. Though I was sorely tempted when you issued the ultimatum and broke our engagement."

"I didn't mean to…Never mind." He shifted from foot to foot uncomfortably. "Is there something I should know about these faerie talents you possess in addition to witch magic?"

"Given your situation, you're probably better off not knowing." Before he could protest, she winked one of her sparkling, emerald eyes at him, tucked the pup under her arm, grasped both of his hands, and ported them to Pixie Magic.

Inside the shop, the sun's rays bounced off the bright crystals hanging in the windows, throwing rainbows around the showroom. The mirrored wall behind the counter gleamed as though Gale had recently polished it. The fragrance of fresh flowers and vanilla wafted in the air. Not so different from Gale's scent and one of the many things he loved about her.

She put Trouble down on the floor and let her scamper off to her crate.

"You know a bit of warning would have been nice." He chuckled, taking the clipboard and pencil she handed him. Flipping through the inventory sheets, he asked, "Where are we starting?"

She winked at him. "The bookshelves and going around the room counterclockwise. The supplies in the back are already accounted for, and we'll move part of them out here so I'm fully stocked in the showroom." She turned and quickly returned to the counter. "I'll fill the orders for lotion and things I have and make extra. So Erin will have plenty on hand. How long will we be gone?"

"I wish I knew." He sighed. "No reason we can't port back here on the weekends." A popular jig played from his pocket. He took out his phone, stared at the screen for a beat or two, then connected the call. "Grandfather, what a surprise."

"Your father was furious when he called here looking for you or Patrice. Claims neither of you can be found. What's going on?"

"An extremely good question. And one I am trying to dig up answers to, but it's not easy when most of the family members are under his thumb. Creating chaos is the only way I can think of to catch him off balance. Do you have any other ideas?"

His grandfather's disapproving voice rang loud and clear. "No, but I thought you'd keep me apprised of the situation. Patrice is safe?"

"As far as I know. We both went off-grid this weekend." Not to be intimidated, he calmly reiterated his intentions. "If you know my plan, the element of surprise in your voice will be missing and Father will pick up on it. Remember you called me in to drain this swamp."

"Aye, that I did. Get to it, boyo. Give our love to that little Irish lass of yours."

"Aye." He rang off neither denying nor confirming his grandfather's fishing expedition. Shoving the phone back in his pocket, he returned to the inventory.

"What was that all about?" Gale paused pouring a creamy lavender liquid from a mixing container into a decorative bottle with a Pixie Magic logo. She popped the cork into the top, tied a purple ribbon around the neck, and turned her attention to him.

"Grandfather let me know Father is looking for me and Sis. So it begins."

He worked silently for the next several hours as he made his way around the room, looking up only when the bells over the door chimed announcing a customer's arrival. Each made their purchases, chatted for a few minutes, then left with bottles of lotion, a few crystals for gifts, dried herbs for potions, and other items. Watching as customers trooped in, he was surprised by the fact that not all her customers were magic folk. Several of the townspeople came to her for remedies, books on gardening, favorite lotions, and advice on their love life.

Children by their parents' sides requested candy from the candy jar on one of the glass shelves on the mirrored wall. While others went to the children's section of books, pulled a favorite book, and plopped down on the floor to read. Still another took a coloring book from the bin beside the bookshelves and a spilled tin of well-worn colors. No wonder she didn't want to leave. This town was her extended family.

Eventually, he crossed the floor and put the clipboard on the glass countertop along with the pen and smiled seductively at her. "I'm finished. How about a reward."

She raised her gaze up to him. Her phone played a merry tune. She picked it up off the counter and glanced at the screen. "Hi ya, Bridge."

There was a pause as she listened intently.

"Aye. He's still here. Sounds like fun. Gotta finish up here, then we'll stop in."

He rubbed his chin with thumb and forefinger. "We going somewhere?"

She snickered and pointed to his chin. "You smeared a black smudge on your chin. Probably from your fingers. Might want to wash your hands. Aye, Quinn's band is playing the pub tonight, and Cori will be joining them. Bridge thought it would be fun for us to pop in. Work for you?" She screwed on the top of the last bottle of lotion. "I have a few bath beads to create, and I'm done."

****

He grabbed the old decoratively twisted brass door handle and jerked the heavy wooden door open. Inhaling deeply, his mouth watered at the yeasty smell of the pub combined with freshly baked bread and lamb stew. He wasn't quite sure what else was on the menu. But it smelled fantastic. His stomach growled loudly.

She turned to peer at him and chuckled. "Sounds like we made it here in the nick of time."

Already up to her ears in customers, Bridge pointed to an empty table in the corner, not far from the stage and bar. "What can I get for you?" She danced her way through the crowd meeting them at the table. "Glad you made it." She looked from Gale to Dillon and back nodding approvingly. "A little time alone did you both a world of good."

"Food, bread, and a pint. Not necessarily in that

order." He grinned but surveyed the room cautiously.

Bridget scribbled on her pad and stuck her pen in her messy bun. "No strangers in the pub tonight. Security tonight will be on the lookout. Doubt that idiot from the other night will show his face around here again. Not after the beating you gave him." She chuckled and flounced off to another table, then to the bar.

The lively jigs and Irish ballads played by Quinn's band had Gale tapping her toes all through dinner.

He popped the last piece of brown bread into his mouth and extended his hand. "May I have this dance?" He gave a formal bow that had her giggling. It felt good to laugh and enjoy the company of friends. This was where he belonged. Not Scotland. Not rubbing elbows with the Scottish elite, his parents' friends, or clients of the firm. He wasn't cut out for that life no matter the outcome of the current situation.

"I never thought you'd ask." She took his hand and whirled into his arms. The band switched to a lively jig with Cori taking lead on the fiddle. How her cousin could play the instrument and bounce never missing a step of the dance nor a note to the tune on her fiddle, she'd never know.

After several fast-paced tunes, Quinn slowed it down with a favorite ballad, then put the mic back in the stand. "Thanks, everyone! We're going to take a short break. Be back in a bit."

Quinn stole a kiss from Bridget as he made his way to Gale and Dillon's table. "Whew, rowdy crowd tonight." Quinn wiped his brow and shifted his gaze to Gale. "Dillon almost danced you under the table. Fun watching you two compete with each other on the dance floor." He slapped Dillon on the back. "Good try, boyo."

He shrugged. "Did my best, but she's phenomenal."

"Aye, she is. Only people to outdance her years ago were Mary and Brandy. Even then it was close. But our own Cori does a good job of the dance." Quinn stole a chair from another table, swung a leg over the back, and straddled it. "So what's the story? Get things straightened out between you?" His friend eyed him. "You staying this time?"

"Wish I could. Family matters are demanding my attention and time in Scotland. Only this time Gale is accompanying me. Between the two of us, we should get things settled. Then I hope to be back permanently."

Bridget crossed purposely to the table and set down another round of drinks. Quinn snatched a pint and downed nearly all of it. She fisted hands on hips. "Who's driving home?"

Quinn looked sheepishly at his woman. "You. I hope."

Bridget slapped him upside the head affectionately. "Aye. Appears so." Turning her attention to Gale, her gaze slid to her friend's left hand clicking her tongue. "How long the boyo staying?"

"Dillon and I are having Sunday dinner at Tim and Mary's, then…" Gale glanced at him. "We'll probably take off for Scotland early part of the week."

"Aye. I'm expected at the law firm on Monday morning. Gale will follow as soon as Erin has everything in hand at the Pixie Magic."

"Putting Erin to work, huh? Bet Tiarnan isn't happy." Quinn eyed his empty mug, turning it around in his hand, checked his watch, and motioned to the other members of his band toward the stage. "Gotta go. If I don't see you before you leave, good luck. Hope you'll be back soon. Town could use a decent solicitor. The only one we had was ancient and finally retired a few years back." Quinn kissed Bridget soundly, swung his leg over his chair, and bounded up on stage.

"He sure makes everyone aware you are his woman." Gale snickered watching the drummer count off the beats with his sticks.

"Wish it worked in reverse." Bridget jerked her chin toward the group of women crowded around the stage reaching for him. "Same group every night they play. But he never looks their way off stage." She shook her head.

"He's a keeper. When you two tying the knot?" Gale leaned over to Bridget.

"A Sunday very soon. I'll let you know. Just a small get-together. Tim and Mary are letting us use the pub. Mostly friends, a few of his family, and avoiding mine." She waved her hand in the air brandishing her new engagement ring.

"Wow. Let me see. Nice rock." Gale nodded approvingly. "Thought you didn't want…"

"Quinn insisted. I relented. Give and take makes a good marriage." She eyed Dillon before grinning at Gale. "Gotta get back to work. I'll have another round for you soon."

"Make mine orange juice straight up, please." Gale laughed and snuggled next to Dillon, laying her head on his shoulder.

He leaned over and kissed her, wishing this evening would last forever. A foreboding settled in his stomach like a rock. Dealing with Tristian was never easy, especially when you weren't in his inner circle, though Gale seemed comfortable with the enforcer. Determined not to let his family affairs put a damper on today's fun, he tuned into the cheerful conversations swirling around him, snaked an arm around Gale, and smiled.

****

Sunday arrived with a clear blue sky and bright sunshine. *A good omen.* The delicious aroma of freshly brewed coffee greeted him as he padded down the hallway to the kitchen. Gale had breakfast on the table. Her long wavy ginger hair hung loose to the middle of her back the way he liked it. The long brightly colored skirt she wore stopped at her ankles, and her feet were bare. His heart skipped a beat.

"I wasn't in the shower that long." He grabbed her around the waist and spun her into him, kissing her soundly on the lips, then nuzzling her hair. "I love the floral citrusy scent to your tresses this morning.

"Why thank you, kind sir." She braced her hands on his bare chest and gazed up at him, her eyes warm and dreamy. "Breakfast won't cook itself. We're due over at Shaughnessy's place in little over an hour."

"About that. Maybe we should try to work out my family situation without intervention of the warlock kind. How about we enjoy good food, great company, and fun before I head back to Scotland?" He pushed his fingers through his hair leaving neat little rows.

"Getting cold feet, are ya?" She snickered, raising an eyebrow. "Tristian isn't as big and bad as he lets people think. Being married to Hannah has mellowed him. She doesn't take any of his shit."

"Still he wields great power and the influence of the Demon Overlord of the Western Hemisphere."

"True, but if something illegal is going on with magic folks, Tristian will find out sooner than later. You'll want to be on the sooner end. Later will involve Bruce and consequences you don't want to be involved with. Covering up something isn't the way to go. Even if Mary may box your ears for talking business on Sunday." She giggled.

"This is no laughing matter." He narrowed his eyes at her.

With her fingertips, she caressed the contours of his chest muscles. "Not laughing at the situation. It's serious. I know it without even being in Scotland. But your fear of Tristian is unfounded. Speaking of Scotland. You're going back alone?"

Her touch had sent spirals of lust through him, making it hard for him to concentrate on what she was saying. "It's not fear." He crossed his arms across his chest, capturing her hands, and stared down at her.

"Sure it's not, boyo. Keep telling yourself that." She pulled her hand free and waggled a finger in his face. "We best get a wiggle on. Not advisable to be late to Tim and Mary's invitation." Sitting down, she forked up scrambled eggs and slipped it in her mouth.

"As to the Scotland matter, I was up most of the night going over the logistics. Aye, I'm going back alone on Monday. You will join me Monday night or Tuesday depending on how things shake out."

"Engaged or not?" She wiggled the bare fingers of her left hand at him.

"Engaged, but not wearing the ring. I want to keep them guessing. Especially when I confront Father about your stalker. Nothing is set in stone until we have Tristian's opinion. Maybe he's heard rumblings of something. I don't want to get crosswise with him or Bruce under any circumstance. For that matter, something occurred to me last night. What if Father is setting Royce up to be his fall guy? I can't see him stooping that low, but I'd never believed he would take magic cases under the table either. Guarantee their disposition to the detriment of the client. Not good business practice."

Her eyes went wide. "Are there more than the one you told me about?"

"I hope not. But I can't be sure until Patrice and I get a look at all the firm's files. By now the outcome of the O'Sullivan case will have caused a backlash if the client was expected to be found guilty. Railroaded in my opinion." When his phone chimed in his pocket, he yanked it out and stared at the screen frowning, then put it to his ear. "Patrice, I thought we agreed…"

"You'll be returning to a hornets' nest. Father is furious—on the rampage. From what I can discern, some kind of deal was agreed to that included the client would take a fall."

"About what I figured. Hence our disappearing for the weekend. The client is long gone now too. He won't be found. Did Father find you?"

"No. Boyfriend and I took off for the Highlands when I heard Father was looking for me. Neighbors said some guys came knocking and crashed the door in. Father is going to pay for that too." Patrice's voice reached a fever pitch.

"Calm down, Sis. Thanks for letting me know. I figured this is how it would go. We need to provide a unified front tomorrow morning. Remember that tree house we built as kids in the woods way behind the family home?"

"Aye. It's falling down but still there."

"Meet me there about five tomorrow morning. We'll port to the firm from that location. Don't want to involve Ian in our arrival." He rubbed at the back of his neck.

"Don't know if Father sent people your way. He probably suspects you disappeared to Ireland."

"Causing trouble where we'll be today would not be in his best interest." A smug smile turned up one corner of his mouth.

"Why, what have you done?" Patrice's voice quivered a bit.

"It's better you don't know. I'll explain it all when I see you tomorrow. Check in with Grandfather if you get a chance. Make sure Father isn't harassing him."

"Now that's a battle I can't see Father engaging in. But…"

"Gotta go. Expected at a friend's house for Sunday dinner and I haven't eaten breakfast or gotten dressed yet. Stay safe and out of Father's way."

"Will do."

He ended the call and explained to Gale what was going on. He buttered a piece of toast, took a bite, and washed it down with a gulp of coffee. After breakfast was finished, the dishes washed, and set in the rack to dry, he rushed to finish getting dressed, shave, and comb his hair.

Gale padded into the bedroom, slipped her feet into strappy sandals, and glanced at him worriedly. "It's going to get bad, isn't it?" She glanced over at the sleeping pup snoring softly. "Not sure how Tim and Mary feel about a pup in the house. I'll leave Trouble in the crate while we're gone. If necessary, we could always come back and get her."

"Best to err on the side of caution. Let's take the pup for a quick run over the cliffs. She'll sleep for a while. Put the crate in the car. As far as the Scotland situation, I certainly hope not. But it's not looking good."

Chapter 11

Sunday Dinner, Good Friends, A Quiet Conversation

Gale knocked on the screen door of the Shaughnessy house. Dillon waited beside her, shifting from foot to foot.

Mary hollered, "Come on in. Glad you could make it."

With a beer in his hand, Tristian sat next to Hannah at the kitchen table. Hannah sipped a glass of iced tea while visiting with Mary as she prepared a Sunday dinner of colcannon potatoes, lamb chops, carrots, and soda bread.

"Fixing a little of everyone's favorites today. Tristian enjoys lamb chops, Gale loves colcannon potatoes, Hannah can't get enough of my soda bread since hers doesn't turn out." Mary snickered and glanced in Hannah's direction. "There's smoked salmon cheese spread on the table with pretzels, chips, and veggies to munch on." She waggled her finger. "Don't spoil your dinner."

"Never said I couldn't get the bread to turn out. Don't have time to try." Hannah frowned, tossing a napkin in her mom's direction.

Tristian snorted behind his napkin. "Easier to get you to make it."

Hannah punched her husband in the arm. "Nobody asked for your comments. You'll be doing the cooking if you're not careful."

Grinning, Tristian rubbed his arm, snatched a kiss from his wife, then leaned back in his chair, two front legs off the ground, and switched his attention to Gale. "So how's it all going? Erin and Tiarnan doing well?"

"Aye, right as rain and happy they are." She leaned over the table, spread creamy smoked salmon blend on a cracker, popped it in her mouth, and closed her eyes. "Oh, yum. Best in Ireland." She slathered more spread on another cracker, took a bite, and offered the rest to Dillon, who declined. She sighed, glancing over at Mary, then back to Tristian. "But there is something we need to talk to you about."

Mary whirled and shot Gale the stink eye while shaking a wooden spoon at her. "Remember what I said. Sunday is the day of rest for all. No business discussions." She slapped her hand down on the counter for emphasis. The wooden spoon popped out of her hand and flew up in the air. "I'll not have it."

With ease, Tristian reached up and caught the spoon. Ignoring his mother-in-law, he leaned forward. The two front legs of the chair banged on the gleaming hardwood floor. "Must be serious if Ma doesn't want you talking about it. Let's take a walk." Tristian pushed up from his chair and plopped the spoon on the table. Picking up his beer, he took a long swig and winked at Hannah.

At Mary's disgusted look, he swung his arm around the older woman's shoulder and kissed her on the cheek. "We won't be long, Ma. Promise. Dinner smells fantastic." He snatched a fresh-out-of-the-oven soda bread loaf, tore off a big piece, failed to avoid Mary's hand slap, stuffed part of the bread in his mouth, and sauntered outside. "Coming?"

Gale patted Mary on the shoulder. "We won't take much of his time. But it's important." She grabbed Dillon's hand and scurried after Tristian.

"Way to piss off your hosts," Dillon whispered.

"Don't worry about it. She'll be fine. Hannah will set things to right. Now, what is the problem?" The crunching of rocks underfoot was the only sound until Tristian turned and stopped halfway up the path overlooking the jagged cliffs. He sipped his beer and nibbled on the bread looking out at the ocean waves crashing below. "Beautiful, serene place."

"How'd you get away with that?" she said, eying the bread. "Mary would have grabbed the bit of bread right out of my hand."

"Gotta be quick." Tristian grinned. "Ma and Da have grown fond of me—after a rough start. I'm an expert at difficult family dynamics." He shook his head. "Tell me what's going on."

Dillon's shoulders slumped. "It's my family's law firm and Father's bizarre behavior. I hate to admit it, but my gut says something unsavory is going on. I don't know how to…"

Narrowing his eyes, Tristian rocked back on his heels his facial expression unreadable. "That be Bram Dunlop's family firm. Thought you left there?" He paused, took another bite of bread as if waiting for Dillon to speak. When Dillon stood staring at his shoes, Tristian continued. "Law firm employs numerous solicitors, both mortal and magic kind for over a hundred years, if I'm not mistaken. Your firm only takes on mortal cases to avoid the sticky magic/mortal dynamics. Correct?"

"Well…not exactly." Dillon swallowed hard. "That's the way it has been for years. But when I was…forced…called back to the firm a few weeks ago, things were not as expected."

"Quit beating around the bush, boyo. Spill it." Tristian's gaze razor sharp. "I won't terminate you on the spot." The warlock chuckled. "I have teams that do that for me now."

"He won't judge or do anything to you at all." Gale put her hands on her hips and glared at Tristian.

The warlock raised his hand in surrender. "What she said." He paused and appeared thoughtful. "You know the world was so much easier to navigate before I married into this family." Tristian slapped Dillon on the back. "Let me guess. Bram is taking magic cases on the sly. Maybe delegating them to his eldest with instructions that didn't sit well with—you."

"How did you know?" Dillon sputtered. "Not his eldest, Aiden, but Royce."

"It's my job. One of the reasons for our little vacation trip. Hannah gets to visit with her parents for a while. I pop over to Scotland and check out the rumors. A win, win." Tristian focused on Dillon. "You didn't know anything about it until you took that case from your brother, won it, sent the client packing, then disappeared along with your sister. Did you? There'll be hell to pay when you return, just so you know."

"No. But I couldn't let an innocent man be punished, so I stepped in." He paced up the path and swore. "This whole bloody thing started when my father called and demanded my return—" Dillon glanced in Gale's direction. "—amid threats. A frigging nightmare. Then Grandfather called indicating family problems in the firm."

"You broke Gale's heart and fled to Scotland. Then involved her in your mess. Now you return, need my help figuring out what the hell is going on and what your next moves should be?" He paused. "First off, not a good way to treat our sweet Gale. It happens again and there will be extremely unpleasant consequences."

"Just wait a minute. Gale suggested that we talk to you. I can handle my affairs." Dillon straightened.

"I can see that." Tristian smirked. "Tell you what. I'll do a little more poking around. Scotland was on my agenda Monday afternoon or Tuesday anyway. Things are getting mighty hot for Ella Mallory, a reporter. Suspect your family or firm are behind it. Keep me informed as to the fallout on Monday."

"Fair enough. Thanks. Wait. You know Cork, I mean Ella?"

"Aye. She's a source of reliable information. I arranged for her recent assignment away from Glasgow."

A door slammed in the distance. Tristian glanced at his watch. "That's either my lovely bride or Mary. Either way, we better get back to the house. Dinner is probably done, and you know how Tim is about dinner time."

Gale picked her way down the path along the cliffs. "Didn't realize we'd wandered so far."

"This is one of my favorite places on earth." Tristian shoved his hands in his pockets and started down the path.

Dillon followed close behind his woman with

133

Tristian ambling along behind them all. Halfway down the path, they met Hannah.

She huffed out a breath. "Ma's furious. Dinner's been ready for several minutes. Da was washing up when I left to find you. You know how he is about punctuality at mealtime."

"Funny we were just discussing that fact." Tristian draped his arm around Hannah and kissed her affectionately. "I'll take the heat," he said nonchalantly. "Important matters. Did you tell your parents this was a vacation mixed with business?"

"Aye. But Ma hears what she wants." Hannah shrugged. "Very protective of you, she is."

"Turns out, my business in Scotland seems to be tangled up with our friends Gale and Dillon. I'll need to move my schedule up a bit, but good news, we can stay longer."

"Which may keep you in Ma's good graces." Hannah turned on her heel and marched back the way she'd come.

When they all trooped into the house, Mary and Tim were already seated, as well as Synn who was sipping on a tall glass of iced tea. Gavin smirked, taking a swig of his beer. Storm thundered toward them all wiggles and barking with excitement.

"Storm, sit," Synn commanded, and the pup's butt hit the floor a few inches from Gale. The dog's bright shining eyes looked back at Synn, then up at Gale. Storm's purple tongue lolled out the side of her puppy grin. "Hey, where is Trouble?"

She laughed and scratched the pup behind the ears. "Wow, has she grown. It's only been a few weeks since I've seen her. Trouble is crated in the car sound asleep

I'd bet. Took her for a long walk before coming over here. Didn't know you'd be bringing Storm."

Mary waved her hand in a dismissive gesture. "Pups are always welcome here. No need to ask, just bring her—Trouble—no need to leave her in the car."

"Greetings, oh troubled ones." Gavin chuckled. "Forgotten about house rules already?"

Synn glanced up and raised an eyebrow but said nothing.

"Sorry. As it turns out, Dillon and Gale appear to be embroiled in a situation I came over here to investigate. Ma, I'm sure Hannah told you part of our vacation would be a working one for me. Good news, we'll be staying a bit longer than anticipated. I hope you don't mind."

"Don't like business on Sunday." Mary snapped. "But…if you're through?" She raised an eyebrow and stared him down. "If we can devote the rest of the day to family time, I'm all right with it." Mary's determined expression melted into a wide smile. "How much longer you be staying?"

"Couple of weeks." Tristian took a seat nearest Tim. Hannah sat down beside him, and Mary smiled wide.

"We're sorry." Gale eased into the seat next to Mary. Dillon plopped into the seat between Gale and Gavin.

Mary waved her hand. "Forgiven. We're all here. Let's give thanks and dig in before everything gets cold."

Silverware scraping china plates, the crunch of puppy kibble, and lapping at water were the only sounds for a few minutes.

Tim cleared his throat "There isn't going to be a repeat performance of what happened last year when Synn came here. Right?"

"Absolutely not. The investigation takes me to Scotland. If there's a scene, it'll be there. Nothing to do with this family or Ireland," Tristian assured them.

"Well…It appears that Mr. Dunlop senior has already sent his minions here to harass me." Gale shrugged. "Don't know what lengths he'll go to in order to force me out of Dillon's life." She forked up the last bit of lamb. "Delicious. Mary. You've outdone yourself."

"What? This is the first I've heard of such a thing." Tim shoved up from the table, took the whiskey out of the cupboard, and poured three fingers in a glass. Returning to the table whiskey bottle in hand, he tossed the liquid down his throat and hissed. "Is that what happened the other night at the pub with the stranger that wouldn't leave you alone? What are you going to do about it?" Tim set his glass down on the table harder than necessary and directed his glaze to Dillon, then to Tristian.

"Now Tim, it wasn't Dillon's fault. He didn't know a thing about the incidents until he got here. Then we compared notes and figured out who must have been behind it." Gale took the last sip of her iced tea.

"What? There was more than one?" Tim ran his fingers through his thinning salt-and-pepper hair and rubbed at the back of his neck.

Dillon sighed. "I'm working on it. With Tristian's assistance, the matter will be settled in Scotland. No danger to your family. Gale will be with me." He popped the last bit of roll in his mouth. Butter dripped from his fingers.

"'Tis what I like to hear." Tim settled into this seat set the whiskey bottle on the table and reached for his coffee. "Though I don't like Gale being embroiled in it."

"Gale's a big girl. She can handle herself." Mary put her hand on her husband's arm, raised an eyebrow as she glanced from Tim to the whiskey bottle. "Getting a bit ahead of yourself?"

"No. Don't want demons, witches, and all manner of magic creatures descending upon us without warning. No offense, Synn. You know we love you. But it was a rocky start."

"None taken. It appears this situation is far different." Synn slid a glance at Gale.

"Synn is exactly right. I'll accompany Dillon to Scotland. Erin is going to watch the Pixie Magic while I'm gone. She's also going to keep Trouble for me." She glanced at Dillon for confirmation.

"Not exactly. It's best if I return very early Monday morning alone to see what kind of shitstorm Father has stirred up while I've been out of touch. My sister, Patrice, and I will meet before popping into the law firm. I'll apprise Gale of the situation by Monday evening, and we'll decide when she'll arrive. Don't want to subject her to any more adversity than necessary. Not sure of Tristian's plans."

"We'll play it by ear. It's better if you don't know when or where I'll show up. The element of surprise should be for all. You'll be given time to snoop around—unless things go south quick. Which I've seen happen before, so be prepared. I'm sure he won't want to explain why I'm there to the magical staff. The mortal staff won't be any the wiser. On the other hand, the magic community, including the council, will be aware of my investigation. Just not privy to what or who I'm investigating nor why. Really unnerves them." Tristian chuckled wickedly.

"How about we take the chocolate coffee cake out on the back porch. I'm sure Gavin will be happy to whip up some Irish coffee with mint." She winked at her son. "Then I can get the kitchen cleaned up and we can visit. The evening is so nice. Hannah, I want to hear all about your new house in Colorado. Is commuting between the east coast and Colorado working out for you both?"

"'Tis. We are both more relaxed in Colorado. Fewer interruptions. Long evening walks in the crisp mountain air are a perk. When we do have to return to DC, we're less stressed and able to handle whatever emergencies arise. Always something brewing there. Believe me." Hannah blew out a breath.

Mary started to gather up the dishes from the table, as Tim led Tristian and Dillon out onto the porch.

"How many Irish coffees? Mint or not?" Gavin asked.

"Four, counting you, son." Tim glanced at the men who nodded in agreement.

"Might want to make that five." Tiarnan's voice boomed from the bottom of the stairs to the porch.

"Well, to what do we owe the pleasure of the King of Faeries and his wife?" Tim gave a slight bow.

"Knock off the nonsense, Tim," Tiarnan teased. "We'd turned down your original invitation to Sunday dinner. Erin promised to prepare fried chicken, mashed potatoes, and gravy. A great Yanks Sunday dinner."

Tiarnan licked his lips. "But my favorite."

"We're on our evening stroll and saw everyone gathering on the porch. We're taking you up on dessert and Gavin's Irish coffee. I'll take mine with mint, light on the whiskey." Erin padded into the house and sent Mary a sweet smile.

Grinning from ear to ear, Mary wiped her hands on her apron and hugged Erin. "You're welcome here any time."

"Thank you, Mary. We don't get by as often as we'd like, but with Gale's well-being at risk, we'll be staying close. Your family has always been a wonderful resource." Erin smiled as Tiarnan nodded his head.

"Mary, let me take care of this for you. It'll only take me a minute or two. I know where everything goes." Gale made a whooshing motion with her arms and murmured a few words. In the blink of an eye, the large wooden dining table and kitchen were spotless. Chocolate coffee cake sat in the center of the table surrounded with small plates and forks. "All set." She brushed her hands together and glanced at her aunt. "What? The magic wasn't used for my benefit. Want to cut and serve the cake, Mary?"

"Aye. Thanks so much, Gale." Mary cut the cake, slipped the pieces on the plates, and handed them off to Gale, Synn, Erin, and Hannah.

Once everyone had a piece of cake and coffee, they settled into the chairs available on the porch and chatted about recent events, gossip going around the town, including Hannah and Tristian's plans while they were in Ireland. No mention was made of the trouble brewing in Scotland. Though from the underlying concern emanating from Tiarnan and Erin as they sipped their coffee and nibbled on the cake, she was sure they were aware.

Dillon helped Gavin gather up the dessert plates and coffee mugs. Juggling the china and silverware, Dillon followed his friend into the kitchen, bobbling the plates as the silverware clattered to the floor. He quickly bent down and picked up the utensils.

Gale's hand flew to her mouth to cover a snicker. Dillon wasn't used to performing domestic tasks, though he tried when he was with her. She could hear voices in the kitchen but couldn't make out the conversation. Slipping from her chair, she padded toward the voices. When her shadow fell across the kitchen's entrance, the voices ceased.

Dillon greeted her at the doorway. "Guess it's time for us to get going. Need to get an early start tomorrow. It will be a long day, for both of us."

Chapter 12

Best Laid Plans of Witches and Warlocks—A
Surprise Visit

Up long before dawn, Dillon had spent most the
night tossing and turning. He took Gale in his arms,
kissing her long and hard before reviewing the tentative
plans they'd discussed long into the night. His last
words were smothered against her lips, and he was
gone.

Patrice was pacing behind the treehouse when he
materialized. There were deep dark circles under his
sister's wary hazel eyes. Her dark red hair was pulled
back in a messy bun with a few curls around her face.
The sea breeze caught the curled strands, and she
brushed them out of her eyes.

"He stationed guards at my apartment. Did you
know that? Of course you didn't." She paced some
more. "Scoured my usual haunts questioning my friends
as if I was a wayward teenager." Fury reflected in her
eyes. She sucked in a breath and blew it out. "I'm ready
to kill him right now. No explanations. No clandestine
searches or confrontations."

He let her continue spouting off for a good ten
minutes. "I don't want to be defending you for murder.
So we need to be going if we are to arrive before
Father."

"Bloody hell, with our luck, he probably spent the night waiting for us." She swallowed hard, tears glistened in her eyes. "Never in my wildest dreams did I imagine he could behave like this." Pausing for a moment, she stared at him. "Where's Gale? You're not going to let Father…"

"No, he won't get at her. She'll be along later tonight. Besides, Gale can hold her own against Father if it comes to that. Another barb in his side that we'll twist tomorrow. If we're still employed. If not, I've another trick up my sleeve Father is not going to like."

Calmer now, Patrice took in a deep breath and let it out slowly. "With the upcoming switch of power, I don't think he can fire us." She straightened her tailored suit jacket and tossed her head back. "I'm ready."

The law office was quiet. The interior was dimly lit with only the overnight emergency lights still on when Patrice and he ported into his office. He listened and risked magic in opening his third eye searching the office for anyone. "There's no one here." He set his personal laptop on the desk, tapped a few keys in an attempt to circumvent the firm's antiquated security and encryption systems. He let out a low whistle. "Someone's updated the security systems—recently."

A deep dive into encrypted files he could get into netted nothing out of the ordinary. Then he opened files that contained nothing but the name, case number and notation of guilty verdict, and date. No charges were noted. No accounting or hours billed sheet, no law firm file number, but each time the attorney assigned was Bram Dunlop or Royce. One file had exchanged Aiden's name for Royce but wouldn't open with Dillon's code. He jotted the name down. *I'll ask Aiden about this one.*

Patrice leaned over his shoulder and watched as the information scrolled on the screen. "That's not the way we do business. If we were audited—" She pushed his hand out of the way and moved to another section of files assigned to her. "Look here." She punched in her code, the files opened and contained the routine documentation. "This is my most recent case. No additional security or encryption. As a senior partner, I have a master code that should open any file in the firm." She tried it to access Royce's and her father's without success.

"It appears that only Father's and Royce's files are encrypted with the new security. Wait." Going further back in the database, she tried again. Her master code opened any file two years old or older including those assigned to Royce and her father.

He pointed to the intake dates. "It appears this started about eighteen months ago." He pushed back from the desk and craned his neck to look at her. "Anything earth-shattering happen eighteen months ago that you know of?"

She shook her head, walked around the desk, and plopped into a chair. "Nope. Father was still doing a lot of estate cases at that time. Civil and criminal cases were handled by associates. Since then, all the cases are divided equally by Aiden or myself and deciding who gets what depending on the caseload of that solicitor."

"Wow, Father simply gave up micro-management just like that." He snapped his fingers.

"Didn't think of it that way. Figured since Mother left the firm, that Father was preparing to retire too, leaving us to run the firm." She paused and rubbed her chin. "Now that I think about it, the action was abrupt. One day he's his usual meddling self, the next, he's basically handing the firm off to Aiden and me." Patting her hair as if checking to see her bun was still in place, she shrugged.

He tilted his head to one side as one eyebrow quirked up. "Royce didn't object?"

"Not to our faces. We heard him grumbling to others, and Aiden confronted him. Shut him down, if you know what I mean. But we all knew Royce wasn't… well…you know."

"The sharpest scholar in the family?" He snorted a laugh.

She chuckled. "That's a nice way to put it."

"Actually, according to Grandfather, the firm was never to be left in the hands of Royce. It was Aiden because he was the oldest and you. Grandfather had long known I didn't want to be in the firm. We had long conversations when I graduated from the prestigious law school in America. He claimed the Yank culture ruined me. Always thought you two would step in equally."

"Yep, you still sound like a Yank. Muddled your brain, it did." She snickered and dodged her brother's playful slap. "I want the record to show that I do a bloody good job at litigation."

"So noted, counselor. Never said you didn't. You love to argue." He patted her on the back.

She batted her long dark eyelashes at him. "Got to go with what you know." She paused pursing her lips. "Still there are cases I didn't know about within the last eighteen months. I'm betting Aiden didn't either. They're all assigned to Royce or Father and encrypted so we don't have access."

A beep echoed through the lobby and up the stairs as someone disengaged the alarm. Stiletto heels clicked across the entranceway and quieted in the plush carpeting of the lobby.

Patrice frowned and eyed the office door. "Shall we play innocent in our respective offices? Since the whole world is aware he's looking for us. Or present a united front here?"

Shoving his hands in his pockets, he hesitated considering. "Play it by ear. Go on to your office. I'll be the first he confronts."

He walked her to the door, glanced up and down the hall as she sauntered to her office. The receptionist clinked coffee mugs in the client lounge area and the aroma of freshly brewed coffee wound its way to his nose. His mouth watered. Still no sign of the head of the firm. He shook out his hands and tried to relax. A cup of coffee and a pastry sounded pretty good right now. There were always pastries in the client lounge first thing in the morning. He leaned over the banister to confirm his suspicions, then took the stairs two at a time and helped himself to the food. Hot mug in one hand, a plate of lemon pastry in the other, the brisk morning air whooshed through the lobby accompanied by the booming voice of his father, nearly causing him to drop both.

Eyes bulging, face purple, and a vein pulsing in his temple, his father stood one hand clenched at his side the other shakily pointing at Dillon. "I could have your license for the stunt you pulled Friday. Involving Patrice in your escapades was unconscionable. Risking her license as well. Where in the Hell have you been all weekend?"

He took a sip of his coffee, set his plate down on the counter, and glanced calmly at his red-faced father. "Didn't know I had to account for my whereabouts on my personal time." Picking up his pastry, he took a bite, set it back on the plate, and chewed. "I'm not sure which escapade you are referring to. Couldn't possibly be the one where I got an innocent man acquitted of the charges that never should have been brought in the first place.

"Not to mention a case that never should have been taken by this firm. How many others have you misrepresented in the last eighteen months? Ten, twenty, more? Dragging Royce through the muck with you. Now let's talk about your license and this firm's reputation." He stood there, figuring his face was as flushed as his father's. He'd let his temper get the best of him and spilled information he didn't mean to. Now he'd have to backtrack.

Aiden waltzed into the lobby, his mouth set in a thin line, and shoulders stock straight. "Airing family dirty laundry in front of the employees? Let's take this conversation in Father's office."

"I second that idea." Patrice sauntered up behind Dillon and put her hand on his shoulder. "What have you gotten us into this time?" She smirked at her father.

His brother turned on his heel, stalked up the stairs, down the hallway to the carved wooden double doors at the end. A brass plate screwed to the door was engraved Bram Dunlop, III, Managing Partner. Aiden thrust open both doors so hard, each bounced off the wall stop and swung back at him. Dillon caught one door and eased it against the wall. His father bulldozed his way past

Aiden and stood behind his huge mahogany desk.

Once everyone entered the office, he closed both doors gently. "Quite a show you put on there, Aiden."

"What in bloody hell is going on around here? I take a few days off and return yesterday to Father on my doorstep in a fit of rage because he can't find you or Patrice. Then I walk into the office this morning, the two of you are going at each other. lobbing accusations apparently questioning the other's ability to practice law? What the Hell?" Aiden paced the length of the office, returning to the front of the desk.

Dillon hitched his hip on the corner of his father's desk. "I could ask you the same thing. A lot of things have changed since I left and not for the good." He directed his next question to his brother. "Are you aware the firm is taking on magical cases? Railroading innocent clients?"

"Absolutely not. You must be mistaken. It's against our charter. Not in over a hundred years have we taken a magical case. For God sakes, we employ mortal solicitors, clerks."

"Better check again, bro. Friday I tried one such case because our brother, Royce, was unprepared to go to trial and was willing to let our client, who by the way was innocent of the charges of using magic in front of mortals, plead guilty."

Aiden narrowed his eyes and switched his gaze from Dillon to his father. "Is that true?"

"It's my firm. I can take the cases I see fit. If Royce had done his job, none of this would have happened," his father blustered, pounding his fist against his stately wooden desk.

Shoving his fingers through his hair, Aiden's

mouth hung open for several minutes as he stared in disbelief at his father.

"While your impression of a codfish is impressive, it's not the decorum of a respected solicitor." Dillon coughed to disguise a chuckle.

Finally, Aiden closed his mouth giving Dillon an eat-shit-and-die-look. "Where the feck is Royce?"

"I sent him on an errand. He'll be back tomorrow. Or the next day—depending on his success." Bram leaned forward on his desk with hands flat on the polished top. "Got a problem with that?" His lip curled in a sneer and eyes laser focused on Dillon.

"I do if it's business you have no right sticking your nose into. Sending spies to Ireland, stalking Gale, scaring her half to death is wrong on so many levels."

"Wait." Aiden's eyes widened. "You sent people to Ireland to intimidate Gale, Dillon's former fiancée?"

"No, just making sure the relationship was over. Our family doesn't need her kind wheedling her way into our ranks." His father eased into his high-back leather chair and tented his fingers together.

"What are you talking about? She is a nice girl from a well-respected family in Ireland." Aiden stared at this father in disbelief.

"She has more magical power in her little finger than all the members of this family together. That's what was wrong with her. And my relationship with her is still none of your business." His temper yanked at the end of its tether, but he reined it in before saying more he'd regret.

Patrice sat in the navy and cream leather chair in front of her father's desk, one leg crossed over the other, examining her bright red polished nails. "If anyone's interested in my opinion, I think it's about time someone else takes over the reins of this family and law firm. I'd nominate Dillon, but I don't think he'll be here long." She looked up at Aiden. "Guess that leaves it up to you and me."

Bram slammed his fist down on the desk. "No one is going to take this firm away from me. I'm the head of this family and firm, like it or not." His voice rattled the walls of the office.

"Now Father, settle down before you pop an artery. We will discover what you've done eventually, and your fall from grace will be much more public."

Voices outside the office caught the attention of the family.

"You can't go up there without an appointment. What did you say your name was?" The distraught voice of the firm's receptionist rose.

"I didn't say. But I'm well known to the Dunlops," a female voice with an Irish lilt calmly answered. "Believe me you don't want to get involved in what is about to happen in the next forty-eight hours. My advice—go back to your desk duties, and keep your head down. You might survive."

There was a pause. The click of of heels on the stairs subsided. "Come along, Royce, let's get to the bottom of your assignment before my friend makes an appearance."

The blood drained out of Bram's face as his gaze locked on the office door. Dillon rose from the chair in front of his father's desk and walked toward the door. *Why is she here? This wasn't part of the plan. Could be interesting.* He reached for a door handle, but it turned and Royce shoved into the room. Gale sauntered in

149

behind him. She caressed Dillon's cheek, then brushed her lips over his and whispered, "Change in plans." Royce paused halfway into the room. Gale encouraged him forward with a little push.

"Now Bram, did you or did you not send this sniveling coward to threaten and accost me in my place of business?" She paused, surveying each face in the room. "He claims to have acted on his own volition." She tilted her head and glared at Bram. "He's a rotten liar, just so you know. After the last idiot I sent scurrying back to you tail between his legs, I'd thought you'd get the hint. Apparently, that famous legal brain of yours lacks any common sense. Whatever is between Dillon and I is absolutely none of your business." She jabbed her left index finger in the air toward him for emphases.

Dillon's lips twitched, but he kept the smile at bay. She wasn't wearing her engagement ring as discussed. Pride welled up inside him as he watched her performance. He pushed all thoughts of the ring to the back of his mind. More important things demanded his attention. *What a mess.* He glanced around the room.

His father and Royce were screaming at each other, pointing fingers. Aiden was lecturing Patrice who looked bored with a smirk etched on her face. Gale was leaning against the far wall enjoying the melee. "Enough," he bellowed. Swinging his arm up over his head, he cast a soundproofing spell. It was one thing to have the family at odds with one another. However, they had to present a united front to the employees and clients. "Quiet," he roared.

Shock registered on everyone's faces except Gale. She smiled and nodded encouragingly. Patrice looked as if she was about to clap. He sent her a stern glance to discourage such antagonistic behavior. Although he appreciated the support.

"What brings you to Scotland, Gale? Since you could have sent Royce packing the same way you did the other unwanted suitor. Is there another reason you accompanied my brother to Scotland?" Patrice asked.

Gale smiled sweetly at Bram, then winked at Dillon meandering toward his father's desk. She traced an imaginary line along the front edge of the desk with her finger. "Well, Bram's sending Royce to mess with me didn't sit well with my aunt and uncle, nor another high-ranking friend with the council." She shrugged.

"If I were you, I'd put my house in order, or come clean as to why the secrecy and sudden representation of magical cases. In the hundred years this prestigious law firm has been in business, it's never swayed from its roots of representation in nonmagical cases. Isn't it in direct conflict of the magic councils' directive that a law firm can't do both? Especially with mortal employees?"

"You meddling bitch." Bram came up over his desk, his eyes nearly popping out of their sockets, and his arms extended toward Gale's neck, magic current popping and snapping from his fingertips.

With a flick of her finger, she flattened him against the wall behind his massive desk. He slid to the floor with a thud, dazed. "I don't believe you want to spar magic with me. You'll lose every time. Which if truth be known, my magic was the reason you didn't want Dillon to marry me." She raised an eyebrow and peered over the desk at Bram.

"Aye, figured that out a long time ago. Though

your wife, Iris, is a pleasant lady and was always nice to me. Much better than you deserve. Now get to your feet, you sorry excuse of a warlock, and explain what's going on around here. I don't like anyone meddling in my personal life."

Bracing himself against the wall with both hands, Bram got up shakily and made a spectacle of brushing off his suit, then straightening his tie. Slowly he brought his dark eyes to hers. Emphasizing each word, he said, "I have no idea what you are talking about, bitch. You'll live to regret your accusations. Or not. Witch." Pausing for a beat, he slicked his hair back. "Get out of my office. All of you. There's work to be done. Dillon and Patrice, you're terminated. Clean out your desks and leave immediately."

Aiden straightened and took a couple of steps forward. "You can't do that, without my consent or Patrice's. Since I'm assuming she won't give it, I won't either. We'll get to the bottom of this fiasco with or without your help."

"Was that a threat, Bram Dunlop? We can add that to the other offenses. I'm sure my friend will have no problem sorting things out." Gale sighed as her eyebrow arched as if to accentuate the statement. "Too bad about this firm's reputation after his investigation is through. Not to mention yours."

"You're bluffing," Bram thundered.

"Am I? Don't think so." She touched her index finger to her lip and appeared thoughtful. "We'll find out soon enough." Wrapping her arm around Dillon's waist, she leaned into him. "Ian is waiting in the limo outside with my luggage. Where are we staying?"

"I'll need to delegate my case files to a few trusted

associates in the firm before I can leave." He turned to glance at Patrice and Aiden. "Any problem with my delegating?"

"Nope." Patrice shook her head.

"It's fine. We need to have a board meeting—soon." Aiden scowled. "I've a full calendar this afternoon. Tomorrow morning?"

"Might want to consider tonight, if what Gale says is true. Which I don't doubt. Visited with our friend and the Shaughnessys on Sunday over dinner. The warlock enforcer indicated he had business in Scotland, which is what brought him across the pond besides a chance for his wife to visit with her parents."

"Tonight it is. I'd like Mother's input into this situation. Meet at the family home?"

"As would I." Cocking his head, Dillon raised his eyebrows glancing at his brother. "Not sure that's a good idea. But if things don't work out, we'll port elsewhere."

"So you were in Ireland cavorting with this trollop." His father pointed at Gale.

He tilted his head. "Now there's a word I haven't heard in years. Better watch it, Father. You'll not talk about her like that or... I'd hate to see her turn you into something—more fitting for your recent actions."

He wrapped an arm around Gale's waist and guided her toward the door. After only a few feet, he turned and crooked a finger at Patrice. "Come along, Sis. Some of my cases will need your attention." When they reached the door, Aiden yanked it open.

Holding the wooden door for them, Aiden pushed Royce out behind them. "We've got a few things to discuss, brother." Aiden jerked his chin in the direction of his office, towing Royce along with him. "See you three tonight."

Chapter 13

Trouble, Trouble, Toil and Power Bubble Over

Inside Dillon's room at Blythswood Square, he nuzzled Gale's neck. "I take it Royce's visit pissed you off?"

She tilted her head allowing him more access. Enjoying the attention, she wrapped her arms around him feeling his heartbeat against her. "Oh, aye, but not as much as it did Tristian. Royce appeared out of nowhere into the showroom at Pixie Magic. Luckily, there were no customers that early in the morning. He began acting aggressively, grabbed my hair, and yanked when I refused to go with him. I asked him to leave. He threatened me. As if he has enough power to follow through." She sniffed and raised her head to meet his gaze. "I conjured a bit of fire in the palm of my hand touched his arm and hand holding my hair. He squealed like a little girl, cursed up a blue streak, but let go of me. Scorched a good size hole in that expensive shirt he had on."

He interrupted. "Where was Erin while all this was going on?"

"She'd stepped out to run a few errands for me. It was a quiet morning." Easing away, she toed off her shoes and plopped on the bed. "Been quite a day." She wiggled her toes and tucked her legs underneath her.

"Unfortunately for him, Tristian and Hannah were passing by the shop and witnessed the altercation through the front window. They entered the shop, and in a blur of movement, Tristian backed Royce against the wall. I intervened."

"Why?" He quirked an eyebrow. "Should have let Tristian handle it."

"The dangerous gleam in Tristian's eyes worried me. He doesn't get physical anymore, mainly manages his teams from the home office. He took on this case so Hannah could come to visit her parents. Hannah and I both thought Tristian was spoiling for a fight. So I defused the situation by offering to port Royce back to Scotland and the firm." She paused. "When Tristian released Royce, he whispered better not set eyes on him again, or they'd never find the body." Her lips curved into a wicked smile. "One of Tristian's favorite catch phrases. Royce didn't have any idea who he was dealing with nor did he say anything afterward. We ported to the firm without incident. Only a constant stream of threats flowed from his foul mouth."

"You've had an interesting day. And it's not over yet." After kicking off his shoes, he sat down beside her. "Just enough time to have a good romp in bed before…" He leaned her back on the bed, covered her mouth with his, then trailed kisses along her jawline. Fumbling with the low neck of her peasant blouse, he snaked his tongue along her cleavage and slid his hand under her blouse to cup her breast through the lacy bra. When he flipped open the closure of her bra, he smiled as her breasts spilled into his hand.

She arched up against his exploring hand. "This seems a little one-sided." Her lips nibbled along his neck and breathed a kiss at the pulsing hollow of his throat. Reaching for the button on his pants, she unbuttoned it and pulled the zipper down. "Now that's a bit more like it." She slid her hand inside and stroked his arousal. "Missed me?"

"You bet," he murmured against her firm stomach and swirled his tongue around her belly button.

Bringing her leg up, she wedged her foot in the crotch of his pants and shoved them off his body. "Much better." She purred.

He caught her foot, pulled her long broomstick skirt up, and slid his hand up her leg until he reached her center. Slipping his fingers inside her panties, he teased her center with feathery strokes. "All ready for me, huh?" He kissed his way lower and spread her legs wider.

She arched against him and moaned. "So ready for you."

"I like it when we leave your skirt on. Maybe you shouldn't wear any underwear at all. Easy access for me."

"Not happening, boyo." She giggled.

He raised his head to look at her and grinned, then thrust two fingers inside her quivering channel and moved his body up hers. Screaming his name, she crashed over the edge of ecstasy. Stars and streamers exploded in the air above the bed. Not waiting for her sensations to subside, he slipped inside and began a rhythm extending her pleasure as she writhed beneath him. When she was pliant like melted wax, he increased the rhythm and brought both of them to the pinnacle of fulfillment. Once again stars winked across the ceiling as she cried out his name.

Tena Stetler

"I love when you do that," he murmured against her lips. His watch chimed. "Time to get dressed and meet our obligations."

She reached her arm around his neck and pulled him to her. Tracing his lips with the tip of her tongue, she teased inside, caressing his tongue. "Not yet." Her legs twined around his waist.

He settled himself against her. "I guess we'll be late." In a sudden movement, he picked her up off the bed, legs still wrapped around him, and carried her into the shower. "We'll finish this in the shower."

She giggled. "You're so wicked. But…" She raised an eyebrow. "Exactly what I anticipated." She wiggled against him enjoying his warm hands on her bare butt cheeks. *And why I love you.* But the last part she couldn't say out loud…yet.

****

The lights blazed in every window of the Dunlop family home. The lanterns atop the lampposts lining the long driveway flickered as if in warning of what was to come. She shook her head to dislodge those thoughts. By the number of cars lined in front of the house, she figured they were the last to arrive.

"Oh, wow, Grandfather and Grandma are here too." He closed his eyes and blew out a breath as the limo rolled to a stop. "Showtime." Stepping from the limo, he offered his hand to Gale. "Ian, park the car next to Grandfather's vehicle and come on in."

"Sir, are you sure? Might be safer out here." Ian eyed the mansion nervously. "If Michael, your grandfather's, driver is out here, permission to visit with him?"

Dillon turned and stared at the vehicle in question.

"There's no one inside. I expect you within ten minutes." He closed the door, tapped on the limo's hood, and strolled up the massive stairs with Gale's hand through the crook of his arm. Hand raised to knock on the ornate door, he turned to her. "I apologize for putting you through this."

The brass handle turned, and the door *squeaked* open. A man dressed in a black suit with dark hair, silver at the temples, gave a little nod as his gaze wandered to Gale, then he smiled. "Good to see you, sir, miss. Everyone is in the banquet room." The butler offered his arm. "May I take your jackets?"

"No, thanks, Jackson. We'll keep them with us—if that's all right."

"As you wish. Follow me." Back ramrod straight, Jackson led them down the polished white marble hallway.

Family crests hung on the walls. She surmised the crests must be from both his parents. Though, usually only the patriarch's was displayed. A knight's armor polished until it gleamed, even in the low light, stood guard at the right side entrance to the banquet room. Hesitantly, she reached her hand toward the knight's helmet. *I always wanted to lift the facemask and see if anyone or thing was inside.* She stifled a giggle and lowered her arm. *Not the best time.*

Sucking in a breath, she passed through the tall arched doorway, and her hand flew to her mouth. Two long wooden tables split the room. Several serving dishes were arranged in the center of one table. Place settings lined the upper half of the table. Two large warming pots, mugs, and snacks lined the other table. Against the far wall appeared to be a fully stocked bar complete with a bartender.

"I thought this was a meeting, not a dinner party. I'm underdressed." She glanced down at her patchwork broomstick skirt and embroidered peasant blouse she'd worn to work this morning before all Hell broke loose. *Seems my life is not my own recently. Stirring the pot and taking part in a wee adventure isn't completely out of my wheelhouse.* A feeling of foreboding washed over her, making her shiver. Her wrists warmed with the threat of the gauntlets making an appearance. *No, won't allow that. What if it turns out to be much more?*

Dillon drew her close to his side. His hand on her waist. "Are you cold? This house can be a bit drafty even on the warmest of nights."

"No, no, I'm fine. But this house…Wow." She blew out a breath, surveying a massive stone fireplace occupying one entire wall. Orange and blue flames snapped and crackled, racing up the logs in the hearth though the summer evening was still warm. She touched the stones with her fingertips. They were cool. The floor to ceiling windows captured her attention and offered a spectacular view of the rolling hills against the colorful sunset of oranges and pinks darkening on the fringe to maroon and purple. This was the first time she'd been in the Dunlop home, and it was impressive. It could have been considered a modern-day castle, minus the moat of course. A quiet giggle escaped her lips as her imagination took flight. She swallowed hard and schooled her features. Iris, Dillon's mother crossed the floor to greet them.

Dillon turned to Gale, his eyebrow winged up looking almost like a question mark. She shook her head whispering, "I'll tell you later."

"Mother, so good to see you. Missed you at the office." Dillon kissed his mother's cheek.

"I don't go into the firm often anymore. Much more pleasant atmosphere in my gardens." She pointed out the towering windows. Scottish heather bloomed across the rolling hills as far as you could see in the dusky evening light.

In the lighted gardens up close to the house, there were brightly colored blooms that Gale couldn't identify. "The heather is beautiful. The flowers next to your house are fantastic."

"I'm sure you are missed at the firm. Although, Grandfather alluded to possible…"

His mother cut him off. "Your father indicated the board had some matters to discuss. I insisted we enjoy dinner before tackling business. Are you agreeable to that arrangement?" She glanced at Dillon, before turning her attention to Gale. "So good to see you again. Too bad it's under such dismal circumstances. Dreadful that your engagement was called off."

"The status of our engagement has yet to be decided." Gale smiled sweetly. "Dillon dear, I'm going to visit with Patrice." She withdrew her arm from the crook of his elbow. "There are a couple of matters I'd like to discuss with her. If you don't mind."

"Not at all. I'm sure she'll be delighted to chat with you." His phone chimed. He frowned at the name that popped up on the screen. "Excuse me, I need to take this."

Gale drifted across the floor and waited for Patrice to finish her animated conversation with an older woman.

"Gale. How wonderful to see you again. Did you

get my message?"

"Aye. The crystals and herbs you inquired about are in stock at my store. I can have them delivered by next week. Will that work?"

"I think so. Maybe I could visit your store? Pick them up myself?"

"Sure. Next time you are in Ireland, stop by. Not sure when I'll be back, but my Aunt Erin is running the store while I'm gone. Are you needing these for a specific purpose?" She eyed Patrice suspiciously. "If you are in a hurry, I'm sure they can be found here in Scotland."

Dillon breezed into the room, tucking the cell phone into his pocket. "Shall we be seated and get dinner over with?"

Patrice raised an eyebrow and glared at her brother. "Interrupt much?" Turning her attention back to Gale, she said, "I'll need those items sooner than later. I'd hate to be caught unprepared." She hesitated for a moment or two surveying the room. "Would it be possible to pop over to the shop in the morning to collect what I need from—Erin?"

"Of course. I'll let her know tonight. Your order should be ready shortly after the shop opens, say around ten tomorrow morning. That will give her time to prepare your items. Will that work?"

"Aye, should be fine. It's been a while since I…Never mind." Patrice floated off toward the table, stopped to whisper to one of the servants, before joining Aiden at the bar.

"What was that all about?" Dillon watched his sister order a drink.

"I've no idea. Patrice wants crystals and a few rare

herbs that I happen to stock. The items, two of the nightshade family, probably can be found here too. But she totally ignored me when I suggested acquiring them here."

He shrugged, then nodded toward the bar. "Want something? Patrice always has an agenda."

"Wine would be nice. Take the edge off. Pretty intense in here." She followed him to the bar.

"Father likes to control through intimidation. One of his character flaws. Won't work tonight," he said easily, then requested two glasses of wine. He handed one glass to her, and they padded back to the table. She picked up a plate, selected salad, a salmon dish, and a piece of freshly baked soda bread. "This smells heavenly."

The corner of his mouth quirked. "Helena is a fabulous cook. She's been with the family for years."

Soon everyone followed suit, selected their meals, and sat around the table. Patrice eased into a chair next to Gale and farthest from the head of the table, where Bram was seated, Iris to his right, Royce to his left. His paternal grandfather and grandma sat across the table from him and Gale.

"Aren't you going to introduce this lovely lass to us?" His grandfather smiled at Gale.

"Sorry. Gale, this is my grandfather, Sturgen Dunlop, and grandmother, Olivia."

"Pleasure." He stood and winked at Gale. "Dillon's intended?"

Olivia smiled. "Nice to meet you."

Dillon blew out a breath. "It's complicated."

"Life is complicated, boyo. Don't let it stop you from obtaining your heart's desire before it's too late. I can't imagine that you are this lovely lass's only suitor." His grandfather sent an appreciative glance in Gale's direction.

"Stop it, Sturgen." His wife touched his arm. "You're embarrassing the lass. Sit down, you old flirt."

****

Heat rose in her cheeks. "Do you live close to here?" She took a sip of wine.

"Aye, just down the road at Pemberly castle. It's been in my family for centuries." Olivia smiled, giving Gale a knowing wink. "All this land belonged to my family. A falling out between my brother and my father left me the owner of the land when he passed. Cost my brother, Chadwick, everything. Yet when I offered to split the land with him, he refused." She shook her head. "Scottish men are so stubborn. When Bram married, we gifted him the land this house is built on and a couple more parcels as a wedding gift."

"I see." Relieved to have help steering the subject away from her and Dillon's relationship. She smiled at Olivia and relaxed against Dillon's arm.

"Do you? It takes a strong woman to keep a Scottish man on the right path. Know what I mean?" Olivia's eyes sparkled with mischief as she forked up salmon and slipped it into her mouth, indicating the conversation was finished.

Gale was happy to turn her attention to her own food. *How had that introduction gone completely off the rails? Olivia was as sharp as the men in this room with more finesse. She couldn't help but feel there was a secret between them.*

The room was devoid of conversation as sounds of silverware scraping plates and the chime of crystal

A Witch's Quandary

glasses being set on the table nicked the china plates. Finally, the staff cleared the table, and they got down to business. The board of directors consisted of Sturgen, Bram, Iris, Royce, Aiden, Dillon, Patrice, and Todd, a warlock who'd been at the firm longer than Bram.

****

"It's been brought to my attention that my favor for a friend has been blown completely out of proportion." Bram's voice boomed in the high-ceilinged room. "It was a slam dunk. The defendant needed representation in the court procedure. I saw no harm."

Dillon narrowed his eyes at his father. "But it was against…"

Bram held up his hand. "Let me finish. Figured I'd have Royce handle it."

"And no one would be the wiser. How could you let an innocent man take a fall like that? This firm has never railroaded its clients." His grandfather broke in. "It's not done. Not in my time or now. You put the firm at risk, the employees mortal and magical at risk. Now we wait for the council to discover what you've done."

"Not I. Dillon. His first day back, he failed to recall we didn't represent magical people. Took the damn thing to trial, instead of taking the plea, and now we have the council to contend with. His fault, not mine. Had Royce done as instructed—None of this would have happened. Then there is the issue of involving the press and a slam dunk." Bram's hands made the sign of exploding.

"Press? What are you talking about?" Dillon kept his calm.

"Don't play coy with me. You enlisted your former girlfriend, Cork? To twist the facts to get our client released." His father turned his gaze full of malice to Gale. "You did see the picture of him kissing his old flame. Right?"

A slight smile curved the corners of Dillon's mouth. *And another piece of the puzzle slides into place. Cha-ching. Did Father use company funds to have me followed?* Gale's annoyed voice drew him out of his thoughts.

"Again you are sticking your nose where it doesn't belong, Mr. Dunlop. Personal affairs have nothing to do with the business of your firm. I strongly suggest you keep this meeting on track, or your board will be here all night." She placed her hands flat on the table.

"This meeting has nothing to do with you." His father's face turned beet red, the muscle in his jaw was working overtime.

"Exactly. I need some air." She excused herself from the table and walked toward the doors leading to the veranda. Olivia got to her feet and followed.

"Now, let's get back to business. We all have an early morning tomorrow," his father directed attempting to regain control of the meeting.

"I don't." Patrice glanced at her long polished fingernails. "You fired me. Remember?"

"Which brings us to another point of this meeting. You and Patrice didn't clean out your desks as ordered but defied me in front of the staff. Insubordination."

Gale and Olivia quietly slipped back into the room and their respective seats.

"We did no such thing. We were all in your office with Dillon's silent spell preventing prying ears." Aiden blew out a breath in frustration. "Your leadership is in question. I contend that you are relieved as managing partner effective immediately. Patrice and I will take over."

"You did what?" Sturgen whirled around and glared at his son. "Of course that action will not stand. Both will be reinstated immediately." He glanced around the table, all heads nodded but Bram's. "Further, I second Aiden's action removing Bram as managing partner and add that position temporarily be shared by Aiden and Patrice." Once again, Sturgen glanced around the table at affirmative nods.

"This is an outrage. It's my firm," Bram bellowed slamming his fist down on the table. Sparks flew in all directions, creating a red-hot spiderweb of power crackling across the tabletop. Everyone at the table scrambled back or stood. Dillon caught the malevolent spark in his father's eye a split-second after Gale. She had already brought her hands together, the room sizzled as she conjured a ball of fire and with a few words sent the witchfire and spell at him.

"What have you done?" Bram screeched as the fire and spell hit him center mass. "Witchfire too? Bitch." He slid to the floor.

Iris ran to his side, tears spilling her cheeks, she wiped his sweat-soaked brow with a napkin. "You just couldn't stop, could you? What did you do? Make a deal with the devil? We should have put a stop to it. To you. But..." She helped him into a chair.

"I'm afraid you've messed with the wrong witch, this time. Brought this on yourself. You did. But I won't let you take this family—the firm—down with you." Giving his shoulders a little shake, she gazed into his shocked eyes. "What have you done?"

Bram slowly shook his head and murmured, "It's

my firm." He raised his gaze and glared at Gale pointing a bony finger at her. "You'll pay for this." Then turned his attention to Dillon. "I told you nothing good would come from aligning yourself with this witch. Her blood is not pure. Diluted by the Fae power of her..." He broke off.

Dillon stood at Gale's back, his hands steady and supportive on her shoulders as she said nothing for several beats. Eventually, she turned her emerald green eyes to him and held his gaze. "I couldn't let him divide the family with that dark magic. I tempered my deadly witchfire with the spell. I couldn't kill him." She tore her gaze from Dillon's, touching her fingertips to the scorched marks radiating across the table, stopping an inch from the edge all around. "If he'd succeeded, there'd have been no turning back. If the tendrils of that spell had left the table and reached one of you..." She shook her head.

Appearing to gather his wits about him faster than the rest of his family, Sturgen surveyed the scene, wiped his brow with a monogrammed handkerchief, and sucked in a breath. "The firm is no longer yours." He squeezed Olivia to him, starting for the door. "We've had enough for one night. Let's adjourn until a full audit of the cases and firm can be conducted."

Chapter 14

Fireworks Erupt—A Surprise Guest

Gale leaned against Dillon, his strength and calm flowed into her. "I felt your father's intentions. The intentions he was able to disguise from his family. He planned to destroy all of you."

"I know. I felt him…hmm…something evil. Only my reaction was a second too late. I'm glad yours wasn't. How long will he be spellbound? That is what you did. Right?"

"Aye. Among other things. Indefinitely… I hope. He's got a lot of power that isn't his. I've no way to bind what I don't know."

He raised an eyebrow. "I don't understand."

She glanced around the room at the family members still staring open-mouthed at her. "This isn't the time or the place to explain. We'll talk later," she whispered against his ear.

Sturgen paused, his hand shaking on the door handle, and turned his attention to Gale. "Young lady, I don't know what kind of talents you have or magic you wield—I'm certainly glad you're on our side." His grandfather winked at her, then turned a stern gaze to his grandson, Dillon. "She's a keeper. Don't you forget."

"Understood." He grinned at her and reached for

her hand, linking fingers with hers. "On that note, we're going to take our leave. See you all sometime in the morning at the firm. Business as usual until we get this all sorted out?"

Patrice closed her mouth and nodded emphatically. Then grinned at Gale. "You got a lot of 'splaining to do, girlfriend."

"After you set your own house in order," Gale shot back. "I'd say you have your hands full with him." She jerked her chin toward Bram.

Patrice puffed out her cheeks as her face flushed, then blew out a breath. "You're probably right. The boys can handle him. I've a feeling we'll need your magic to delve into this mess. Which is the reason all of us sat here with our thumbs up our arses while you did the heavy lifting. Unfortunately, we're no match for our father. At one time or another, we've all challenged him independently and together. Usually—" She surveyed her siblings still gathered around the table and cleared her throat. "We get our hats handed to us, so as to speak. But you…wow!"

She smiled shyly. "Just lucky." Deciding not to expound on the situation until she'd had a chance to talk with Dillon, she glanced at her hand in his, warmth raced through her, and she followed the elder Dunlops.

When she and Dillon stepped out on the porch behind his grandfather, they were met by Ian.

"See, I told you it wasn't safe in that house. Mike and I decided this was as close as we wanted to get. Rhona, the housekeeper, offered to bring food out to us." Ian glanced at the dirty dishes and half-empty pitcher of lemonade resting on the little table in front of the porch chairs. "Tried to convince her to bring us a beer, but she wouldn't hear of it." Ian finished off his drink in a big gulp. He waved to Mike, Sturgen, and Olivia, then returned his attention to Dillon. "Ready to leave?"

"We are," Gale and Dillon said in unison.

Once inside the limo, Gale blew out a breath and collapsed against the back seat. "I'm sorry. Didn't mean to disrupt everything. Couldn't believe what he had in mind—to his own flesh and blood. Something is seriously wrong with that man."

He chuckled then sobered. "Not a problem. No one else was going to act, as Patrice stated. I was a split second too late. Your premonition was spot on. Father has always been difficult, but now he's downright dangerous." Dillon rubbed his chin and narrowed his eyes. "It's like something or someone is pulling his strings."

"Kinda what I thought. Reminds me of Synn when she had to learn to control the evil demon power accidentally transferred to her during a fight with the now-deceased Baltizar."

"Synn has quite a colorful history with you and the Shaughnessys." He cocked his head at her in question. "Is it true Gavin met her after a failed attempt on his sister's life?"

"Aye, but Synn was under the influence of Baltizar, a high-ranking demon. Took a lot of guts to do what she did for her freedom. You know Baltizar killed her family and kidnapped her as a child. Then forced her into service as a warrior. He was after the unique guardian power she didn't even know she had until after she fled. All that is Synn's tale to tell. What's your next move?"

He leaned over brushed his lips over hers. "Get you into bed."

She giggled. "No beating around the bush with you. What I meant was…"

"I know what you meant," he murmured against her lips, then deepened the kiss.

Her heart beat a tattoo in her chest as the pit of her stomach went into a wild swirl of desire. *How is it he can do this to me time and time again?* She returned his kiss with reckless abandon. *Will it always be like this?*

I certainly hope so. He answered in kind.

Her head shot up, eyes as big as saucers, she blinked at him. "You can read my mind?"

"When you let me." He smiled seductively, buried his face in her soft hair, and pressed a kiss to the pulsing hollow at her throat as his hand snaked under her blouse.

"Ahem…You two have a room. Just let me get you there." Ian's eyes twinkled at her look of surprise.

In all honesty, she'd forgotten where they were and that Ian was even there.

The limo slowed. "Here we are." Ian glanced in the rearview mirror.

"Just in the nick of time." Dillon laughed straightening her blouse. "I'll call you tomorrow when I want you to pick us up. Going in late."

"Got ya." Ian slipped out of the driver seat and opened Dillon's door slowly. "Everyone decent?" He chuckled. "Pulled up to the back entrance, since I knew you had a key or code to get in and kept you away from prying eyes."

"Love the way you think, Ian." Dillon offered his hand to help her out of the vehicle, wrapped an arm around her waist, and waved at Ian. Dillon slowly surveyed the area.

She followed his gaze. "Anything wrong?"

"No, not really. Making sure no one pops in if you know what I mean." He slid the key card in the slot, tapped in a code, and the tiny red light turned green. Before yanking the door open, he peered down the wall at the delivery dock and out onto the grounds. Apparently satisfied there was no one around, he tugged the door open and held it for her. Slipping in behind her, he pulled the door closed and jiggled it to make sure it was secure.

Her gaze flicked from him to the surrounding area. "You're making me nervous. Your father is spellbound. He'll not be using his magic anytime soon. Is there something you're not telling me?"

He escorted her to the elevator, pressed the button, and turned to her. "Not really. You mentioned his magic. But also you can't account for other magic he may have obtained. It also bothers me that he twice used strangers to discourage you from our relationship. Hired henchmen. How many more does he have set up and why? Are they on the firm's payroll, or does he have a whole other life we don't know about? His recent actions are not the man I've known all my life. After his intended actions tonight, I'm concerned. What if you'd not been there?" He shivered.

"I was. If not for me, none of this would be happening. Stop looking for trouble." She took his hand in hers and brought it to her cheek. "He didn't expect what happened. It'll take him a bit to regroup. I've no doubt he's got underlings that will do his bidding. But we have Tristian. He'll help us get to the bottom of this." The elevator doors *whooshed* open, and they stepped inside.

"You're right." Dillon released a breath inside the elevator. "Alone at last."

"Aye." She snickered, sliding her arms over his shoulders, and nuzzled his neck, inhaling deeply. His scent was fresh, clean yet held an intriguing spice to it. Her fingers caressed the contours across his upper back. The sculpted muscles were tight, flexing as he moved her carefully to his side, stepped out of the elevator, then led them down the hall to his room. *He's on edge.*

When he unlocked the door to his room, he cautiously pushed the door open. Blew out a breath and relaxed. "Just like I left it." Using his foot, he pushed the door closed.

"What did you expect?" She toed off her shoes then glanced around. "Nice place."

"Beats staying at the family compound. With my family, you never know. Halfway expected to open the door to a brooding Patrice or Aiden demanding an explanation for what went on. Your performance probably held them at bay for tonight."

"Good thing, I'd hate to have had to kill them." She trailed kisses down his neck, unbuttoned his shirt, and let the tip of her tongue tease down his muscular chest. "No more interruptions tonight." Her breathing ratcheted up a couple of notches.

He swept her, weightlessly, up in his arms. She squealed but slid her arms around his neck and buried her face against his heavily muscled chest. His strength made her weak-kneed and wildly aroused for him. Finally, they arrived in the bedroom. He lowered her onto the bed. With a flourish of his hand, he had them both naked. Easing down beside her, he traced his fingertip between her breasts and leaned into her. "Oh, that's so much better."

His breath was warm and moist against her face, her heart raced, and her body tingled all over in anticipation.

****

The bedroom was still dark when Dillon's phone chimed. Sleepily he rolled over and patted the nightstand in search of his phone. When his fingers touched the device, he accidentally knocked the phone onto the floor. Cursing, he leaned over the side of the bed, stretching to reach the phone, nearly slid out of bed, and landed headfirst on the floor. Ignoring Gale's snickers, he checked the screen and answered on speaker. "This better be good, Patrice."

"There's some guy here. He's making all kinds of demands. Wants to see Father immediately. I tried a freeze spell on him. Bad idea. Help."

Gale sat up and glanced at the clock. "Bet it's Tristian. Said he'd be around. Didn't think it'd be this soon. Need to let him know what happened last night." She got out of bed, padded over to her backpack, and dumped it out on the chair. Picking through the items, she located her phone. "I'm going to give him a call to confirm."

He nodded, leaning over to listen long enough to confirm Tristian picked up.

The warlock picked up on the first ring. "Tristian."

"Hey Tris, you don't happen to be at Dillon's firm?" She glanced over at Dillon trying to calm Patrice.

Listening intently for several minutes, she blew out

a breath. "Figured. We'll be there within the hour unless I can talk you into meeting us for breakfast? Last night there was an incident you need to be aware of." She turned to Dillon. "Anywhere we can get a good meal around here?"

"Aye, a couple blocks down from the Register newspaper. Bet Tristian knows where it is."

She relayed the information and disconnected the call. "Tristian will meet us there in an hour. He's leaving the firm now before he terminates someone. Your family didn't impress him."

"Didn't expect they would. But advance notice would have been nice," Dillon grumbled, pulling on jeans. He paused to watch her parade naked around the bedroom. "If you don't stop that, we'll be late…real late."

Her eyes widened, and she batted her long eyelashes at him innocently. "What?"

In one fluid movement, he grabbed her around the waist, swung her around in a circle, then brought her tight against him. "You know what and why. The when would be right now if we had time. Now get dressed." Kissing her soundly, he released her.

She giggled, glanced over her shoulder at him as she sashayed across the room, snatched clothes she'd set out last night off the chair, and sprinted into the bathroom.

"Tease." Laughing, he popped his head out of the light green polo shirt he'd yanked on and called to her, "You're not safe in there."

A few moments later, she emerged dressed in black jeans, a lilac and black striped pullover, and tennies. She whirled in front of him. "Too casual?"

"Doesn't matter. You look good in anything. I favor your long flowing skirts, but the way those jeans fit, I may change my mind." He raised an eyebrow. "I like your hair cascading down your back in a swirl of curls."

"Ahh, you silver-tongued devil." She circled her arm around his neck and smooched his cheek. "I'm starved."

"Well, let's go eat." He led the way out of the hotel. They walked at a brisk pace to the cafe where he and Cork had met. Seemed as good a place as any to meet with Tristian, and the food had been delicious. As they passed by the front window, he paused to glance inside. "Doesn't look like Tristian has—"

"Oh, but you'd be wrong," a deep voice cajoled behind him.

"Tristian." Gale gave him a quick hug as the door to the cafe swung open.

Dillon offered his hand in greeting. Tristian clasped it. "You've got quite a mess brewing at your place of business." He eyed Gale. "What did you do?"

"What makes you think it was me?"

Tristian raised an eyebrow and stared at her.

"Okay, it was me. I spellbound Bram before he could do major harm to his family. That's all." She waved her hand in dismissal. "Believe me, that was his intention."

Tristian nodded his head as the waitress showed them to the corner table in the back where Dillon had pointed.

The waitress put menus in front of them. "What you be drinking? Coffee, tea?" She eyed them. Her gaze lingering longer on Tristian. "Something stronger?"

"Coffee," Tristian said from behind the menu.

"Tea." Gale smiled, setting the menu on the table.

"Orange juice, please." He glanced at Tristian and Gale. "We're ready to order."

"Shoot." She took out her pad and pen.

"Ham and cheese omelet, pan boxty, toast." Gale grinned at the waitress. "You do have pan boxty, right?'

The waitress smirked. "We can manage it."

"I'll have fried eggs, bacon, toast." Tristian handed his menu to the waitress.

"Fried eggs, sausage, toast." Dillon held the waitress's gaze. "Last time I was here, you indicated you didn't have anything stronger than coffee, tea, soda, and juice."

"Things change," she said primly, then flounced away. Halfway across the floor, she turned on her heel and stalked back to the table. "Aren't you the one that was in here a few weeks back with Ella Mallory?"

Dillon nodded. "Yes. Old friends. Why do you ask?"

"Ain't seen her around since that meeting." She paused and tapped her pencil to her lips. "I take that back, she had one meeting after you. But it was you and her that caused the tussle with the photographer." Leaning in, she lowered her voice. "He came back in here skulking around after you two left—asking questions. Tossed him out on his ear, I did. Don't need his kind in here. Is Ella all right?"

"Far as I know. She's on assignment out of town." Dillon smiled reassuringly.

"Good to hear. I was worried. Rumors, ya know. I'll have your food up in three shakes of a lamb's tail."

"Nothing to be concerned about." He smiled ending the conversation.

Tristian raised an eyebrow. "Was that the infamous photo sent to Gale?"

"'Fraid so. Father's doing."

"Your father appears to be quite a piece of work," Tristian observed. "I did visit with Ella—Cork. She's doing fine. Her assignment is nearly over, but there's a young man that seems to have caught her attention in Wales. It appears he's taken a shine to her also. I believe she'll be staying on for a bit. Probably for the best."

"Piece of work, that's putting it mildly. Father's recent escapades have been out of character even for him." Dillon scratched the top of his head, then ran his fingers through his hair. "Wait, you saw Cork?"

Tristian's lips twitched. "That's what I said. Kinda got off on the wrong foot, but we straightened it out. She's a real spitfire."

"Oh, that explains a lot. She called me in a panic, said someone was following her. Then hung up. I was dealing with my own things at the time. When I tried to call her back, she'd left a message everything was fine."

"You might want to be a little more attentive to your friends." Tristian narrowed his eyes. "Especially where Gale is concerned. Your father doesn't seem to be hitting on all cylinders at present."

"Understood. Cork never would have hung up if she was in imminent danger. She has a sixth sense about those things." He returned Tristian's glare. "How do you want to handle this?"

The waitress returned with steaming mugs of dark

liquid. Eyes sparkling, she grinned, handed Dillon a mug, then sat his glass of orange juice on the table. He took a sip and winked at her. "Ahhh, that's so much better."

Tristian relaxed, picked up his cup of coffee, sniffed, stared into it, then back at the waitress.

She took a step back, chewing on her bottom lip. "I wasn't sure if you'd like Irish coffee or not. No history with you, but I can remedy it for you." She batted her eyelashes at him and smiled coquettishly.

Ignoring the come on, Tristian held his mug for a moment, then handed it back to her. "Yes, please. Going to be a long day." He turned his attention back to Gale. "First I want to know what transpired before I arrived. There was an altercation last evening?"

Gale nodded and filled Tristian in on the events of the night before as they ate their breakfast.

When she was finished, he nodded thoughtfully and pushed up from the table. "Good thing I moved up my timeline. If he's using dark magic on his family, no telling how much farther he'll go. We need to show a united front and see what we can discover. You are probably going to need to send out a memo or make a statement of explanation for the changes taking place at the law firm. Don't want the staff lawyers snooping around."

"It's none of my business, as an outsider looking in, maybe you should include his mother, sister, and brothers in a quick meeting outside the firm before we address the changes to the rest of the staff. Are there other lawyers that are partners but not family?" Gale glanced at Dillon as she stood.

"Aye, but only family are the managing partners,

or were. Not sure where Mother stands now." He reached for the check a second too late. Tristian had already snatched it from the table.

Tristian motioned the waitress over handing her the check and ninety-three euros. "Keep the change."

"Thank you, sir," the waitress gushed and tucked the currency in her apron pocket.

He turned toward the others whose jaws dropped. "What? Waitressing is a tough job. Never hurts to reward great service."

"Especially when she's got her eye on you," Gale teased.

Tristian stiffened and glared at her. "I'm a happily married man. End of discussion."

Gale grinned and gave a sloppy salute. "Yes, sir. But admit it, attention like that strokes your ego."

"Again, I'm a married man. I don't have an ego." He nearly choked on the last bit of his statement. "I do my job well."

"Right." Gale snickered. "And there's no magic in Ireland."

"Let's get back on track. There is a park around the corner from the firm. We could ask them to meet us there, maybe walk around a bit to keep our conversations private. Though there's usually not a soul around until midday. And the canopy of trees would keep our meeting out of sight of the law firm." Dillon slipped out the cell from his pocket, then raised a brow. "Agreeable?"

"Fine with me." Tristian pushed the door to the cafe open, holding it for Gale and Dillon.

****

Half an hour later, Tristian, Gale, and Dillon

strolled into the park. Patrice, Royce, Aiden, and Iris were huddled together near a bench in animated conversations. All parties were dressed in business attire except his mother. Iris seated on a bench had opted for brightly colored casual gardening clothes. His sister's voice was low, but her wild hand gestures and stiff body language indicated a conflict she was adamant to win.

Iris calmly watched her daughter, then switched her gaze to her sons. His brothers appeared to be listening intently with Royce shaking his head vehemently at times. Aiden stood with his hands in his pockets surveying the area when he caught sight of them ambling across the green grass toward them. Tapping Royce on the shoulder, Aiden pointed and the rest of the family's heads swiveled in their direction and conversation stopped.

"Well, we've been spotted." Dillon stepped up his pace and took the lead. Deciding to take a tongue in cheek approach, he grinned. "Guess you all are wondering why I've called you here."

"You knew the demon overlord's henchman was coming. Didn't you?" Royce accused, his hands fisted at his side. He took a menacing step toward Dillon. Aiden blocked his brother's advance.

"Stands to reason, if you and Father are involved in illegal activities at the firm, attention would be drawn." He switched his gaze to Tristian and jerked his chin toward the others. "I believe you've already met Tristian."

His mother stood up from the bench and offered her hand. "We've met. As you know, I'm Iris, Bram's wife and semi-retired partner in the Dunlop and

Associates Law Firm."

Tristian nodded his head and clasped her hand. "Wish it was under better circumstances."

"Am I to assume that you are here because of purported wrongdoing?" She allowed a fleeting glance to linger on Royce before returning her gaze to Tristian.

"Afraid so. To set the record straight, my business here was scheduled before I ran into Dillon and Gale. I've opened an investigation and would like your family's cooperation. Thought it would be best to explain the situation to the managing partners away from the prying eyes of your employees."

"While we appreciate that, they will become involved in the investigation correct?"

"Probably. However, how much do you want them to know? We could use the excuse of Bram stepping down, semi-retiring and Patrice and Aiden taking over his duties for the intrusion into the firm's business and cases," Tristian suggested.

"Are you insinuating your snooping around won't violate attorney-client confidentiality?" Royce paced around the group. "And you." He shoved a finger at Gale. "You're the cause of all of this. Know the enforcer on a personal level do you? Or does it run deeper."

"No need to be obnoxious, Royce. Returning you to Scotland merely gave me a reason to visit with Dillon. Nothing more."

"I saw you and Tristian being chummy in Shaughnessy's Pub in Ireland." Royce jerked his chin in Tristian's direction while keeping his eye on Dillon.

"Shaughnessy's Pub is a popular place." Tristian shrugged. "But none of this had anything to do with why I'm here, or the reason you failed to provide adequate representation to your client. Leaving your brother to step in and see that justice was served. Might I also mention you or your firm had no business being involved in a magical case when you have mortals working for you?"

"It's none of your business who our firm represents. We are licensed and in good standing."

"Shut up, Royce, before you dig yourself a hole we can't bail you out of." Iris's stern glance had Royce closing his mouth though his eyes reflected a burning rage.

"Now that you know why I'm here, I'd like to interview each of you separately before we return to the office. It won't take long, only a few questions. Meanwhile, I'd like Dillon to return to the firm, gather all the cases that Bram and Royce have handled in the last eighteen months as well as access to both men's computers. Gale can run interference with the staff." Tristin paused narrowing his eyes. "Do either of you work from home or on personal computers?"

"Bram has a desk computer at home, a laptop, and his work computer," Iris volunteered. "I imagine Royce has the same. But I didn't hear an answer for maintaining client confidentiality."

"As of this morning. Tristian is part of our investigation team. Therefore, he is privy to any and all files while still keeping the client confidentiality intact." Dillon glanced at his watch before taking Gale's hand in his. "Tristian, I'll leave you to it. Aiden and Patrice, could I have a minute of your time before I head back to the office?"

Tristian motioned to Iris. "Let's take a walk around

the park. Royce, I'd prefer that you still be here when we return. Understood?"

"Aye. I'll be here."

Chapter 15

The Hunt is On, Surprising Discoveries, and a
Permanent Change in Command

After Dillon explained the reason for making
Tristian an investigator for the firm to Patrice and
Aiden, they were firmly on board. Gale accompanied
Dillon to the law office where they scoured the files on
his father's computer. Gale hit a brick wall after
searching the first layer of files. It was apparent that
there were several layers of encryption with a few files
having their own encryption.

Dillon watched over her shoulder as she blew out a
breath in frustration. "We are going to have to get an
expert in here to decode the layers of encryption. Are
the files on your computer set up with this type of
security?"

"No, I don't think so. Obviously, we have security
and passwords to get into our files, so the responsible
party can be tracked, but nothing like this."

"Any idea who set this up? Or is your father a whiz
at computer security?"

He roared with laughter. Wiping his eyes, he
finally sucked in a breath and met her gaze. "Unless
things have changed, turning on the computer,

negotiating the desktop and necessary files he needed was a challenge in itself. You can bet he hired someone to set up this kind of security. It would have cost a pretty penny too."

"Then there should be an accounting paper trail to who he hired. Right?" She tilted her head back to look into those large, deep blue eyes. Getting lost in those baby blues was something she'd done often when... She sighed. *Will things ever be the same between us? Long walks on the beach, talking until dawn, making plans for the rest of their lives. That's what I miss the most.* Touching her finger to her lips, she remembered the warm lingering kisses they'd shared. Before his family intervened. She straightened her shoulders. They would not control her life or happiness. She would win.

"Hey, Gale, you okay?" He waited a beat before he placed fingers at her temple and gently massaged. "Such a frown."

Loving his touch, she paused to enjoy it before snickering. His blue eyes were snapping now. "It's frustrating to sit here and be unable to penetrate the security. And I'm no slouch with computers."

"We should be able to find out who he hired and get them in here to access the files." He picked up the desk phone punched in the extension for accounting. "Jeana, I need all the outside contractor requisitions for the last twenty months made by Father. Specifically, I'm looking for a computer security specialist. Yes, I'm authorized, but if you feel more comfortable, contact Patrice or Aiden. I'll need this information by mid-afternoon." He listened for a minute or two. "It's up to you, but time is a wasting." He replaced the receiver in the cradle.

She snapped her fingers. "But I know someone who can get into these encrypted files."

"Who?" He held up a finger as he pulled his phone out of his pocket and looked at the screen. "Tristian, what can I do for you?" Dillon listened for a couple of beats. "I doubt he'll come willingly. But we can stop by the house after you've talked with the rest of the staff." Another pause. "Oh, okay. We could do that. Gale's not making any headway on his computer. There are layers and layers of encryption and security. But she…Okay, see you soon." He ended the call and stuck the phone back in his pocket.

She raised an eyebrow and rested a hand on her hip. "What was all that about?"

"Tristian has a cybersecurity specialist he's going to call in."

She smiled wide. "Of course he does. It's his wife, Hannah. She came with him to visit her family in Ireland. Hannah works in cybersecurity for the United States government and loves a challenge. This will be child's play for her. No need to involve another outside vendor."

"Still I want to know if Father hired this guy by normal channels or another one of his under-the-table deals on the firm's dime." He glanced at the phone on his desk. His finger hovered over the intercom button as it buzzed. "Aye?"

"Aiden would like you and Gale to meet him and Mrs. Dunlop in Patrice's office. Now."

"Sure, happy to." He tapped her on the shoulder. "Shall we go?"

She pushed up from his father's desk, gave the computer a withering glance, and clasped Dillon's hand as they strode out of the room.

He knocked lightly on his sister's office door.

"Come in." Patrice's voice had an edge to it.

Not something he'd heard often, he tugged open the door. "We were requested to report here."

"Aye. Join the party." She waved her hand at the group standing around her desk. "I believe Tristian is on his way too. Have you had a chance to shuffle through Royce's computer?"

With a nod, he acknowledged his two brothers and mother, then turned back to Patrice. "Not yet. It's on the agenda next. Father's computer is layered with security and encryption. Going to need an expert. Do you know who he hired to do that? He didn't have the skill to install that kind of security, and it doesn't come cheap."

"Not aware of any security specialist hired by the firm." She turned to her brother. "Aiden, did you know about hiring a computer person?"

Aiden shook his head. "Check with Jeana, she'd know if the firm hired an outside computer person or security company."

"I already did. She wanted to know if I was authorized to make such inquires. Told her I was, but she could check with you or Patrice if she wanted. But insisted I needed that information by mid-afternoon."

His brother's mouth turned up in a wan smile. "Didn't give her much time. Did you?"

"Nope. Figured she'd call either you two or Father. Since you suggested it. Apparently, Sis didn't know anything about additional security. It's fair to assume Jeana contacted Father. Didn't we send out a memo that he wasn't to be contacted under any circumstances?"

"Aye, first thing this morning. There's been so much going on, Jeana may have missed it. Even though, she's been with the firm for a long time."

"My point exactly. Some of the long-term employees may need a nudge as to where their allegiance falls." Dillon studied his brother.

"Let's call a meeting right now. Tell 'em the reins of management have changed. Father has stepped down. All questions are to go through Patrice or me."

"Isn't that what the memo said?" Dillon glanced at his brother.

"Aye, it was worded a bit softer so as to not raise questions."

"Didn't work." Dillon glanced at the door a minute before there was a soft knock.

Gale closest to the door opened it. Jeana rushed in.

"I'm sorry. I just saw your memo." With a deer-in-the-headlights expression, Jeana handed Aiden two memos, then walked to Dillon and handed him two invoices. "I found these. No request forms and only Mr. Dunlop's note to pay the invoices. Not much information on the company doing the work."

Aiden glanced at the memos and smirked. "Father beat us to the punch." He handed the documents to Dillon.

Dillon perused the documents and smirked. "At least our memo indicating the change in leadership and whose directive will be followed was the last one to come in. Therefore, technically it's the one that the firm should be going by."

"A...sir. The employees don't know what to do. One memo contradicts the other." Jeana shifted from one foot to the other nervously.

"We were about to announce a company meeting. Have all employees meet in the large conference room. Patrice and I'll be there in a few minutes." Aiden glanced at the others. "This shouldn't take long. We'll be right back."

"Aye, sir." Jeana turned on her heel and all but ran for the door. As she yanked the door open, she nearly crashed headlong into Tristian. "Oh, so sorry—wait—who are you and how did you get in here?"

Tristian coolly glanced at Jeana then Dillon, Patrice, and Aiden. "I believe the partners will vouch for me."

Jeana surveyed Tristian from head to toe doubtfully. "Weren't you in here this morning?"

"I was. And I'm here again." Tristian's lips twitched.

"It's okay, Jeana. Go ahead and arrange for the meeting." Aiden motioned for Jeana to leave. She scurried out the door and closed it behind her.

"What's he doing here again?" Were the first words out of Royce's mouth since Dillon and Gale had entered the office.

"He's doing the audit of the business while we transition to Aiden and Patrice taking the helm of Dunlop Law Firm." Dillon glared at Royce. "And you will assist us as we scour the contents of your computer. Understood?"

"This is an outrage. Father will never allow this." Royce crossed his hands over his chest in a defiant gesture.

"Father has no say in it. If you are hiding anything, it would be best to come forward now," Dillon suggested. "Do you have any unauthorized encryption on your computer?"

"Father authorized the security programs on my computer." Royce sneered.

Lips set in a thin line, Dillon nodded. "We might as well wait until our expert arrives. No need spinning our wheels."

"On that note, Patrice and I will address the employees and be back." Aiden opened the door waiting for Patrice.

"I couldn't agree more." Gale stepped away from the door.

Tristian glanced at his watch. "Interviews and scouring the computers ate up a lot of the day. It's nearly quitting time. I'll contact my expert and meet all of you back here tomorrow morning."

Gale breathed a sigh of relief. She had no desire to remain here any longer than necessary. Her nerves were frayed "If it's all right with you, I'm going to pop back to Ireland and check on my shop." She paused a moment. "Patrice, would you like to accompany me? Since you do have a shopping list."

"You bet." Patrice picked up her suit jacket and tossed it over her arm. "Let me take care of our meeting first, and I'll be along later." She sauntered through the open door Aiden held for her.

"Wait a minute," Tristian and Dillon said in unison. Then Tristian continued. "Let's step outside the building and discuss this matter." He stared at Royce, Aiden, Patrice, and Iris. "We'll reconvene tomorrow at ten a.m."

Iris put her hand on Royce's arm. "Would you please take me home? I've had all the excitement I can stand for one day."

Royce glanced around uneasily. "Of course."

Aiden and Patrice were the first down the stairs and headed to the conference room.

Patrice paused at the entrance to the conference room. "I'll catch you later at Shaughnessy's right? Cute little pub you been talking about. I'll follow your trail."

Gale smiled and nodded.

Tristian led the others out of the building and around the corner to a secluded area. "Last one to Shaughnessy's buys the first round." As the last word slipped out of his mouth, he noticed he was the only one left standing in the area. "Well, shit." With a pop, he disappeared.

****

Dillon and Gale were the first to arrive outside the pub. At least so they thought. Dillon wrenched open the heavy wooden door as it *moaned* in protest. Music, voices, laughter, along with the aroma of mulligan stew and fresh-baked soda bread spilled out into the night.

"I'm starved." She bounced into the pub in front of Dillon.

He possessively wrapped an arm around her waist and nuzzled a kiss at her neck. "Me too, but not for what the pub has to offer."

She raised an eyebrow. "You'll have to make do for now. Later, I'll see what I can arrange once we get to my apartment." She slid him a seductive grin.

"I'll hold you to it." He released her waist and took her hand as they made their way through the crowded pub. Gavin and Tim greeted them from behind the bar. Synn waved as she ducked under the pass-through with a tray full of drinks. Tristian, a shit-eating grin on his face appeared, biscuit in hand, and Hannah appeared from the kitchen and joined their group.

"Let me clear off a table over in the corner." Synn flounced across the floor, dropped off the drinks at a nearby table, and stopped at the only empty one. "This will have to do. I think the booth will accommodate the four of you and more if necessary."

As everyone settled into the booth, Gale laughed and pointed to the front door. Patrice stood in the doorway, glancing around, a panicked expression on her face. Her eyes lit up as her gaze settled on their group and looked relieved. "She's with us. Patrice is Dillon's sister."

Synn gave Dillon's sister the once-over and leaned into Gale. "Looks like she has a stick up her butt." She shrugged. "Like most Scots."

Gale snorted. "Don't let Dillon hear you say that."

"He's the one I was thinking of after what he did to you." Synn tapped her pen on her pad, staring over at Dillon.

"Unfortunately, he had his reasons, which I didn't allow him an opportunity to explain. But that's a story for another time." Stifling a giggle, Gale grinned. "Naw, Patrice's all right. The rest of the family I've mostly won over, except Bram and Royce." She stood motioning Patrice to the booth.

"What can I get for you?" Synn raised a brow as if remaining unconvinced.

Gale hip-checked Synn as she slid into the booth next to Dillon, then made room for Patrice. "Remember second chances, my friend."

Chapter 16

Change of Plans and Unexpected Visitors

It was the wee hours of the morning before Gale
and Dillon left the pub to walk Patrice to her B&B, then
a few more blocks to Gale's flat above Pixie Magic.
She pulled the keys out of her bag and noticed out of
the corner of her eye movement in the bushes at the end
of the building. "Did you see that?" Pointing toward the
edge of the building.

"See what?" He glanced at her, then in the
direction she was pointing. "I don't see anything."

She paused then conjured up a ball of light in the
palm of her hand and held it out to illuminate the
shadowy area.

His eyes widened, and he snorted out a laugh.
"Who would be skulking around at this ungodly hour?"

Erin followed by Tiarnan sauntered around the
corner of the building holding a leash leading under the
bush. "Top of the morn to you. The wee pup didn't
want to sleep after she sensed you were back on Irish
soil."

She bounded over and picked up Trouble. Rubbed
noses and cuddled the pup to her chest. "But I, uh, we
have to return to Scotland later this morning."

"Be that as it may. The pup wanted to see you.
Could be a crowd in Scotland. Seems to me, it's best if

your lad returns alone, leaving you and his sister here to complete her shopping. Hannah and Tristian plan to be in Scotland this morning to straighten out some computer snafu." Erin's tinkling laugh echoed in the silent dawn.

"How would…? Is there anything you don't know?" Hands on hips, she grinned at her aunt.

"Take it from me, the answer is no." Tiarnan chuckled.

"Well then, I guess you've the day off. Trouble and I will handle the shop today." She paused for a beat finger, tapping her lip. "Maybe I should just take her back to Scotland with me."

An expression of pure horror crossed Erin's face. "Absolutely not. That would be cruel to subject the wee lass to such unsavory creatures as you are dealing with. She'll stay right here with me and help run the store."

"Besides she likes our early morning and late evening strolls along the cliffs." Tiarnan reached out and scratched Trouble under the chin. "Don't you, lass?"

"I can see the pup will be spoiled rotten by the time we, uh, I return and settle into a routine." She rubbed her cheek against the creature's soft fur.

"I hate to butt in, but if Gale and I are going to get any sleep, we best be after it." Dillon yawned wide, covering it with the back of his hand.

"Tell you what. Since I wasn't partying until the wee hours of the morning, I'll open Pixie Magic. You and Trouble relieve me later this morning with Patrice." Erin glanced at Tiarnan. "All right with you?"

He nodded his head. "Thought I'd stop in for a cup of the spiced tea in the customer area of the shop.

Maybe pick up a few cakes on our way in?"

She laughed at his hopeful expression. "I guess you two have it handled. If you don't think the townspeople will be shocked at the King of Faerie's appearance in Pixie Magic. See you in a few hours."

"I'll be long gone before anyone comes into the shop," Tiarnan said indignantly. "Don't want to set the whole town a twittering. It's bad enough when Erin is covering for you in the shop." He harrumphed.

"Oh, stop it, you big lug. You enjoy their reaction as much I do." Erin switched her attention to Gale. "Now you two shoo…I've got this." She made shooing motions with her hands, then slid one hand through Tiarnan's bent arm strolling around the building toward the front of the store. "We'll prepare the tea, then get scones and cakes as soon as Lilly's opens," Erin whispered to her husband.

Gale led the way to the back of the building, walked up the flight of stairs to the back door of her apartment carrying the pup. "She not going to enjoy negotiating these stairs."

"Probably not. At least you have an area you can fence off to keep her out of your flower gardens back here."

"Have to do that while she's still a puppy. She'll learn not to bother my gardens. Right?"

He snickered. "Aye, if you want any of your herbs and flowers left for your customers."

She paused halfway up the stairs, snapped her fingers, then pointed to the cleared plot of land at the bottom of the stairs. A tidy white fence appeared, with a latched gate. She brushed her hands together. "That takes care of that."

"So much for not using magic for personal reasons."

"Not for me, to keep Trouble from getting scolded within an inch of her life." She held the pup up to her face. "Isn't that right? Besides, the plants are my livelihood and some of the herbs won't be good for Trouble." Unlocking the door, she trudged inside, put the pup in her crate with food and water. Then she grasped Dillon's hand, lacing her fingers through his, and led him to the bedroom.

He whirled her around to face him and brushed his lips over hers. "Remember our bargain?"

"Aye." She wound her arms around his neck, curving into him, and trailing kisses along his jaw to his collarbone.

****

Bright yellow sunshine streamed in the window spreading across the patchwork comforter as Dillon leaned over the bed, fully dressed, and kissed her, then straightened. "I've got to get to Scotland. You and Patrice have a good time today. I'll call after I meet with Tristian and Hannah. We should have a concrete plan by midmorning. I'll see you at the hotel this evening. Will that work?" He paused for a beat, then snapped his fingers. "Oh, by the way, I let Trouble out to do her business. I checked the fence to make sure she couldn't escape. She's still out there playing with the toys I took out of her crate."

"Thanks." Sleepily, she blinked up at him. A devilish smile spread slowly across her face. Reaching up, she snared his collar with her fingertips, pulling him down and taking his mouth with hers. She lingered, savoring every moment, before she reluctantly released his shirt and attempted to straighten his collar.

"On second thought. Maybe I'll just stay here. To hell with the firm." He bent down and brushed strands of ginger hair out of her face.

The warmth in his eyes was nearly her undoing. She stretched her arms over her head, then scrubbed her hand over her face. "Have we heard from Patrice this morning? Does she know you are leaving without her?"

"I phoned her this morning. The call went directly to voice mail. No surprise there. Prickly in the morning, she claims to be allergic to rising early. So I left her a detailed message indicating you would be waiting for her at the shop."

"She's going to want breakfast. Give me her number, and I'll try a little later. If she shows up at the shop, I'll send her across to Lilly's. Erin and Tiarnan will have eaten up all the goodies they picked up earlier." A giggle burst through her lips. "I guess I'm still a bit tired." She giggled again and sat up running her fingers through her long tangled hair. "Gonna take a bit of a while to brush out this mess," she said more to herself than to Dillon.

"Um…I like it tangled and mussed." He scrolled through his phone, paused, and tapped the screen. "Sent you Patrice's info. See you tonight." With a wave of his hand and a soft *pop,* he was gone.

So much for not using magic for personal gain. But then again, this whole thing is not personal gain, it's about trying to save a family legacy. She pushed up and swung her feet to the floor. Deciding on a long skirt swirled with blues, lavenders, and pinks, she settled the garment at her waist and slipped on a lavender blouse with embroidered pink roses around the neckline. As she toed on matching sandals, several sharp barks came from the backyard.

"I'm coming, I'm coming." She smiled at the thought of the cute bundle of fur and raced through the flat and out on the back balcony. At the bottom of the stairs stood Trouble, paws and face covered in mud, her tail and whole body wiggling, clearly happy to see her person. "Where did you get all that mud?" She clambered down the stairs and stared at a hole dug between the pickets, not large enough for the pup to escape though, but… Snatching up Trouble, she held the puppy paws out and away from her clothes. Turning on her heel, she rushed into the flat and dumped the furball in the sink. With one hand on the pup, she pulled on an apron hoping to keep the mud off her clothes and ran water over the pup. After a good scrubbing, she toweled the pup dry as possible, slipped a pink harness over her head, and clipped on a leash. "Come on, lass, it's time to go to work."

Inside the shop, Erin stood hands on hips grinning. "Pup get into a bit of trouble?" She walked over and rubbed Trouble's ears.

Gale put the furball down on the floor. "She did, but we're all cleaned up and ready to work. Funny she wouldn't climb up the stairs to scratch on the door. Barked at the bottom of the stairs until I came out and got her."

"Aye, she is having a little difficulty negotiating the stairs. We practiced on those." Erin pointed to the narrow winding staircase that led to Gale's flat from inside the store. "Yesterday she got halfway to the top before whining and crying to be picked up. If I didn't know better, I'd say she's afraid of heights. Except on the walks along the cliffs, she barrels her way along. Stops to sniff, look out over the water at the crashing waves, then continues on down the trail at breakneck speed."

"Good morning, ladies." Patrice stood in the doorway dressed in white linen pants, a lavender blouse with matching peep-toe heels.

Smiling, Erin glanced down at her multi-colored skirt and turquoise shirt. "Why didn't I get the memo we were wearing lavender today?"

They looked at each other and burst out laughing. "Same wavelength, I guess." Patrice glanced around the store. "I thought I'd be early enough to meet your uncle. King of the Faeries, right?" She stuck out her lower lip in a pout.

"Tiarnan has been gone for a while. He's a restless sort." Erin waved her hand dismissively. "He usually walks Trouble while I tend to the store until she's worn out, then brings her back, and she naps the rest of the day in her crate in the corner. Today the pup was up with Gale."

"Did I hear someone mention my name?" Tiarnan sauntered into the shop. His straw-colored shoulder-length hair framed his chiseled facial features accentuating one dimple in his cheek. It winked when he smiled. He took her hand and brought it to his lips. "Who is this lovely creature?"

Erin rolled her eyes.

Patrice fanned herself as she stared up into his smiling eyes. "Oh, my. The legends don't do you justice."

"Don't they?" He chuckled.

"Tiarnan, this is Dillon's sister, Patrice. She

wanted to pick up a few things in the shop before heading back to Scotland." Gale picked up a frilly white eyelet apron and tied it on.

"Pleased to meet you." The Faerie King turned his attention from Patrice to Erin. He kissed her cheek and pulled her tight against him. "Lonely walking the cliffs without you or the pup. Are you finished here?"

"Aye. I believe so for today." She glanced at Gale. "Returning to Scotland tonight?"

"Probably. I'll drop Trouble off at your home before I leave. If that's all right."

"Sure. How long will you be gone?" Erin glanced at the pup.

"I don't know. Hopefully, with Tristian and Hannah's assistance, Dillon will get down to the bottom of the treachery and sort it all out soon."

"And you two?" Tiarnan narrowed his eyes at her. "Don't want him playing with your heart."

"I'm a big girl, Uncle. We'll get it sorted out."

"If I could interject an opinion here?" Patrice peered from Tiarnan to Erin and back to Gale. "Dillon never had any intention of breaking things off. Apparently, his Scottish temper got the best of him when you refused to accompany him to Scotland. The man is head over heels in love with you."

Tiarnan nodded and took his wife's hand. "Good to know. We'll see you this evening." He bent down and ruffled the pup's fur. When he straightened, he grinned at Gale. "You too."

"Figures you addressed the dog first," Gale grumbled, then snickered. "Thanks for everything." She stood in the doorway as Erin and Tiarnan ambled hand in hand down the sidewalk, then turned at the end of the block onto the path to the cliffs.

Patrice sidled up behind her. "I'm starved. Where can I grab breakfast?"

"Across the street, at Lilly's. Would you mind bringing me back a bacon and egg plate with orange juice? I haven't eaten this morning either. Dillon was up early and took off for Scotland."

"Aye, he left me a message." She handed Gale a list. "These are the items I need. Do you have them all?"

She eyed the list. "Probably. What are you planning to do with all this?"

Red patches bloomed on Patrice's cheeks as she tried to sidestep the question. "Restock my supplies. In case of an emergency."

Gale raised her eyebrows. "Really. Peppermint, ginger, and lemongrass? Paintbrush, lady slipper, and wild rose? If I were you, I'd let Tristian handle things at the firm. Just say'n."

Patrice shrugged her shoulders nonchalantly and stepped toward the door.

"I should have all these bagged up for you when you get back with breakfast." She took another gander at the list. "Some of these crystals are pricey. You aware?"

"Aye. I'm a well-established solicitor and managing partner. Remember? I can afford them." Patrice laughed and scooted out the door. Trouble padded to the door and sniffed.

"There may not be much to manage soon," she said to herself more than to the back of Patrice, then glanced at Trouble and shrugged. The pup trotted behind the counter to her crate, circled twice on a pink floral hooked rug, and lay down with her head between her paws. After gathering the requested herbs and crystals, she carefully layered them in a bag, then paused in front of the lotion cabinet. Sliding the door open, she studied the array of large crystal bottles containing her recent creations. She finally settled on a bottle with lavender contents and poured the creamy liquid into a decorative bottle, then added a Pixie Magic label on the front. With a length of pink ribbon, she tied a bow around the neck of the container and pushed a cork into the top. After wrapping it in tissue paper, she added the bottle to the bag and left it on the counter for Patrice.

Fifteen minutes later, the door to Pixie Magic banged open. Trouble bounced to her feet and growled.

"Shhh…it's a friend," she cautioned.

Patrice charged inside her arms full of bags. "Didn't want to eat alone. So Julie packaged our meal up and sent me on my way." The woman plopped the bags on the table next to the door, took the insulated containers out, and set them on the table. "We have to return this thermos. It's chilled orange juice. Julie said you hated warm OJ."

"She knows me well." Gale smiled and brought a couple of mugs of steaming coffee to the table. "Hazelnut, freshly ground." She waggled the silverware wrapped in napkins and placed them on the table, then poured OJ into glasses.

Patrice inhaled deeply. "Mmmmm, smells delicious." She plopped into the chair farthest from the door, unwrapped a fork, and dug in.

Gale eased into the seat with her back against the wall so she could see anyone that came through the door. "Tell me a little about your father." She forked up a piece of egg, bit off a piece of bacon, then picked up the orange juice and sipped.

"He's always been a tyrant at the office. At home, he tried to be a loving father—mostly. At least while we were growing up. It broke his heart when Dillon left the firm. Grandfather was none too happy either. I suspect that Dillon was always Father's favorite. Not that he showed any preference until we were adults. From a young age, Dillon was able to grasp complex legal issues. Maybe Father saw himself in my brother. Clearly, Dillon was the best solicitor among all of us.

"Nerves of steel, an intuition that was almost always spot on, and smart. Almost like he knew what the opposition was planning before they did." Patrice shook her head in amazement. "I'm not talking magic. Pure talent. For every star, you must have back up. That is what Royce, Aiden, and I were. Until one day, Dillon said he was through. Walked out, he did. Father blamed you." Spreading butter on the toast, she took a bite, then scooped up a piece of egg.

After topping off her glass of OJ, she motioned to Patrice with the container. "I didn't have anything to do with—I didn't even know what or who he really was, for sure while we were dating. When we got serious, he told me about the firm, his dreams, and desire to live a different life than his father. I visited Scotland once with him, met Bram and Iris over lunch." She sighed. "That was enough. Never met such controlling people in all my life."

Patrice snickered. "We are generations of solicitors. Not sure what you expected."

"Not that. Bram peppered me with questions the whole time. Barely got anything to eat. Iris spoke little but her unwavering ability to scrutinize me was disconcerting. Wasn't prepared for that." She shivered at the thought and scooped up a piece of egg, slid it on a bite of toast, added a bit of bacon, and popped it in her mouth.

"Just our way. Yet, you agreed to marry him." Patrice searched Gale's face. "Why?"

"I love him. Simple as that. And we planned to make a life in Ireland." Trouble snuck out from behind the counter and padded over to her nose in the air. "No, you don't." She picked up the puppy, tossed a treat in her crate, and encouraged the pup inside and closed the gate, then returned to the table.

Patrice chewed while she held out her glass for more OJ. "I know. He was torn. The last time we talked, I told him to do what made him happy. Life's too short. Father broke him with his demands, control, and micro-management. Dillon was strong enough to stand up to him and walk away. I had no idea that was what he was going to do. You meant more to him than the family." She waved her hand in dismissal at Gale's shocked expression. "Don't get me wrong, I totally understand. Now that you've had a go at our family, you do too."

After pouring Patrice's juice, she gulped her own. *It was never my intention to make him choose between me and his family. Was it? No, of course not.* "Why did he come running back to Scotland then?"

"Grandfather. He never was the dictator that Father was." Patrice looked thoughtful for a moment. "Or maybe Grandfather mellowed with age. Dillon always had respect and love for him. Maybe Dillon's intuition kicked in that something was seriously wrong." Patrice shrugged. "He always had a way of knowing things. I was as shocked as anyone when he showed up at the firm. It was apparent he didn't want to be there." With the toast, she wiped up the plate, put the last bit of egg on it, and slipped it in her mouth.

She pointed her last bit of toast at Patrice. "You have your own agenda. Don't you?"

"Possibly. But only as a last resort." His sister put her fork and knife on the plate and wiped her mouth with the napkin.

"You don't know the power of Tristian. He'll take care of the situation."

"So I've been told." Patrice picked up her paper plate and stuck it in the trash. Waving the silverware in the air, she asked, "Where do you want these?"

"I'll take 'em. There's a sink in the back room." She slipped the last piece of toast in her mouth, dumped her plate in the trash, and took the silverware to the sink. The chimes rang over the front door as she returned to the showroom. "Well, it's a party now."

Warm aqua eyes, thickly lashed and sparkling with mischievous energy, glanced up at her from a sculpted pixie-like face. "Just checking on you." Synn smiled brightly and bounced into the shop. "Need bath beads, lotion, and shampoo in that wonderful rose scent you gave Cori." Slight color rose in her cheeks. "Gavin loves the scent."

Gale laughed. "Oh, by all means, let's get you fixed up." Pulling crystal containers of iridescent bath beads from the shelf, she combined the two into a lavender crock. Then took large bottles from under the counter and poured them into smaller cut glass bottles, circled a ribbon around the necks, and secured the top with corks. "There you go." She wrapped the bottles in tissue paper and carefully put them in a bag.

Synn stuck her face in the bag and inhaled deeply. "Wonderful." She peeked over the bag, and her face took on a more serious expression. "One more little thing."

Chapter 17

Meanwhile, in Scotland the Search Begins

Seated at his desk, Dillon glanced up when he heard Tristian and Hannah make their entrance. He smiled at the commotion.

The receptionist squealed, "You can't go up there."

He pushed up from his chair and ambled through his office door. "It's all right. Jeana. They have a meeting with me. FYI, Tristian and Hannah are part of my legal team now. They can come and go as they please."

"An email arrived this morning in which Mr. Dunlop left strict instructions no one was to enter the sanctity of the partners' offices without his authorization."

Dillon pinched the bridge of his nose, taking a moment to gather patience. "Mr. Dunlop is no longer running this firm as we stated in the staff meeting."

"But he called this morning, said things had changed and he'd be in—" She paused and glanced at the huge metal sculpted sunburst clock on the wall. "By now."

He smiled at Tristian and Hannah as they reached the top of the stairs. Then he pointed toward his office. "Be back in a minute." Jogging down the stairs to the main lobby, he paused at the receptionist's desk.

"Nothing has changed. Father's not here, and I'd be surprised if he makes an appearance. However, that shouldn't concern you. Aiden is now running the firm. In his and Patrice's absence, you'll take your instructions from me."

"Yes, sir. But he said I'd lose my job if—"

"No one is going to lose their job. But if he walks through the front door, I want to be notified immediately. Understood?"

"Yes, sir." She stiffly walked behind her desk and sat down in her chair nervously pushing around pencils on her desktop.

"Cut out the sir. It's Dillon."

Yes…sir…Dillon." The phone rang. She hurriedly picked up the phone, obviously relieved to have something else to do besides talk with him.

He bounded back upstairs and sprinted into his office. "Are we ready to get started?"

"Lead the way." Hannah grinned. "I love a challenge. From what Tristian has told me, this should be a good one."

"Don't know about that, but getting access to the files on Father's and my brother's computer will shed much-needed light on the situation we are faced with." As he passed other offices on the floor, doors opened, and firm partners paused in their doorway. "Is there something I can help you with?" He paused at one of the open doors.

"No. Need to do research in the library." The man held out a file. "Not your run-of-the-mill case."

"Good luck, then." Their little entourage made it to the end of the hall. He turned to see people still standing in their office doorways. "Nothing to see here.

If your assistance is needed, we know where to find you."

He tried Royce's door. It was locked. *Strange, I'd thought Royce would be here by now.* Unlocking his brother's door, he showed Hannah to the computer, leaned over the desk, typed in the main password to unlock the machine, and backed away. "It's all yours. There are several more layers of security once you get into the files. The ones labeled RD or BD are the ones we want access to first."

Hannah plopped into the chair, laced her fingers, stretched her arms out, wiggled her fingers, then rubbed her hands together like a gleeful child. After a few minutes of tapping the keys, she snickered. "Child's play." Her fingers continued to fly over the keyboard.

Royce shoved open the door, a thunderous expression on his face. "What's the meaning of this? Get out of my office." He strode to the desk and pushed Hannah away from the keyboard.

The wheeled, high back, leather chair rolled to the side of the desk. She glared at him, scooted the chair back in place, shoving him backward in the process, giving him a warning glance that had him edging toward the door.

In a whisper of movement, Tristian crossed the room, had Royce by the throat, and shoved up against the wall, feet dangling. Royce's eyes bugged out before Tristian shoved him to the ground with a thud. With a deadly gleam in his eye and a sneer curled his lips, Tristian leaned over and yanked Royce up. "If you ever lay hands on my wife again, they'll never find your body."

"You knew we'd be auditing your files today.

Father's is next in line. If there is anything you want to say, now would be a good time." Dillon looked at his watch. "Humm, wonder where Aiden is?" The words were no sooner out of his mouth and his eldest brother popped his head in the door.

"Need me?"

"Nope. Hannah's working on Royce's computer. Father's is next." He paused. "Oh, where are my manners?" He glanced at Aiden, then motioned to Hannah. "This is my friend and Tristian's wife, Hannah. She's one of the top cybersecurity experts in America."

Hannah's face flushed. "I don't know about that. But these files are open now. Where's the other computer?"

"Wow, that was fast." Aiden stepped into the room.

"Whoever set up the encryption and additional security programmed back doors, presumably so he could get in without much time or trouble. It's a common practice. The bad part about doing that is someone else like me can use them too." She giggled and glanced up at Tristian affectionately. He placed his hands on her shoulders and massaged.

The exchange wasn't lost on Dillon. *Anxious to move on, the sooner this thing got settled the better.* "Tristian, do you want to show Hannah to Father's office while I peruse these files for anything out of the ordinary, or do you want to…"

"I'd rather make a copy of these files. We can review them at a remote location unless you have a problem with that."

"Nope. You're part of my legal team. I'll sign a document indicating I've copied and removed the file copies off-premises." He glanced at Aiden. "Any problem with me doing that?"

His brother ran his fingers through his hair, leaving it standing in little rows. "I guess not. What a fecking mess."

"Aye, it is. But the sooner we find out what's going on, the better. Don't you agree?"

Aiden nodded, a frown creasing his forehead.

Tristian rubbed his hands together. "Excellent." He handed the thumb drive to Hannah. "Download all the encrypted files protected with the new security. Then we can go on to Mr. Dunlop's office. I'd rather we all stick together if possible in the event he makes an unscheduled appearance. Dillon, did you say other than this recent security upgrade on Royce and Bram's computers you have remote access to the firm's files?"

"Aye. Most of the partners work from home on occasion." He noticed Royce leaning against the door frame nervously trying to secret a glance down the hallway off and on. "Hey bro, are you expecting someone?"

Royce jerked, clearly absorbed in something else. "No. Waiting for all of you to clear out of my office so I can get to work." He gave one last fervent glance down the hall and strode to his desk giving Hannah a withering look.

Aiden cleared his throat. "Don't mean to cause problems. But I'd rather stay here at the firm. Give the staff and attorneys a semblance of normal routine in the law firm. Otherwise, there'll be no work done today amid speculation and gossip. My presence here will cull that behavior and shore up our explanation of the audit before Patrice and I take the helm. Should Father make an appearance, I'll head him off."

"Okay. But if he does show, I want to be informed immediately. And be careful. Not sure what dark magic he may still be in possession of according to Gale."

"Understood." Aiden pushed off the wall. "I'm going to return to my office. I assume you'll keep me in the loop if you discover anything."

"Of course." Dillon's gaze met his brother's worried one. "We'll get to the bottom of this and right things."

His older brother blew out a breath. "I sure hope so."

After downloading all the files, Hannah removed the thumb drive and dropped it in Tristian's outstretched hand. "Next," she said brightly, then leaned over to whisper in her husband's ear.

Tristian's eyebrow shot up, he grinned, then led the way to Bram Dunlop's office. Again, the door was locked. He glanced at Dillon, who nodded. Tristian then turned the knob. "You'd think entering a locked door would be more difficult, especially when a warlock is trying to keep secrets."

Dillon narrowed his eyes. "Remember those able to do what you just did are a small percentage in this firm."

"Understood. Still…"

As they walked in his father's office door, Dillon cursed. The only thing on top of the dark mahogany desk was a clean spot where his computer monitor had set yesterday. All the files, personal items, and office supplies were gone. He rushed behind the desk and cursed again glancing down at only wires where the computer had been connected. "Father managed to port in here or have someone do it for him and take what he didn't want us to have access to."

"Explains the easy access." Tristian glanced at the desk. "Didn't you say Gale spellbound him?"

He blew out a breath. "Aye. She said he'd be unable to use his magic, but if he's channeling power other than his own—" He shrugged, raising his hand palm up. "So how'd he...or who..." He turned on his heel and raced to Royce's office. It was empty."

On Dillon's heels, Tristian paused at the top of the stairs and glanced around before snapping his fingers. "He didn't get far."

A loud curse came from outside the tall, glass doors.

Tristian shook his head. "I hate it when the doors close faster than you anticipated, come back, hit you on the arse, and catch the heel of your expensive shoe." His lips twitched. "You might want to retrieve your brother before he makes a scene."

A smirk curved Dillon's features but was gone by the time he reached the bottom step. "Royce. Clumsy moment?" His palm warmed the offending door. The release was immediate. Royce pitched forward but not fast enough to escape. "Hey, bro, where you going in such a hurry? We need to have a little chat." Dillon caught his arm and pulled him inside the lobby. "Don't make a scene. You're outnumbered and woefully outgunned." He raised an eyebrow. "Know what I mean?"

Royce glared up to where Tristian, Hannah, and Aiden were leaning leisurely against the balcony railing on the third-floor watching. "Yeah, I get it." His brother's shoulders slumped, and he trudged beside

Dillon up the two flights of stairs.

"Now where is Father's computer?" He gave Royce a little push onto the landing to the third floor. "If you haven't figured out already, whatever you and Father are up to has landed you both in a lot of trouble. Now would be a good time to come clean. Your license to practice law is toast, but at this point, the rest of your life could be salvageable. Think of your wife."

Hannah shook her head. "I took a quick peek at those encrypted files on Royce's computer." She clicked her tongue. "They deal with people charged in magical crimes, found guilty, brought before the Witch's Council a/k/a Magic Council and punished. Now I don't pretend to know the law but reviewing just a couple of case files I'd say the evidence against each one was sketchy at best. Bram and Royce are the solicitors of record, not the firm. But it appears the files were backing up to an off-site server for the firm." She turned to her husband. "Setup is a word I'd use."

Tristian's expression turned from mild annoyance to full-on thunderous. He swallowed hard, and his face went blank. "Guess we better take a look at those files sooner rather than later. Shall we step out back? Looks like your brother could use a little fresh air, then reconvene at your hotel?"

Dillon glanced at his watch. "Sure. I'd like to stop by the family home first. More information could be gleaned there." *I sure hope Mother isn't involved.* Not to mention maybe Father's laptop and desktop

"I'd prefer we stick together," Tristian reiterated. "Obviously, Bram has use of additional magical powers." His eyes narrowed. "I'll remedy that situation when he is located." He moved his jacket slightly, fingered a barely visible crystal collar hanging from his belt as he took the first step off the landing.

Royce's eyes went wide. "That's illegal. The council won't allow you to…"

Pausing Tristian turned to glance at him and shrugged. "It's a good thing I don't need their permission. However, I will contact my boss, Bruce— you know the Demon Overlord for the North/Western Hemisphere—and bring him up to speed." Slipping his jacket back over the collar, he grimaced. "He may take a personal interest in the case. Wrongly accused and punished individuals whether magical or mortal are rather large pet peeves of his. He does enjoy hands-on once in a while." Taking several more steps, he paused to wait for Hannah. "It's been a while since you've seen Angie, Bruce's wife, too, so he'll probably be here by tomorrow."

Hannah smiled wide, catching up to her husband. "After this is all over, we can…"

Tristian gave an almost imperceptible shake of his head."

Hannah's smile disappeared. "All right if I return to the…never mind, we're to stick together." Her lower lip barely slipped out in a partial pout.

Tristian's lips twitched. "It won't take long." He looked at Dillon. "Will it?"

He took the stairs two at a time and stopped beside Tristian. "I hope not. Depends on Mother and whether she admits to knowing Father's whereabouts. Meanwhile, not wise to allow Royce access to Father in the event he's at the house. Especially if Royce is the source of Bram's power."

"Where are Gale and Patrice?" Tristian bounded

down the rest of the steps to the second landing and turned.

One foot on the second set of steps, he gulped. "In Ireland—shopping. Well, Patrice is shopping at Gale's establishment." Dillon's face heated. "Didn't figure we needed them first thing this morning to work on the computer files. I'll contact them now. They'll be here by sundown."

"Good." Tristian reached the lobby floor first and turned, eyed Royce. "What should we do about you?"

"This way." Dillon led the way through the lobby, the tiny kitchen, break room, and out the back door before he yanked his phone out of his pocket, tapped a series of numbers, and put the phone to his ear. "Patrice, we need you at the firm. Now."

"But I'm not done," his sister's plaintive whine rose through the phone.

"Now."

"Be right there. I'll have Erin package the rest of my purchases." She ended the call in a huff.

"Patrice is on her way. We can leave Royce with her at the hotel and…."

A pop sounded from behind a huge fir tree on the back lawn of the firm. "What's so damn important." Patrice sauntered out from behind the pine, a shopping bag tucked under her arm.

He filled her in on the current situation.

Tristian nodded in agreement. "We'd like you to stay with Royce in Dillon's hotel room. If you're comfortable with that arrangement. I'd prefer we all stick together, but… Not wise to have him in the vicinity where Bram may be located."

Patrice glanced in her shopping bag. "No

problem."

To his surprise, he felt a presence in his mind, then heard Tristian's voice in his head. *She is trustworthy. Right? You'd stake your life on it?*

He answered in kind. *Yes, I'd trust her with my life.*

Good enough. I'd like Gale here also. Her many talents will come in handy. Tristian raised one eyebrow.

He nodded. *I agree. I'll make the call.*

Patrice polished her bright orange nails against her cream and tangerine blouse. "By the way, Gale said she'd be here as soon as Erin returned to the shop from taking Trouble for a walk."

"Excellent." he and Tristian chimed in unison.

Tristian cocked his head and stared at him. "More trouble?"

"No, no. Trouble is Gale's dog's name. It's a long story. Best get over to my parents' house before we lose the element of surprise." He strode toward the limo where Ian waited. "We can ride over near the house, then pop in. Not enough time to follow a magic trail, if Father is at the house." *Which I'm betting he's not.*

Ian stepped out of the vehicle and opened the doors. Patrice and Hannah slid in first followed by Royce, Tristian, and Dillon. "To Blythswood Square first. We'll drop Royce and Patrice there, then take the rest of us over to Father's home."

"Yes, sir." The driver closed the doors and slipped behind the wheel.

Once Patrice and Royce were safely at Blythswood, Dillon tugged his phone from his pocket and touched in Gale's number. It rang several times and finally rolled over to voice mail. He frowned but left a message. The knot in his gut twisted tighter as he disconnected the call. As he shoved the phone back in his pocket, it rang again. "What the heck?"

Tristian raised an eyebrow. "Popular this evening, are you?"

The screen lit up with a familiar name and number. Hurriedly he put the phone to his ear. "Cork?"

"Aye. I've accidentally run across something you may have lost." Cork's voice hissed into the phone.

"I'm kinda in the middle of something right now. Can it wait?" He shifted in his seat.

"Not long. I believe you've been searching for this—um—item. Can't talk now. I'll call you back."

"Where are you?"

"Wales." She disconnected.

He looked at the screen, his brows furrowed. "That was really weird—even for Cork." Dillon repeated the conversation for Tristian and Hannah.

"You don't have any idea what she meant?" Tristian rubbed his thumb and forefinger over his chin.

"None." Switching gears, Dillon tried to concentrate on the matter at hand.

****

Ian stopped the limo behind the flowering hedgerows separating the road from the driveway and parking area in front of the Dunlop house. The driver jumped out and opened the doors. "Do you want me to wait?"

"No, thanks. I'll contact you later tonight or tomorrow." As he stepped out of the vehicle, the scent of sweet briar swirled around him on the light breeze.

"See you then." After closing the doors, Ian returned to the driver's seat and quietly drove the vehicle down the lane.

"It's now or never." As twilight fell on the house, only two windows glowed with a warm yellow light. "Port into the kitchen. Should be someone around this time of the day." He started toward the house.

A loud pop came from the other side of the hedgerows. "Dillon?"

Chapter 18

Enlightening Conversation and Secrets are Spilled

"Gale, is that you?" Dillon said in a loud whisper.

Another pop, this one quieter, and she appeared behind him. "Sorry about that. I scryed in on you, but I wound up on the wrong side of the hedgerows. Didn't screw anything up, did I?" She brushed the leaves and twigs from her long patchwork skirt. "Magic signature was disguised."

"But magic trail…We were attempting to make a surprise entrance." He shrugged. "It is what it is. Let's go."

They ported to the center of the kitchen. Cook squealed in surprise. His mother paused her fork of salad halfway to her mouth, then set it back in the bowl. "To what do we owe this grand entrance? Who are your friends, Dillon dear?"

"As you know, Tristian and his wife Hannah are here to help in the investigation of the firm." He turned and took Gale's hand. "You know Gale."

"Nice to see you again, Gale. It's a pleasure to meet you, Hannah." Smoothly, she rose to her feet and offered her hand. "Tristian Shandie, we meet again. "

"The same." Tristian smiled a wolfish grin. "Trying to get to the bottom of this unfortunate situation as quickly and quietly as possible as we discussed at the park."

"Seems you've been unsuccessful. Raised quite a few eyebrows this morning at the firm." Iris pursed her lips. "I received several phone calls early this morning from staff members when you barged into the office."

"Didn't barge. Merely entered and asked a few questions." Tristian's voice held a hint of irritation.

"Be that as it may, you upset the staff." Iris narrowed her eyes at Dillon.

"Mother, that situation has been rectified. The staff is now aware that Hannah and Tristian are on my legal team. You're stalling. Where's Father?"

"I've not a clue. He left late last night and hasn't returned." His mother eased into the chair and pushed her bowl away.

He narrowed his eyes. "Isn't that strange behavior even for him?"

His mother waved a hand dismissively. "No. We've been at odds for several months. I don't approve of his sneaking around, including Royce in late-night clandestine meetings. Did you know Clarisse has threatened to leave him?" Iris clicked her tongue disapprovingly. "After all these years together, your father has gone off his rocker. A late mid-life crisis?"

"When did all this start?" Dillon wanted to know.

His mother was quiet for several beats. "When you started dating Gale. To be honest, he was envious of her heritage and power. He spent an inordinate amount of time researching her. Then when you became engaged—Well…" She turned her attention to Gale. "The Fae in your linage worried him."

Gale released Dillon's hand, took a step forward, and directed her gaze at Iris. "My family is an open book in the magical community, at least in Ireland. I've nothing to hide. As far as magic, heritage, and power, we are what we are. There's no changing that. He even acknowledged that early on. Remember? Wouldn't you say?"

Dillon returned to Gale's side and slid an arm around her waist. "Ultimately, it was none of Father's business."

"Not the way your father saw it. To make matters worse, your grandfather Sturgen took your side. Always favored you, he did. They had a terrible disagreement. Sturgen refused to discuss it further. In fact, they hadn't spoken of that subject since that day." Iris tapped her finger to her lips. "It all happened around the same time frame, eighteen months ago give or take."

"His home computers, laptop?"

"All gone. When I went to his home office door this morning, it was locked." His mother sniffed. "As if that could stop me. Obliterated his magic protecting the door and walked in. Nothing there. You're free to take a look." She motioned down the hallway.

Dillon and Gale strode across the kitchen floor, took a right, and followed the hallway to the paneled double wooden doors. He paused, grasped the knob, and turned to push open the door. Inside things were strewn around, drawers empty and left open, closet door ajar, and the desktop was clear. He walked around the large wooden desk, recalled sitting on it as a child watching his father work. Disconnected wires lay scattered on the floor. The scene was reminiscent of the condition of his office at the firm. "He's gone. But where? Why?"

"I don't know what he's mixed up in, but it's bad.

Involves the Magic Council as well. About the Council…" She directed her statement to Tristian. "I've heard tell that a couple of unscrupulous individuals have been appointed in recent months after a respected witch and warlock retired. Your friend Cork wrote an article about it a while back. Then I believe she was forced to write a retraction. Well, it was mostly a retraction. You know Cork."

He shoved his fingers through his disheveled hair. "Mother, why didn't you bring all this to Aiden or Patrice's attention? Bloody hell, you could have called me."

"Because Aiden has enough on his plate with his family and law practice. Until recently, Patrice would run like a scared rabbit rather than confront him. She's changed since your return." His mother shrugged. "United front, I'd guess. I have to live under the same roof as your father, so I took the path of least resistance. You…you made a life for yourself in Ireland." Her tone was bitter. "Eventually, your grandfather did contact you. And here we are." Her gaze surveyed the room landing momentarily on each individual.

Gale touched the desktop, ran her fingers over the filing cabinets, the telephone, and closet doors. "He's gone. But he wasn't alone when he cleared out this room. The snippets of visions I see—he's trying, I mean he tried to mask magic detection—so I can't get clear impressions, but he's scared and being rushed by whoever is with him. It's not Royce." She closed her eyes. "Clock says two in the morning as he was closing the door."

"Sounds about right," Iris said wearily and sighed. "Might be best to close the firm."

"Best for who? And what happens to Patrice, Aiden, and all those who've worked there for years?" He released Gale, leaned over the desk, and slapped his hand on the top. "No, I won't let that happen. The firm may not hold my interest, but Aiden and Patrice deserve better. Hell, the firm has stood for justice for over a century. We can't just let it crumble under a cloud and walk away."

Tristian took his phone out of his pocket. "I'm going to get a team working on locating your father." He turned his attention to Gale. "Any impression where he was going?"

"Not really, but I don't believe he is still in Scotland."

Dillon stood staring at his shoes, then his head jerked up and he snapped his fingers. Yanking out his cell phone, he scrolled to the call from Cork. "She should have called back by now. Any bets she saw Father in Wales? That's what she was trying to tell me."

"You sure?" Tristian paused in his conversation.

"No. Not until she calls back. But it's a place to start. She said she found something we lost or was looking for. Gotta be Father."

Tristian resumed his conversation. "Wales. I want you boots on the ground ASAP." He ended the call. "Hannah, you have access to the files on Royce's computer?"

Hannah held out the memory stick. "Yep."

"Let's convene at the hotel. We'll get a room, and you can start through the files."

Gale waved her arm. "I can help." She glanced at Hannah. "Not as good as you, but I can hold my own with a computer. Besides, I can help comb through the accounting records, if necessary. Never know what we'll find."

Chewing on her bottom lip, she hesitated a beat glancing at Dillon. "You might want to check on Patrice and Royce. The items she purchased at my shop would make a pretty powerful truth potion, with a few nasty side effects. Patrice was pretty pissed at your father and Royce."

He whirled on her. "Why didn't you say something sooner?"

"No chance. You've been pretty involved with things here," she shot back.

"On that note, I'd better head back to my room. I'll give you a status report as soon as we have one. Gale, would you care to join me?"

"My pleasure." She paused to wave to Hannah and Tristian. "See ya soon." She took his hand, and they disappeared.

They reappeared in his room to find Patrice stretched out in a chair frowning intermittently at her laptop and Royce, who was slouched on the chair opposite her with a silly grin on his face.

"If that's all you got, not going to be much help, so you're on your own, boyo." Patrice jumped up and squealed when Dillon and Gale popped in. "Wow, wasn't expecting you for a while." His sister closed her laptop and eased back into the chair with a satisfied grin.

"What have you done?" Dillon demanded.

"Just gave Royce here a little encouragement."

Gale sniffed. "I smell a truth potion with a trace of herbs given to hallucinogens."

"Maybe…" She glanced at the glass resting in front of Royce. "Someone had to do something. He wasn't cooperative."

Dillon rushed over to Royce. Shook his shoulder. "Bro, I've questions that need to be answered."

"Chill. Why so demanding?" Royce blinked up at him. "Whatcha need?"

Eying his sister with disdain, he turned his attention to Royce. "Were your encrypted files backed up to the firm's server off-site? If so, where? Why did you railroad those clients?"

"Whoa, whoa, not so fast." He leaned to the left on his chair and nearly fell to the floor, then snickered. "Secret files, no one is to know. But I know. Father said I'm the only one he could trust."

"To do his dirty work. What happened eighteen months or two years ago that took Father down this path?" Dillon shook his brother gently again.

"Can't tell you. Can't tell anyone." Royce held his index finger to his lips. Grinned. "Shhhh…But if you research Freestone's estate file you might get lucky. Oh…" Royce wavered from side to side and moaned. "Gonna be sick." He stood wheeled around and ran to the bathroom only to miss the door, run smack dab into the wall, and slide to the floor.

Gale quickly picked up the wastebasket and shoved it under his chin. He spewed his stomach contents into the container, then eyed the glass on the table. "What did you do to me?" Belligerent now, Royce cursed and kicked at Dillon's leg.

"Father will seriously impair your newspaper friend. If he ever finds her. Her article eighteen months ago nearly outed him and—now it's time to pay the piper." Royce got up shakily from the floor and took a swing at Dillon, missed, and face planted onto the floor again.

Patrice snickered. "The spell is wearing off, he's going to be an SOB if you don't let me sedate him. I've got natural…"

"You've done enough, Pat." Dillon glowered at her.

Gale watched the exchange with interest. "He's going to be unmanageable as he comes out of the spell. Scopolamine, poppy, and peyote can be a potent combination mixed with ayahuasca. Also will make him quite sick."

"Wow, you're good. You could tell what I used just by the scent?" Patrice eyed Gale with admiration, then glanced sideways at Royce. "Purging of negative energies is the way I see it." She shrugged and handed Gale a large bottle of pink liquid. "I wasn't going to let him suffer, though he deserves it. Payback for the way he's treated me over the last few months."

"Personal feelings aside, we need to work together to find Cork and your father before he does something he'll regret for the rest of his life." Gale filled the plastic cup with the thick pink liquid, took a vial out of her bag, and sprinkled a small amount of the contents over the top.

"Wait, not more drugs or herbs. Enough damage has been done," Dillon growled.

Gale held up the vial. "It's merely a light sedative sprinkled on something to settle his stomach or he is going to be one sick puppy. Best to let him sleep it off." She paused the small plastic container held in front of Royce. "Unless you want to question him further."

Dillon put up a hand to stop Gale. "Royce, do you have any idea where Father went?"

His brother raised his head and attempted to focus on Dillon. "No. Callum, from the council, was supposed to meet him at the firm to pick up Father's computers. The jig was up, and Callum was going to mitigate the damages." Royce's chin dropped to his chest as he wrapped his arms around his stomach and moaned.

Gale knelt in front of Royce. "Here, drink this. You'll feel better."

Royce swung his arm in an attempt to knock the cup out of her hand, missed, and punched her square in the cheek. Gale reeled back, sparks snapping from her fingertips. Dillon caught her arm and steadied her. He took the cup from her other hand and yanked his brother's head back by the hair. "You do that again, and we'll leave you here alone to suffer until Tristian arrives." Dillon poured the contents of the tiny cup down his brother's throat.

Royce sputtered and coughed spraying pink droplets over his shirt.

He tossed the empty container at Royce, took out his phone, and dialed Tristian, relaying the situation.

"I'll have someone pick him up within the hour and hold him. Not sure we want to trust the Magic Council right now. My team is in Wales searching for Bram. No sign of Cork either."

"She's not answering her phone. How do you want us to proceed?" He rubbed the back of his neck and squeezed his eyes shut.

Gale put a gentle hand on his shoulder. "You're exhausted. Let Tristian handle it from here. He's got the manpower and the means."

"I can't. Gotta find Cork."

"It's handled. You can't do any more than my team is doing." Tristian's voice boomed from the phone. "We have to be smart about this."

"Okay, okay." He paced the floor. "Still, we need to search through the Freestone estate file. I vaguely remember old man Freestone was quite well off, much older than his wife. They had one son, who died while still a teenager. Devastated the family. Mr. Freestone hired our firm to set up trusts for various charities he supported.

"When he passed, though a lot of his estate went to charity, his wife, Matilda, was left with a fairly large fortune again earmarked for non-profits at her death. Rumors swirled in the magical community that she was a witch and dabbled in dark magic when they were married and again after he passed. I was surprised that Father took on the estate case with such innuendos."

Gale raised an eyebrow. "Sounds ominous. How about I go with you and help sort it all out?"

"Great." He relayed the information to Tristian.

"Sounds like a plan. If I hear anything from my team, I'll call you. Meanwhile, Hannah is going to continue to scour the files on the thumb drive. At some point, we may need access to a computer networked with the firm's server and off-site back up. Hold on a minute." Tristian switched to speakerphone.

"If we're lucky, I may be able to access older copies of the files on Bram's computers," Hannah said. "It's a long shot at best. But…"

"We'll need to meet back at the office. I have a laptop. Gale can use it. Hannah can work on Royce's computer while I use my desktop to search for the Freestone file. If that's where all this started, I may need Hannah's expertise to access it."

Gale waved a hand. "How long ago did Mr. Freestone retain your firm? Would there be hard copies archived in a file room somewhere?"

He snapped his fingers. "It's possible. The firm joined the digital age a little over a year ago. Still, a few solicitors liked to keep paper copies of their current files." He narrowed his eyes at Patrice. "Better take Royce with us. He can sleep it off in the staff lounge until Tristian's person comes to collect him."

Glancing at his watch, Dillon blew out a breath. "The workday is over. In a few minutes, everyone should be gone from the firm. Gale and I will pop into my office and check for any stragglers. Give us fifteen minutes, then the rest of you join us."

"Will do." Tristian ended the call.

He reached out for Gale's hand. "Sorry to drag you into all this. I honestly had no idea when I returned to Scotland what the hell was going on. I'm thankful for your help."

She squeezed his hand. "It's what couples do." The words popped out of her mouth before she could stop them. "I mean…"

He smiled. "I know what you mean. We'll get our life on the right path as soon as this is all over." He paused, leaned in, and kissed her, lingering as if savoring every second.

She closed her eyes as her heart did a little flutter and butterflies danced in her stomach. When she opened her eyes again, they were standing in his office at the law firm. "Wow—wasn't quite ready for that. But okay."

"The sooner we get this taken care of, the sooner we can get on with our lives in Ireland." He sighed. "Last I knew the archives were this way." Tugging her toward the door, he opened it to find Patrice and Royce standing there.

"Don't you listen?" Dillon stared daggers at her.

Gale stifled a giggle. Never had she seen him so ruffled, and his sister just didn't seem to give a damn.

"Of course. But the staff wouldn't find it unusual if Royce and I were seen," she protested. "Besides, I'd like to get to work on the accounting audit before all hell breaks loose. And you know it will."

"He's not in any condition to be seen by any of the staff."

"What? I have him upright. I'll tuck him into your office while I check out the staff lounge. Okay?"

"Better. The archives, have they been moved?" Dillon surveyed the area.

"Nope. In the lower level, first door on your right." She gave Royce a little shove. He floated into the office and over to the couch where she settled him. "Be right back, wayward brother." Patrice flounced out and sprinted down the hall.

Dillon locked the office door, descended the stairs with Gale in tow. Pushed open the door labeled files and blinked at the bright light as a female screamed. He sucked in a breath. "Jeana, what are you doing down here?"

"You scared me." She flung her hand over her heart, her breath coming in gulps. "Got an e-mail from Mr. Dunlop, your father, requesting the hard copy of the Freestone case."

"What did I tell you?" he snapped.

"I left a message on your voice mail, Patrice's, and Aiden's. No one called me back. So I thought I'd see if I could find it…"

"Nothing leaves this office without express consent from Patrice, Aiden, or myself. Is that clear?"

Jeana nodded solemnly. "Crystal."

"I'll handle it from here. You can go on home. See you tomorrow."

"I wasn't going to give…You know this is all so confusing. You three tell me one thing. Your father tells me another…and I need this job." Her eyes glistened. A tear rolled down her cheek. "I don't know what to do."

He patted Jeana's shoulder. "As I said before. Father has left the firm. Your alliance needs to be with Aiden, Patrice, or me until further notice. No exceptions!" He pointed to the door. "I'll walk you out. Gale, you'll be all right here for a couple of minutes?"

"Sure. One thing. Is there any order to these files?"

"Oh, sure. They are filed according to years and alphabetically by last name," Jeana offered helpfully.

Gale set her bag down on a chair. "Thank you. I'll get busy." The foreboding feeling that had wavered in and out since she arrived in Scotland was back. The fact that Synn warned her, before she left Ireland, to be careful and that something bad was brewing over here didn't help. She scanned the area, allowing her third eye to open, and still came up empty.

She shook off the feeling and peered at the labels listed on the front of each drawer. Finally, she found a filing cabinet labeled 2018. Sifting through the files, she opened the third drawer from the top, flipped through a few files, and found a fat accordion file.

"Bingo." Grinning, she hefted it out of the drawer and plopped it onto the table. She took out the individual file folders and spread them across the flat surface, noting tabs labeled Will, Assets, Charities, Death Certificates, Instructions, and Miscellaneous. A couple of the tabs had been torn off. Deciding to start with Miscellaneous, she eased into a chair and began shuffling through the papers. Hands reached around her shoulders. She balled up a fist and swung as she screamed, letting loose magic sparks as she whirled around.

"Whoa, there." Chuckling, Dillon dodged the sparks and caught her fist in his hand. "I thought you heard me come down the stairs."

"Obviously not." Drawing back her fist, she slapped at him and blew out a breath. Holding her hand to her heart, she claimed, "Scared years off my life."

"I certainly hope not." He tipped her head back and brushed his lips over hers. "We need some time alone," he murmured against her lips.

Her heart still beating a tattoo in her chest from fright, she relaxed against him leaning into the kiss. She parted her lips, allowing his tongue to sweep inside. Desire spiraled through her pooling in her nether regions. "Uhmm." When he eased away, the tip of her tongue traced her lips, and one corner curved up in a mischievous smile. "You gotta quit sneaking around," she teased.

"Wasn't sneaking. I walked Jeana out of the building after I had her sign me into her computer. When I came back in, I found Father's email, forwarded it to my email, and blocked his email from her computer. Easier on her that way." He spread his arms wide. "And here I am. Seriously, I thought you'd hear my footsteps. I'll not make that assumption again." His sharp blue eyes glittered as his gaze landed on the file. "What you got there?"

"The Freestone file."

Chapter 19

Surprise Visitor! A Whale of a Tale Confirmed. Now What?

Dillon peered at the files spread across the table. "You categorizing them or what?"

"Arranged them on the table after glancing inside each one. This file labeled Miscellaneous seems to have the most information in it. The documents have been well used. Whereas the papers in the other files are not.

"Looks like Bram himself witnessed Mrs. Freestone's death. There's a police report here indicating that he went to check on her and found her deceased in a chair in the downstairs library. No autopsy or investigation. Cause of death was natural causes. On the sheet labeled attorney notes stapled to the left inside of the file is a handwritten note 'coven notified.' All of the attorney notes are written by your father. So he knew she was a witch."

"We need to talk to her coven. Is there a name or anything on the coven?"

"No. Or at least I haven't found anything, but I've just started." She flipped through the papers in the Miscellaneous file, then offered it to him.

He started to reach out for the file, but his phone rang and he jerked it out of his jacket pocket. "Thank God." He touched the screen. "Where are you?"

"Who is this?" an unfamiliar voice responded.

"Where's Cork?" he demanded.

"Who is this?" the voice asked again. "Please identify yourself."

"Not until…ah hell, Dillon Dunlop here. Where's Cork?"

A muffled sound came from the phone as if someone covered the mouthpiece. Eventually, the female voice came back on the line. "Oh, so it is her phone. This is Terra Williams. How do you know Ms. Ella Mallory?"

"I'll ask the questions," he said firmly.

"Then you'll not be getting any answers. Contact Tristian." She disconnected the phone.

Furious, he shook his phone and glanced at a concerned Gale. "Who the hell is Terra Williams?"

"I'm sure I don't know. What did she say?" Gale placed a hand on Dillon's arm. "Calm down, you're not thinking rationally. What—"

"What is she doing with Cork's phone? And how does she know Tristian?" He scrolled through the directory on his phone, tapped the screen at Tristian's name, and put the phone to his ear.

At the mention of Tristian's name, recognition dawned in Gale's eyes. "Terra Williams is a team leader for Tristian's security force."

Tristian answered on the first ring. "What's up?"

"What is Terra Williams doing with Cork's phone?" he demanded.

"I don't know." Tristian paused. "But I may find out. She's on the other line. I'll call you back." The line went dead.

He stared incredulously at his phone. "He hung up

on me."

"Well, you were pretty obnoxious. Tristian doesn't tolerate that kind of attitude," Gale said mildly. "Slow down, and tell me what's going on."

He filled her in on the conversation.

"Then you need to wait for Tristian to call you back. You've alienated one of his top security officers. Don't make it worse."

His phone rang, he tapped the screen. "Dillon."

"Way to go, boyo. Terra tells me you were uncooperative among other things."

"Where the hell is Cork?" Sheer panic was reflected in his voice.

"Calm down. We don't know. Terra found her undamaged phone outside a coffee shop Cork's known to frequent. No sign of her. Now think, why would Cork leave her phone tucked under a bench outside of a coffee house she frequents? She's a shrewd newspaperwoman."

"Shit, I don't know." He shoved his fingers through his hair, then rubbed the back of his neck.

"You know her better than we do. My guess, she wanted us to know she is all right and that coffee shop is where she'd been. Terra is going to stake out the business. If Cork was in trouble, wouldn't you think her phone would be smashed? Certainly wouldn't be left in the last place she was seen."

Slowly, he nodded. "Aye, I agree with your assessment. How can we reach her to make sure she's okay? I shouldn't have involved her in this."

"Wait a minute." Gale grabbed his shirtsleeve. "She was involved long before you enlisted her help. Didn't your mother indicate Cork wrote a newspaper article that angered your father a while back?"

"True. Royce said Father was out to get her."

"Not to minimize your fears, but Cork is a seasoned reporter on the crime beat. Bet she can take care of herself and will contact you when it's safe. Meanwhile, my finest team is on it. Terra will find her. Gotta go, we'll meet you at the firm." Tristian disconnected the call.

"Better gather up all these files and take them upstairs to my office. I'll take half and you take half. We need to find out the name of Freestone's coven. Also, we need to dig into the Magic Council members, especially the new ones."

"Bet Tristian is on that. I have a better idea. Let Tristian do his job, and we can return to Ireland for a couple of days. You're wound so tight I'm surprised you haven't exploded."

"Hey, I'm not the one that showered sparks all over us a few minutes ago." His shoulders stiffened as he gathered up the files. "I can't believe you'd even suggest such a thing. Grandfather is counting on me."

"I meant after we've gone over all of the files, compared notes with Hannah and Patrice. Find out what they dug up. Of course, I wouldn't expect you to drop everything and leave now." *Like you expected me to do.*

"I'd like to know the whereabouts of Cork, too, before we leave the country. Knowing the lengths that Father went to with you, I'm afraid he's capable of anything." He shook his head as his brow furrowed.

"But he didn't hurt me. Only tried to scare me. I, like Cork, didn't scare easily. But I understand." She hefted several of the files spread across the desk and glanced expectantly at him. "Ready?"

"Aye." He signed out the files and placed the markers where the Freestone files had been, gathered the remaining files, and headed toward the stairs.

****

Upon reaching his office, the door was open and Tristian stood in the doorway. Hannah was hunched over the computer typing away.

"I'm in." Hannah leaned back in the chair and looked sheepishly at Dillon. "Figured you were still in the archives, so I borrowed your computer. It's much faster than Royce's because it's not bogged down with all the encryption and extra security software."

She pointed at the screen. "I managed to circumvent the security to your firm's off-site backup and found several files assigned only to Bram Dunlop. The news isn't good. Have a look for yourself." As she flipped the monitor around, his phone went off.

"Dillon."

"Hey, little brother, you'll never believe what I found in the accounting files. I've already sent a copy to Aiden. Thought you might want to see what our father has been up to over the past couple of years." She paused momentarily.

"Mind if I put you on video chat?"

"Go ahead. Aw hell, Dillon, it appears someone's been blackmailing Father, but only recently. Or he's paying large regular sums of money for services rendered. At least that's the category being charged. Found the computer expert he used. Apparently, the man was recommended by Callum Addiar from the Magic Council." Patrice tapped her finger to her lips. "Never heard of him. Have you?"

"No." He shifted his gaze to Tristian.

"Name is familiar. Believe he is one of the new members of the council. Callum replaced a warlock that retired a couple of years ago. Don't know much about him. Not been on my radar. Seem to remember he was born in Ireland to an Irish lass and a Scottish father. Left Ireland abruptly years ago. Parents retired and travel between the UK and the US. His sister married an American and lives across the pond."

"Geez, that's a lot of information for not being on your radar." Gale snickered.

"It's my job to keep up with shifts in the Magic Council membership. Don't need people with a personal agenda holding a seat on the council. Still trying to give them the benefit of the doubt until proved otherwise." He shrugged. "Guess this one wasn't vetted properly."

Gale's mouth dropped open. She made an exaggerated motion with her hand to close it. "Wow, what have you done with the tough enforcer I used to know?"

Hannah put a hand on his arm. "He's mellowed in his recent management position."

"Hell, don't have time to be as thorough as I used to be. Bruce delegates some of his responsibilities to me." Tristian's voice had a snarl in it.

"And he expects you to delegate part of your duties to your trusted team leaders." Hannah flicked her thumb toward him. "That part, my husband is still struggling with." She stifled a snicker with the back of her hand.

"Oh, do tell," Gale said with a grin.

"Enough about me." Tristian slapped his hand on the desk. "Back to the task at hand."

Hannah held up one finger and batted her eyes at Tristian. "One more thing. Talked to Angie this morning. She and Bruce will be visiting Ireland in the next week or two. They may pop over here if the case is still ongoing."

"Then we need to close this case before they arrive," Tristian said with determination.

Patrice cleared her throat. "Bruce…as in the Demon Overlord and his wife?" Her eyes went wide. "Time to get back to business." She ended the call.

Dillon gave a slight chuckle. "I don't think she relishes that idea."

"Not many do." Tristian narrowed his eyes at Hannah. "So are we done here?"

"Yep, I've opened the files. Dillon or Aiden can peruse them. From what I can tell, it's as we suspected. But I'm not a lawyer, uh, solicitor or barrister." Hannah pushed up from the chair. "Have a look." She motioned to Dillon.

He eased down in the chair and pursed his lips as he scrolled through the files. "Need to get Aiden in here. These are his and Patrice's babies now."

As if on cue, Aiden knocked on the door and strode into the office. "What did I miss?" He closed the door behind him.

Dillon brought him up to speed and pointed to the files listed on the screen. "You might want to bring Patrice into the loop after she's finished with the accounting audit."

"That bad?" Aiden asked hesitantly.

"Aye. You're probably going to end up reopening these cases." Dillon scowled, rubbing at his temple. "If I were you, I'd quietly contract an independent firm that

243

specializes in magical cases to straighten this mess. Then Father and Royce will have to pay the consequences. Distancing the firm from both of them would be a good start."

"See, that's why Father always said you were the legal genius of the family. A solution is always on the tip of your tongue no matter the difficulty of the situation. Sure you won't stay. The three of us could…"

He held up a hand. "My heart hasn't been in this firm for a long time. I came here because of Grandfather and to find out what Father had gotten himself into. His threat was never the end deal for me." He glanced over at Gale. Reached for her hand. "Though my handling of the whole situation nearly cost me dearly. I've made a bundle on my own in real estate and investments. Don't need family money." An alarm sounded on his computer. He tapped a couple of keys. "It can't be. I'm standing right…"

A soft knock, followed by the doorknob turning, and a click of the latch made all eyes turn to the sounds. Cork slid in the door and closed it quickly behind her. "Heard you were looking for me." She grinned wide and slumped against the door blowing out a long breath. "Been a real eye-opening adventure. I hope you can explain."

Dillon rushed to the door and flung his arms around his oldest friend. "We thought the worst after your phone was found."

"No, wait a minute." Tristian walked over to Cork and shook her hand. "I figured she was up to something and would resurface on her own time."

"Right you are. But I encountered extreme bizarre behavior and overheard conversations you wouldn't believe." She cocked her head to look up at him. "Or maybe you would."

Dillon studied his friend. Her eyes were bloodshot with dark circles under them. Her face was drawn. She appeared exhausted and ready to drop. "When is the last time you ate? Slept?"

She waved his concern away. "Been a while. A friend arranged a charter flight out of Wales for me under an assumed name. Your father and his friend were a major pain in my arse. Caught me once…well, I let them catch me. I escaped and decided it was time to leave. That's when I heard…Your father has lost it, talking crazy about witches, faeries, magic, contracts, and…paybacks." She waved her arms around as if to dismiss the ideas.

"Once on the ground, I was sure I had a tail, but either I was wrong or lost them. Tried to catch you at your hotel. But heard Patrice and Royce arguing in your room, so I disappeared. Then decided that the obvious place might be the last place I'd be expected. Took a chance, used your old security code to enter the back stairs. You really should change your code more often. Not providing much security." She spread her arms wide. "And here I am."

"First you need food, rest, and a shower." Dillon wrinkled up his nose.

Corked sniffed. "That may well be, but you need to hear what I have to say first." She caught and held his gaze. "There was always something a little different about you. But I learned to overlook it. Now…Well, we'll see.

"And you're normal?" he teased.

"Not one of you, but…You gotta let me tell my

tale."

"Fair enough. Then we get something to eat and you get some sleep." He led her over to a chair and motioned for her to sit.

She plopped in the chair as if her legs wouldn't hold her anymore. "Okay. First I saw Bram skulking around, following me, sitting close, listening, or attempting to listen in on my conversations."

Forehead creased, Dillon opened his mouth as if to speak, but closed it again without interrupting.

"I met this guy, you know, in Wales. He's cute, treats me like a princess, and my nosy nature doesn't bother him. Although, he wasn't impressed when I needed to get out of the country quickly. Still, he arranged it." She waved her arms around, then sighed.

"Probably the end of that relationship. Too bad. He was a nice guy. But that's a topic for another time. Bram never much cared for me after I wrote that article a while back. He threatened to get me fired. I placated him and my boss wrote a retraction, well, partial, but kept my job. Didn't sniff around the Dunlop family anymore. Had you been here—I'd—But you weren't." She lifted one shoulder in a shrug.

"What does that article have to do with this current situation?" he shoved his hands in his pockets.

"Don't know. While your father and his friend thought they had me captured, they talked about stolen dark magic, a broken marriage contract to an Erin Booher. Apparently, the friend had been engaged to Erin and she ran off with, now get this, King of Faeries in Ireland. I mean, really."

He cocked an eyebrow. After glancing at Tristian, he nodded for her to continue.

"Erin's father cursed her, so she would never see the light of day. Would have to spend her days inside the Faerie King's Sidhe for eternity. Now how does one do that?" She fisted her hands on her hips. "Is that crazy or what?

Holding one finger in the air, she grinned. "But wait, it gets better. The guy claims that a group of magical creatures in Ireland was able to break the curse a few years back, freeing Erin. Now the guy wants to avenge this Erin's father. Guess the guy can't get to Erin but can get to her niece, which by the way is supposedly your girlfriend, Gale." Cork shook her head. "Have you ever heard anything so far-fetched in your life?"

Dillon cleared his throat. "Tristian, a word?"

"Wait don't you want to hear the rest of my story? My escape?" Cork protested. "It's riveting. I promise."

"Of course. Just a little business I need to take care of. We'll be right back." Dillon led the way out of the office. Glancing up and down the hall, he motioned to a conference room. Once inside, Dillon touched a couple of buttons. "Soundproofing and privacy screening. Comes in handy on high profile cases." He blew out a breath as the windows turned opaque. "I'm sure Cork knows of magical creatures. She suspected me when we were dating, but I never confirmed. You indicated you knew of Cork. Did she know who you are? What you are?"

"No. She was a trusted source for information in the mortal world. But you're right, she never questioned things a mere mortal should have."

"We should—She deserves to be let in on our secret. I'm positive she'll never divulge such information, but this time she's in too deep for her own good. Who knows what my father and his companion have planned."

"Agreed. It won't be a surprise to her. Probably confirmation of what she suspected since dating you." Tristian chuckled. "And I thought my family was dysfunctional. Yours takes the cake. Who the hell is the friend of your father?"

"Don't know. Could it be Callum? The time frame fits."

"Gonna ask Terra to run an in-depth background on him right now." Tristian yanked out his cell phone. "Go ahead and bring Ella...Cork into the light. I'll be right in."

"Will do." Dillon skated out of the conference room and returned to his office. Upon opening the door, four sets of eyes stared at him expectantly. "Tristian had a business situation come up, he'll be back in a few. Meanwhile, need to bring Cork up to speed. The conversation you overheard while disconcerting on many levels to us, it's not at all as crazy as you seem to think."

He paused, shoved his fingers through his hair, and sighed. "There's no easy way to say this, so here it goes. I'm a warlock as are my father and brothers." He nodded in Gale's direction. "Gale and my mother are witches. Gale is the niece of Tiarnan, King of Faeries, and her aunt is Erin Booher, the witch in the conversation you overheard. Hannah is Tristian's wife and a gryphon shifter. Tristian is the enforcer for Bruce, the Demon Overlord of the Western Hemisphere. Angie, Bruce's wife and Tristian's sister, is a witch." He sucked in a breath and blew it out. "There you have it all in a nutshell, and no, you can't reveal any of this information to anyone ever. Any questions?"

"Just one," Gale squeaked.

He couldn't be sure, but from the silence that followed Gale's squeak and the facial expressions, everyone was more surprised than Cork. "Go ahead, Gale."

"Obviously, the people in this room are aware, but do all these other individuals know they've just been outed to a mortal? I assume you had permission." Gale glanced around the room.

"Aye. Tristian and I thought it best to bring Cork into the loop. However, you probably better have a talk with Erin in light of the information Cork relayed. See what she remembers of a Callum Addiar from her youth. He could be dangerous if we don't get them stopped."

Tristian breezed in, surveyed the room, and pinned Cork with his stare. "Any chance you know where Bram Dunlop and his friend are holed up these days?"

"Yoohoo, guys. I'm standing right here." Cork gulped in air, then exhaled drawing in a slow deep breath appearing to calm herself. "It's anyone's guess. I believe he was still in Wales when I departed. Did he know I left? Can't be sure. You can bet as soon as he finds out…" She paused.

"You know what? I've no idea. Given my recent enlightening—" Cork leaned back in the chair. "—I need time to process…" She closed her eyes and drew in another breath. "Guess my escape escapade won't be as riveting as your revelations." Her lips turned up in a weak smile. "But the story of the century drops in my lap and I can't write a bleeding word of it." She pouted.

"Probably better that way or my boss would think I'm radge. Maybe I am."

Dillon slapped her lightly on the back. "Don't play coy, you suspected something."

Chapter 20

Winds of Change Bring a Multitude of Adjustments

Gale glanced around the room again as if making up her mind. "Given the situation, I have a few suggestions." Her gaze settled on Dillon, then bounced to Tristian.

"Go ahead. You never hesitate to speak your mind." Tristian snickered.

Directing her attention to Tristian, she said, "If you can handle the Bram Dunlop situation without Dillon and myself, there's a bit of family history I've been left in the dark about. It's time light be shed on it. I'd like Dillon's help. I am asking, not issuing an ultimatum."

Dillon nodded his head. "Understood. I'm happy to assist.

"Emma, may I call you Cork?" She turned to the reporter.

"Of course," Cork responded with a smile.

"I'm sorry all this got dumped into your lap, but if you're the tough reporter your reputation claims, you'll hit the ground running without any help from us. Nothing has changed, only confirmed your long-time suspicions. Am I right?" Gale raised an eyebrow.

Cork nodded a devilish smile curving the corners of her mouth. "It's nice to have my suspicions confirmed. But what about all those defendants that were wronged? Who's going to tell their stories?"

"After I've done a little housecleaning in the Magic Council, I'll put you in touch with someone who will help you get their stories out to the magic community." Tristian held up a finger in warning. "It'll be a delicate situation to report the transgressions, leaving the firm out of it, as most were innocent of any wrongdoing, then point the finger to those convicted of illegal behavior in the magic court."

Dillon nodded solemnly.

"So it will be a long process. I'll see that whatever penalties were assessed on the wronged will be reversed. The first order of business is to find Bram, his cohort, and get to the bottom of this mess." Tristian pinched the bridge of his nose.

She turned to Dillon. "We should bring your mother and grandparents up to date before we leave for Ireland. From all I've seen and heard, Patrice and Aiden can help the firm weather the storm that is coming." While she paused to gather her thoughts, the silence was deafening.

An ominous tune shattered the quiet. Tristian yanked his phone out of his pocket, scowled at the screen, then put the phone to his ear. "Terra, what ya got?" A short pause. "Whoa, slow down. Hold on a minute." The warlock walked toward the door, paused glancing at the anxious expressions of the individuals in the room, and held up a finger. "Give me a minute." He sauntered through the door and shut it behind him.

Patrice popped into Dillon's office. "Sorry about the magic. Didn't want to deal with Jeana and her questions. I can't blame her, but…" She paused eyes wide like a deer caught in the headlights, then switched her attention to Dillon. "Did I miss something?"

"Jeana is gone for the day. Not really.. Felt it necessary to bring Cork up to speed on all things with this family's magic. Our secrets are safe with her. Now, let me see what you have?"

In her hand, she gripped several sheets of paper. "These spreadsheets document all the discrepancies I found in the firm accounting, along with backup. I've put payments on hold unless Aiden or myself approve the expenditures. Accounting will be none too happy about being kept in the dark."

The door whooshed open, and Tristian strode inside tucking his phone in his pocket. "I've called an emergency meeting of the Magic Council for tomorrow morning. The best interests of the firm would be served if Patrice, Aiden, Royce, Dillon, and Iris were to attend. Hannah and Gale should participate as witnesses. Terra and her team have captured Bram Dunlop and Callum Addiar in Wales. They are being transported to Scotland as we speak." Tristian eyed Gale. "I'm afraid your trip to Ireland will have to wait. I'm sure you understand."

Gale nodded. "I need to get my thoughts in order anyway. We won't need Erin at the meeting?"

"No. She's in no danger, and Callum hasn't had a chance to act on what Cork told us. Right now, all we have is his encouraging Bram to harass you to assure a broken engagement to Dillon. Which has certainly backfired." Tristian chuckled.

"I'd like a chance to question Father prior to him going before the council. He was always a strict parent. However, his dabbling in dark magic, taking magical cases only to dispose of them without the clients having proper representation is difficult for me to understand. At one time, the firm was his pride and joy. Now it appears he's disgraced the Dunlop firm."

Tristian shrugged. "Shouldn't be a problem. I plan to have a chat with Callum before the council can get at him." He paused for a beat. "You have to realize that sometimes the desire for power is an all-controlling factor in people's behavior. Which may be the case with your father. Still no excuse. Royce is neck-deep in this situation too."

****

A crescent moon rose in the sky with Jupiter shining bright to the lower right. A few lacy clouds floated over the Big Dipper. *What a beautiful night.* Dillon and Gale hurried after Tristian as they followed the path to the Magic Council's chambers. The iron gate leading to the building was locked.

Tristian frowned, touched the lock, and a *screeing* sound echoed through the courtyard as the tumblers in the lock turned, then the gate slowly swung open. He shook his head. "Unnecessarily formidable and dramatic."

Dillon glanced around. The ancient stone building stood on a large parcel of land. The blooming flower gardens around the building were impressive even now, despite the cold nights. Their footsteps clicked on the stone pathway leading to the huge wooden door with a large brass knocker. As they approached, chimes sounded, and the door opened smoothly into a foyer.

"Good evening, gentlemen...lady. We've been waiting for you." A thin woman with her hair pulled back in a long gray braid waved them in. "I'm Gillian, a council member at large. Tristian, we understand from Terra that you want to talk to Bram and Callum before any hearing is commenced?"

"Correct. I'll speak with Callum. Gale and Dillon will visit with his father, Bram. If that suits the council." Tristian's eyes locked on the woman's.

"Well, we have no problem with Bram. But Callum is one of our own. We'd like to question him first."

"Understandable." Tristian pulled out a document from his briefcase and handed it to her. "Witness statements and charges. He kidnapped a mortal in Wales. She escaped unharmed, but that was not their intention, or according to what she overheard. Not to mention in Ireland, he harassed Gale Booher, niece of Erin, wife of King Tiarnan of the faeries apparently in an attempt to settle an old score. Therefore, my jurisdiction takes the lead in this case."

The woman's eyebrows rose nearly to her hairline behind her wire-rimmed eyeglasses. "Mr. Addiar has been busy. We were only aware of his misguided deeds with Bram Dunlop. I'll have to clear your visit with the council's head." She switched her gaze to Gale and Dillon. "I'll escort you to your father's quarters first. Follow me. Then we'll see about Mr. Addiar. Is that agreeable?"

"Of course." Tristian indicated for her to lead the way.

Gale leaned over to Dillon. "Are you sure you want me involved in this? Bram doesn't like me and will more than likely be quite uncooperative bordering on combative with me present."

He slowed their pace considerably. "Probably. This arrangement will allow you to determine any dark magic he may still be able to wield. Want to read his reaction when I confront him with Cork's allegations regarding your family and his actions against you."

She switched to nonverbal communication. *We both know he wasn't present in Ireland. He sent his minions and your brother. But remember, solicitor, we don't have any proof, only hearsay from me.* She smiled smugly.

He followed her lead. *This isn't official. I just want to see what he has to say. He won't be able to falsify his statements with you there to encourage the truth.*

A wicked smile lit up her eyes. *Am I to understand the encouragement can take any form I desire?*

"Aye." He took her hand and strode quickly to catch up with Gillian and Tristian who were impatiently waiting in front of a scarred wooden door.

Gillian touched her hand to the iron pad on the wall next to the handle, then indicated that Dillon do the same. The door opened to reveal Bram pacing around the small room with a bed, table, and two chairs. He lunged toward them only to run up against an invisible shield that appeared to run the entire length of the room. "Mr. Dunlop, you have visitors." She turned toward the door. "Dillon, your handprint on the metal plate next to the door will allow you to leave when you are ready."

"Contact me when you're ready to leave." Tristian standing outside the door tapped a finger to his temple.

"Understood." Dillon turned to face his father with Gale at his side as the door slid shut. "Father, we're here to listen to your side of the story before I advise you of the charges you are facing."

"I've nothing to say to the likes of you." Bram

jerked his chin toward Gale. "Or her. Your witch's family has a habit of not complying with contracts made in good faith."

Gale studied Bram, narrowed her eyes. "Where'd you get the dark magic?"

"It's mine. You miscalculated in your effort to spellbind me." Bram glared at her. "Embarrassing for a witch of your talents. Huh?" He sneered, then raised his arm over his head, conjured a dark maroon fireball, and viciously lobbed it toward his son and Gale. The ball hit the shield with a bang, fractured into several pieces, and bits of it streaked across the room impaling him in the leg and abdomen. He shrieked letting out a stream of curses and fell back into a chair nearly toppling it over.

Without sympathy, she waggled her finger back and forth. "Dark magic doesn't recognize a master as white magic does. Especially when it doesn't belong to the wielder. In fact, it could kill you given the right circumstances." Shrugging one shoulder, she glanced at Dillon. "Better lay out the charges we have proof of before he incinerates himself."

"Good point. Father, we have proof that you stole the magic from Widow Freestone when you went to visit her at the hospital the day she died. It's the only way you obtained the power, but you were caught. Callum found out, didn't he? Blackmailed you. We also have been able to gain access to your and Royce's encrypted case files. Not only did you take magic cases, which is against the firm's policy, you railroaded those clients. The only thing we don't know is why. You'd always been proud of our family firm, and now you've brought scandal to it. Why? Patrice and Aiden may not be able to save it when all is said and done. What a family legacy you've left."

Bram raised a bony finger shakily and pointed it at Gale. "It's all her fault. She used her great power to lure you away from the firm, me, your mother, and your duty to take over the firm when I retire. I was only trying to compete with her. Did you know her family possesses ancient Fae magic? That's why she is so powerful. How was I supposed to compete with her for you?"

He raised an eyebrow. "Not true. I've voiced my desire to leave the firm long before Gale came along. Do you think so little of me, that I'd allow magic to influence my decisions or my feelings? You don't know me at all.

"Her family had nothing to do with power. I wanted a life outside the firm. I don't live and breathe the law and this firm. None of us wanted that. Wasn't going to get it staying in Scotland. I'd made my decision long before Gale came along."

"You are no match for her powers. Her family—"

Dillon held his hand up, palm out. "Her family is not on trial here. You are. How could you do this to Mother, Sis, and Aiden? Even Royce? Why? How did Callum find out? Bragging, were you? Flashing your newfound power around? Callum did a little research and discovered what you'd done and blackmailed you into doing his bidding? Isn't that what happened?"

Bram's eyes flew open wide, then narrowed. "What did he say? It was all his idea. Did you know he was engaged to Erin? Then she ran off with Tiarnan." A slow evil grin spread over Bram's face. "Her father couldn't force her to marry Callum, but he punished her. She was never to see the light of day—until those meddling creatures broke the curse, allowing Erin to go free. Her father had to be avenged. It was only right. Don't you understand? Erin's father went to the grave knowing his firstborn daughter would pay dearly for her wrongdoings."

"That had nothing to do with you or me or Gale, for that matter." He shoved his hand in his pockets. "We aren't getting anywhere." He glanced at Gale. "Father will have to defend himself. Let's go." Dillon stood, took Gale's hand, and ambled toward the door. "You're not the man I thought you were."

Crossing his arms, Bram leaned back against the chair. "You're not the son I deserved. Running off with the likes of her." Bram snorted, then stared daggers at Gale and began muttering to himself. The air in the room stirred. A thin gray cloud formed on the ceiling and spread.

Gale glanced at the mist and back at Bram. She waved a hand in the air and pinched her fingers together. The cloud folded in on itself and with a snap disappeared. A light stench of sulfur remained in the room. "Bram, you realize that magic would have poisoned you as well as your son."

Keeping eye contact, she snapped her fingers. Black tendrils floated out of him. She pulled them toward the middle of the room, then set them on fire. White threads appeared out of thin air, wound around him, and faded into his body.

Bram watched in horror. "What have you done?"

"Not me. You. Gave me a peek at your ill-gotten magic, enough to bind and destroy it too." She brushed her hands together.

He jumped up and lunged at them. This time he

stopped before the magic barrier. "I'm not going to take the fall for Callum. He forced me to take those magic cases. They were people who wronged him in business. They deserved what they got. Cleaning up the magic community was his mission. One day he'd run the Council, and then we'd both be unstoppable."

"This was all for personal gain, power, prestige, and money? Wasn't holding the reins of the oldest, most prestigious firm in Scotland enough?" Dillon shook his head.

"Aye, until she came along. Lured you away, she did." He hung his head, and his shoulders slumped as if what he'd done began to register.

"Shame on you for dragging Royce through the muck with you." Dillon touched his palm to the metal plate, and the door opened. "We're through, old man." He walked out into the stone hallway, still holding Gale's hand like a lifeline. *Tristian, I'm finished. The council can have him.*

Chapter 21

The Aftermath, Rebuilding, and a New Beginning

Gale walked silently beside Dillon down the long stone hallway. The wall sconces were converted to electricity and flickering red and orange shadows of light on the walls and floor. Yet the black soot from flame and maybe gas fuels of years gone by remained. Why hadn't they simply used magic to light the chambers? Maybe this building hadn't always been home to the council.

Her mind circled back to the crisis at hand. Dillon would have to help pick up the pieces of the family. Somehow they'd have to come together, deal with the betrayal of the head of the family, and move forward. She longed to talk with Erin about everything but knew it would have to wait. The Dunlop family and Dillon would have her immediate attention.

"Dillon, I need to let Erin know I won't be home for a bit of a while."

"Of course." He turned to her as tears glistened in his sad blue eyes.

Never had she seen him in so much pain. It was overwhelming as she embraced him. Though engaged, this was the first time she'd seen a vulnerable side to him. He was always the warrior, protector, joker, happy-go-lucky sort. Rubbing her hand up and down his back, she hoped the family could come together somehow, as he laid his head on her shoulder.

"We can return to Ireland if you wish," he said softly.

"No. You've family business here. I'll help where I can. Where will we be staying?"

He raised his head off her shoulder and stared off into space for a few moments. Took a deep breath, blew it out, and straightened his shoulders. "Possibly at the family home until Mother is settled and things are on even ground again. I don't imagine she'll return to the firm. Though she enjoyed her work with charities contracted by the firm, she'll leave the business to Aiden and Patrice." He gave a half laugh. "They've got their work cut out for them."

"You'll not stay and help them rebuild the reputation, the firm?"

"No. It would look like I came back to rescue the firm, then stayed to bail them out. Not the image we want to project. Which couldn't be further from the truth. After the fallout, resurrecting the firm and its reputation will fall squarely on Aiden and Patrice's shoulders, where it belongs. They're strong and will weather this storm just fine." He took her chin between his thumb and forefinger and lifted it. "I love you."

"I know." She brushed strands of reddish-brown hair from his handsome face. Gazing into those fierce blue eyes, she rose on her tiptoes, and brushed her lips over his, then wrapped her arms around his neck.

He smiled against her lips. The Scottish warrior was back. "We're all right then?"

"We will be." Suddenly glad she'd brought the ring with her to Scotland. *This is where things should be settled for all to see.*

Footsteps echoed on the stone floor. Dillon turned to see Tristian striding toward them and sighed as Gale glanced at him. "On to the next problem."

"All settled?" Tristan's gaze flipped from Dillon to her.

"Aye. How about Callum?"

"He'll take the majority of the blame for this fiasco. Except Bram's stealing of Freestone's magic. Your father must take responsibility for that and let the chips fall where they may. A better deal than he deserves, in my opinion, after ripping his family apart at the seams." Tristian's eyes were cold as steel.

"Will you be staying for the hearing?" Gale rested her hand on Tristian's arm.

"Nope. My job is done here. They've been brought to justice. It's up to the Magic Council to decide punishment. They have my statement and know how to reach me, if necessary." He grinned at her. "Hannah and I will be returning to Ireland to meet with Bruce and Angie. I'll give the boss my report, then it'll be on to more pleasant events. They arrived this morning and are staying with Tim and Mary."

He scrubbed his hand over his face. "There's not much left for you here. Wrap it up with your mother. Afterward, why don't you and Gale pop over to Ireland for a few days? The diversion will do you good. Besides, Gale has a few loose ends she needs to tie up with Erin. Your absence would allow Patrice and Aiden to sort things out. Then you can see what help they need from you."

Gale pursed her lips then smiled. "Not a half-bad idea." She tilted her head up to Dillon.

"Aye, we'll see you in a few days." Dillon took Tristian's outstretched hand. "Thanks for all your help and support."

"It's my job." Tristian shook Dillon's hand vigorously. He reached out and gave Gale a hug. "See ya soon."

****

Dillon and Gale walked slowly up the cobblestone path to the front door of his family home. He raised his hand and knocked, then waited. Rhona, the family's housekeeper, opened the door.

"Well, it's about time you showed up. Your mother—well—she's not herself." Rhona motioned them inside, then continued to peer out the door. "Where's your brothers and sister? Didn't they come with you?"

"No. I thought they'd be here. Except for Royce. He's got himself in a spot of trouble. He'll need to work through it before making social calls." Dillon shoved his fingers through his hair and rolled his tight shoulders. "Has anyone heard from Clarisse, Royce's wife?"

"Not that I know of. Just me and Iris have been here all day. Something bad happened, didn't it?"

He placed a reassuring hand on the housekeeper's shoulder. "Afraid so. Where's Mother?" Dillon took Gale's hand and walked through the foyer.

"I'm in the sitting room," his mother called out. As he walked into the room, she lifted her eyes to him. There were dark circles under her red-rimmed eyes. "So it's over? He's alive?"

"Aye. But Father's got a lot to answer for. It's out of our hands. Tristian saw to it that Callum will take most of the blame. Except Father will have to answer for stealing Freestone's magic at her deathbed." Dillon shook his head. "No way around that. He let greed take over his better sense…knew better."

His mother held his gaze for a beat more, then turned to Gale. "It's not your fault. I understand that now. It's just that the power you and your family wield, he couldn't…In his eyes, you spirited Dillon away from him. I guess he felt more and stronger magic could win his son back." Iris rubbed a hand on her chest over her heart. All the anger gone. This was still her family and had to be pieced together beginning with her. "We all know better."

"Thank you for that, Mrs. Dunlop. I had no idea he was even aware of my heritage. Not that it would have mattered. I fell in love with your son, and that was the way of it. I won't apologize for my feelings. Nor would I change them. Wish things would have turned out different."

"Nor would I." Dillon stepped closer to Gale, drew her to him. "The important thing now is to repair the family bonds and get through this. It will take all of us, but we'll be stronger for it."

"So you'll be staying in Scotland?" His mother glanced hopefully up at him and took his hand in hers.

"No. I don't belong at the firm. My place isn't here, hasn't been for a while. I'll stay as long as you need me. But eventually, I'll return to Ireland with Gale to make our home. You must come visit."

"You'll be marrying her?" His mother looked at Gale's bare left hand and back to her son.

He smiled at Gale. "*Mo ghràidh*. Pull that ring you've been carrying around out of your pocket and put it on. Don't want people getting the wrong idea. You belong to me."

After removing the ring from her pocket, her hand paused in midair. "Now wait just a minute. Scotsman. I'll not be anyone's property. Not now. Not ever."

His deep blue eyes sparkled with mischief. "Simmer down, lass." He put his hand over hers, turned it over, and plucked the ring out of her palm. Dropping to one knee, he grinned up at her. "I'm meaning that I give myself over to only you as you will do the same. I want to spend my life with you. Will you do me the honor of becoming my wife?" He paused for a moment. "As soon as possible."

"Well, since you put it that way. Of course, I'll marry you. But let the record reflect your first proposal was much more romantic." She smirked.

He shrugged. "Same outcome."

His mother sat quietly, her gaze shifting from her son to Gale. "Welcome to the family, Gale. Sorry those words have been so long in coming. You will inform me of your wedding plans?"

"When we set a date. We'll let you and the rest of the family know." He turned his gaze on Gale. "Sooner better than later, if it's up to me."

"Men. Always in a hurry when there are months of planning to be done." His mother gave a wan smile.

"Actually. I agree with Dillon. We've waited long enough."

"So be it." Dillon frowned and whirled toward the foyer. Voices and footsteps grew louder. "What the bloody hell?" He strode toward the hallway.

Patrice and Aiden burst into the room. "Sorry we're late," his brother and sister said in unison.

"Had to calm Clarisse down before I could head over here. I assured her she'd be taken care of while Royce pays his debt to the council. At the moment, she's not sure she'll keep his boots under the bed. Can't blame her. But perhaps after the dust settles, she may give him another chance." Patrice turned her attention to her mother and put an arm around her. "You all right?"

Her mother nodded. "Dillon explained everything. Wasn't much of a surprise. Knew he was mixed up in something bad. He of all people knows the consequences of bad and illegal behavior."

"The firm's employees have been informed about the sordid events. Only told them what they needed to know to start the firm moving in the right direction." Aiden glanced at his brother. "You'll be resigning from the firm again…correct?"

"Aye, you'd be in the way of the right of it. I have the necessary documents to start a small firm in Ireland when I'm ready. Thanks to you and several of the other partners."

"There'll always be a place for you in the family firm," Aiden assured him. "Provided we weather this mess."

"I know and thanks for that. It's never been a good fit. The firm will be fine with you and Patrice guiding it."

Aiden switched his attention to his mother. "Did you want to return to the business? To your charities? You're welcome. We could use you in an advisory capacity with all your charities."

His mother chuckled and waved her hand in dismissal. "Heavens, no. I like my life as it is." She paused a couple of beats. "Well, maybe, let me think about it. I'm so sorry that you have to clean up after your father."

"Not a problem. We got this." Aiden glanced over at Patrice for confirmation. But she was otherwise occupied.

Patrice stared at Gale's left hand. "Is there something you want to tell us?" She leaned forward and tapped her foot.

"Like what?" Dillon acted confused. Then he roared with laughter. "Didn't take you long. Always were the nosy one."

"Observant, dear brother. I'm observant. Been watching for the ring to reappear. You two are meant to be together. It was your stubborn streak that caused you to nearly lose her. I believe you've wised up, little brother."

He raised an eyebrow and glared at her.

"Okay, so it was family interference too. So when is the wedding?"

"There are a few things to take care of before we can turn our attention to wedding plans. Be assured you'll be among the first to know." Dillon tented his fingers and touched the tips to his chin. "But it will be soon. Very soon."

Chapter 22

Return to the Emerald Isle, and Erin's Story

In the flat above Pixie Magic, Trouble snored softly at the foot of the bed as the sun rose through the mist. Gale relaxed with her head on Dillon's shoulder, her gaze on his chiseled face, full lips, and eyelids fringed in long, dark, thick eyelashes any woman would kill for, covering his expressive wild blue eyes. Those wild eyes blinked open.

"Good morning, *ghràidh*." He rolled over and enveloped her in his arms. "Sleep well?"

"Aye. And you?"

"Better than expected. Must be your home." He lifted one arm above his head and stretched, letting out a jaw-popping yawn. "What's on the agenda today?"

"I'd like to have a conversation with Erin. It's Sunday so the shop is closed. We'll have to walk the cliffs to find her. Trouble will enjoy the romp." She reached for her sweater and swung it around her shoulders.

A knot formed in her belly. *Just not sure I should even bring up the subject of Callum. Is it my place? Happened so long ago, maybe best to leave it alone. What if he only gets a slap on the hand because of his influence. Would he continue on his vendetta against*

Erin or me? Gotta warn her. Probably Tiarnan too. She refocused her thoughts and gaze to find Dillon staring at her.

"What's on your mind? Seems like you were having troubling thoughts. Aren't we past all that kinda stuff? Anything I can do?" Concern clouded his brilliant blue eyes as little lines dug into his forehead.

Nonchalantly, she waved his worry away. "Nothing. Concentrating on where Erin is. That's all."

His brow remained furrowed as if he wasn't buying her excuse. "It's long past sunrise when they're out and about. Erin isn't walking the cliffs?"

"She's aware when I want to talk and will appear where I'm walking along the cliffs. I've never bothered her in their Sidhe."

Disappointment flashed across his handsome, but he quickly covered it up. "I see. Here I was hoping to get a look at a Faerie Sidhe."

"Oh, no—We never—Considered the height of bad manners." She glanced at him again. This time the disappointment had changed to a mischievous glint in his eyes. "You're yanking me chain."

He drew back looking aghast. "Who me? I'd never do that." With a chuckle, he kissed her long and hard. "So wanta have shower sex, *mo ghràidh,* before we get this day started?"

"Sure." She leaned over, brushed her lips teasingly across his neck, then trailed kisses to the corner of his sensual mouth.

A whine came from the bottom of the bed along with clicking of dog nails on the hardwood floor. The sound quickly escalated to a series of barks.

"Hold that thought." Gale slid out of bed, shrugged

into her robe, and reached down to scratch Trouble behind the ears. The dog promptly rolled over for a belly rub. "You don't have to go that bad." As if contrary to her mistress's words, the pup flipped back over and rushed to the door. "Okay, okay. Let's go." She opened to back door.

Trouble thundered down the stairs, across the small yard, and did her business, then turned as if expecting praise.

Laughing, Gale raced down after her and swept her up in a fierce hug. "What a good lass you are." She carried the pup back upstairs and closed the back door. "Now don't you get in any trouble. Understand?"

The dog tilted its head and blinked dark brown eyes up at her, flipping one ear back and forth as if trying to figure out what her human wanted.

Gale returned to the bedroom to find Dillon already in the shower. "Hey, boyo, you made me a promise." She untied the belt to her pink robe, tossed it on the bed, and pushed open the bathroom door. Clouds of steam billowed out as she heard his baritone voice singing an Irish ballad about a wild rose.

Smiling, she quietly closed the door and slid open the shower curtain to take in the view. She grinned at her Adonis. Wide shoulders, muscular chest, strong arms, narrow hips, long legs, and the sexiest round bum. She couldn't help but reach out and stroke it. The man was built to satisfy. Best of all, he was all hers. She liked that part the best. A glance at her left hand, she wiggled her fingers and watched the stone shimmer in the light and sighed.

He yelped and whirled around. Fluffy soap suds flew through the air. A wide smile curved his luscious lips. "I didn't hear you come in, darl'n." He gathered her tight against him.

"I noticed. Never heard you sing before." She slipped her arms around his neck and wrapped her legs around his waist. "You have a talent for song."

He tilted his head. A puzzled expression slid across his face. "Guess I've always been caught up in trying to make a living or to impress you. To be honest…" He groaned as she ground into him and closed his eyes for a moment. Then he eased her against the shower wall and flipped off the water. "Warmed it up for ya."

"Looks like that's not the only thing warmed up for me." She giggled and leaned back. When she slipped one hand between them, teasing his impressive erection with her fingertips. He groaned.

"Now don't be doing that. Don't want you spoiling the fun." He encouraged her arm back around his neck and slid into her. "I'm already in the way of wanting you something fierce. But first…" He moaned and pushed farther inside.

His tormented growl was a heady invitation. She sucked in a breath as he nibbled on her neck, braced her against the shower wall, freeing his hands to roam over her firm breasts, fingers to tweak the little bundle of nerves between her legs, making her squirm. Ducking his head, he teased and caressed her nipples with his tongue, before sucking first one then the other into his warm moist mouth until they were hard little berries.

She could feel his heart thudding against her own as she bucked against him, taking all of him, then screaming his name when she crashed over the edge of ecstasy. Multi-colored stars sparkled across the ceiling and bright streamers danced in the air slowly fading away.

"Now that's what I like to hear and see from my woman."

She wiggled and ground against him again. Letting out a long moan, he grabbed her arse. "You're going to kill me." He pumped into her until pleasure flowed through them, then pressed her a little longer against the wall until the waves of ecstasy subsided. He slowly lowered her feet to the floor, turned on the water, and directed the spray away from them. "Better give the water a chance to warm up."

"Uh-huh. Mmmm." She reveled in the feel of him inside her and let out a little sound of displeasure as he pulled away.

With a little chuckle, he stroked the side of her breast. "Don't worry. There's plenty more where that came from, but right now someone is coming up the path to your back stairs. Don't want us to get caught—" He paused. "—like this. Do we?"

"Don't really care," she murmured as her lips found his. "Spent too much time stressed, worried, upset, disillusioned, and in fear of what others might think. I want to feel like this forever." She wound more tightly around him as the warm water splashed down on them.

"Okay. Not sure Tiarnan will be in the way of impressed." He snickered.

"What! Who?" She backed away, then unceremoniously shoved him out of the shower. "I'll finish my shower. You entertain my uncle." She yanked the shower curtain closed. "I'll be out in a minute. Just let him in. He'll play with Trouble. Unless he's here on business. Then…"

Dillon stumbled back, then surged forward and shouldered open the curtain again. "But I don't know him that well. To me, he's been more in the way of a legend, myth, not man—ah— king."

"Don't worry. He's just a lovable teddy bear."

"To you, maybe. But I'm the one banging, ah, marrying his…almost daughter, niece… at least. Not to mention breaking her heart not long ago. Nope, not sure this is a good idea." Snatching a towel from the rod, he quickly dried off and scooted into the bedroom leaving the bathroom door wide open.

"He knows the trials of love and family. Don't worry." She yanked the curtain closed again, shampooed her hair, rinsed, and snatched a towel. Hurriedly, she towel-dried her hair, ran a comb through it, and dashed into the bedroom. Shimmying into underwear and a long patchwork skirt, she pulled a turquoise sweater over her head, then braided her hair and toed on tennies.

When she walked out into the living room, Tiarnan sat with the dog on his lap laughing about something with Dillon. The scene warmed her heart. This was just what he needed. What they needed. Family the way it should be.

"Hi, Tiarnan. What brings you here without Erin?" She scooted over to hug him and kiss his cheek.

"Well, that's as good a reason as any." Tiarnan squeezed her. "There's a big *cèilidh* at the pub tonight. I've been tasked to make sure the two of you attend." His chest puffed out just a little.

Dillon studied the king. "All the tales I've been told certainly don't do you justice. You're no different than Gale or me."

Tiarnan met his gaze with a smirk. "I'm not sure that's a compliment. However, what did you expect, son?"

"Someone more stuffy. Not the right word. More unreachable, legend like. Mysterious, smoke-and-mirrors type thing. That's the word. Myths and legends abound about you, but until this fiasco with Gale, no one ever saw you except walking the cliffs alone, then after the curse was broken, with Erin. Stephan suggested that you appeared and disappeared at will in the form of mist. You know the vampire."

"Aye, aye, I know Stephen. Great guy for a vampire." Tiarnan snickered. "It was a dark period in mine and Erin's life back then. Appearances were a great effort and only in the dark. So no one saw us. We still walked the cliffs but only after midnight." He paused his voice wistful. "Seems a long time ago, but it was only a couple of years ago. Now, my bride and I are free to roam wherever we want, whenever we like. So no need for magic, mystery, and melancholy. The townspeople have gotten used to seeing us."

"Why a party at the pub?" Gale wanted to know.

With a twinkle in his bright green eyes, he shook his head. "I'm only the messenger. What I suspect 'tis a happy homecoming." He laughed. "You know Mary and Tim, any excuse for a celebration." Tiarnan glanced down at her left hand. "Looks like they're in the way of the right of it."

She blew out a breath. "Word sure travels fast around here. We were planning a nice quiet evening at home. In recent days, we've had enough excitement for a lifetime. Except I need to have a few words with Erin. Sooner rather than later." She closed her eyes and soon located her aunt finishing the inventory downstairs in Pixie Magic. "She likes it here."

The King of Faeries shrugged. "I suspect she rather likes the interaction with the customers in your shop."

Trouble squirmed and wiggled until Tiarnan released the pup to the ground. "Better take her outside, less she leaves puddles. And I'd best be on my way, with your promise to be at the pub tonight." As his words faded, so did Tiarnan into a thick mist.

Gale laughed. "We'll be there." Her words fell on the mist. She turned her attention to Dillon. "You know he did that just to humor you."

Dillon grinned. "Nice of him."

"I'll take her out and catch Erin in the shop. Figured I'd go over sales and reorders with her tomorrow. But…" She clipped the harness on the pup and bounded down the stairs. At the bottom of the stairs, she noticed the door to Pixie Magic was open and a melodic voice sang quietly. Gale handed the leash to Dillon. "I'll be right back."

"Hey, I don't know anything about dogs." Dillon backed away as Trouble began chewing on his shoes, then tugged at the leg of his jeans.

"Time to learn." She flounced off toward the open door. Once inside the doorframe, she watched Erin flip through the ledger, then polish the tops of the glass cases. "Erin?"

Her aunt whirled around, hand to her chest. "Lass, you gave me a fright. Didn't hear you come in."

"You shouldn't turn your back on the open door when you are here alone."

Erin waved a hand dismissively. "No danger in our little town."

"Maybe not from the townspeople, but they're not the only ones that pass through here."

"Aye. I'll be more careful. Don't need to be here now that you are back to stay. Isn't that the way of it?" Erin smiled wistfully.

"Aye, but…" She sauntered over to the book section of the store, sat down on the sofa, and patted the spot next to her. "Erin, we need to talk."

"Oh, about what, dear?"

Rather than ease into the conversation, Gale put it all out there. "Callum Addiar."

"Who?" It took a couple of minutes for the name to sink in. Then Erin's eyes widened. "How…where did you come across him? Callum is ancient history, long gone."

"Not as long as you think. He has serious issues with you running off and marrying Tiarnan. Then the curse being broken."

"Why?"

Gale filled her aunt in. "Don't believe he'll be a problem, but you might want to tell your husband and keep an eye out, should he at some time be released from whatever punishment the council sees fit to impose. He's not…not all there anymore…"

"He wasn't as a young man either. Something about him didn't feel right. He worshiped the ground my father walked on. No way was I going to marry him. Figured he was harmless enough. Obviously, I was wrong." Erin clasped her hands in her lap, then reached over and put a hand on Gale's arm. "I'm so sorry you paid for my actions so long ago. Yet, I'd not change a thing."

"Don't blame you." She winked at Erin. "Tiarnan

is quite a catch. No harm done. It was a puzzle to figure out the motive, other than his father attempting to make sure Dillon and I were over. Kinda stupid when you think about it. Money and power were the driving forces in this whole fiasco. So much heartbreak."

"As acts of revenge usually are. Enough about ancient history. I see we've a reason to celebrate. When is the wedding?"

Gale beamed. "As soon as arrangements can be made. Dillon and I are ready to start the next chapter in our lives."

"Your young man is staying in Ireland?"

She sighed. "Aye. He'll open an office here in Ballycotton, help people with real estate and business transactions, minor infractions, estate planning, and charity work. Set his own hours and have a life."

"Won't he have to return to Scotland to help out? What about his family?"

"Not sure. It's a tangle right now, but his siblings and mother are certain they will be able to straighten it out. They don't want the appearance that he came back to bail out the firm, then in a few months, he leaves again. Of most concern is the firm's reputation." She paused as Trouble tugged Dillon through the door.

He raised one shoulder in a shrug. "She wanted to come in here." Dillon let the leash go, then sauntered over to Gale, slipping an arm around her waist, and brushing his lips over hers.

She smiled up at him. "Thanks for watching her. Thought she'd want to play outside longer."

All wiggles, the pup made a beeline to Gale. She scratched behind the creature's ears and the furball rolled over for a belly rub. Once she stopped, Trouble flipped to her feet, thundered across the floor, and pounced on Erin's shoes.

"Don't let her chew on your leather shoes. Tell her no. Trouble needs to learn manners."

"Oh, she's teething. Sweet baby's gums hurt." Erin bent down and picked up the pup careful to stay clear of the sharp-as-needles puppy teeth.

Gale rolled her eyes, took a chewy out of her pocket, and tossed the chew strip to her aunt. "If she's going to be here in the store, she's got to learn manners. Can't have her chewing on customers' shoes and tugging on pant legs."

"Got it." Erin put the pup down, rubbed its tummy, and handed Trouble the chewy. "We'll do better, won't we?" she cooed to the pup. "She's just so sweet. Smart too, potty trained already. Maybe we should stick a few of her toys in the freezer. Bet the cold would feel good on her gums."

"Great idea." Gale picked up a couple of toys.

"So Erin what do you know of the *cèilidh* at the pub tonight?" Dillon rocked back on his heels.

"Time for celebration. Bruce and Angie are here for a week or so. Tristian and Hannah are staying an extra week. You and Gale are here and engaged. Not to mention Mary and Tim are excited the timing worked out since they'd recently returned from their travels. Synn and Gavin do a wonderful job running the pub with the help of Bridget, Katie, and the new girl, Brenda."

"Brenda's been working there for several months. She's hardly new." Gale snorted.

Erin sniffed. "She's a yank. Married Joseph Conley first of the year. They moved back to Ireland as soon as her paperwork was straightened out. Bought the old O'Brian place, they did."

"Keeping up with the local gossip, huh?" Gale laughed.

"People talk when they come into Pixie Magic. You and Dillon gave everyone a lot to talk about. Came to the shop to get the updates, they did. Not that I told anyone anything. But steered the conversation back to the town and learned all kinds of things. It was fun."

Erin buffed her light pink polished nails on her blouse. "Tiarnan joined me off and on too. Gave the townspeople even more to whisper about. I think some of the townswomen came here to ogle him. Still has an air about him, he does."

Gale shook her head. "I'll bet you two did. For years, the two of you were thought to only be a myth or legend." She paused putting her index finger to her lip. "How would you like to work at Pixie Magic a couple of days a week permanently? We're going to take a week or so for a honeymoon after the wedding. If you can, I'd like you to cover for me at the shop during that time. After that, a couple of days a week?"

"I'd like that. Of course, I'll take care of the shop while you're on your well-deserved honeymoon. It'll be soon?"

"Aye, as soon as we can get a place and a person to perform the ceremony," Dillon interrupted.

A wide smile spread across Erin's face. "Well now, you have lots of options. Tiarnan could perform the ceremony, he does it all the time for faerie folk. Or Bruce. His overlord position gives him the ability to do the same. They're both here and accessible."

Dillon rubbed his hands together gleefully. "Great

ideas!"

She shifted from one foot to the other. "I'd hoped Tiarnan would walk me down the aisle."

"Oh, honey, he'd be pleased and honored. Just ask him."

She nodded. "I will."

Dillon grinned. "Leaves Bruce, we'll catch 'em at the *cèilidh* tonight."

Chapter 23

A Good Old Irish *Cèilidh*, Wedding Plans, and a Venue.

Dillon yanked open the heavy wooden door to the pub. Laughter, voices raised in song, the aroma of freshly baked bread, and yeasty scent of ale burst into the evening air. "Wow, the *cèilidh* must have already started."

"Oh, they've been celebrating since the pub opened, I'll wager." The happiness in Gale's voice was contagious.

He smiled wide, caught her around the waist as they strode through door. Cheers and whistles greeted them.

"There's the reluctant couple," someone in the crowd called out. "Finally convinced her to marry a Scotsman. What a sad day!" a male voice hooted.

"We want our Gale to be happy, so if it's a Scotsman she wants, a Scotsman she'll get." Tim's deep voice rose over the crowd, then raucous laughter erupted.

Dillon pushed and shoved his way through the rowdy crowd. Making an effort to broadcast his finest Scottish brogue—he'd lost a lot of the accent when he attended college in America—he shouted, "Fine. Outnumbered but not outwitted by a bunch of Irishmen.

In the end, I still got the lass." He pointed both thumbs at his chest and roared with laughter. Then he swung Gale around and planted a smacking kiss on her lips, lingering a couple of beats.

Loud whistles, shouts, and a call to kiss her again emitted from the pub patrons.

He spotted Tristian and Hannah perched on stools at the end of the bar next to Angie and Bruce. Tim and Gavin were busily serving pints of stout to those lined at the bar, while Mary filled mugs and placed them on a tray Synn was waiting on. At the same time apparently, Gale saw them too, grabbed his hand, and wove deftly through the crowd where two empty bar stools were saved.

Synn hoisted the tray and expertly negotiated through the throngs of customers to a table. She served the pints without spilling a drop and turned back toward the bar. Pointing to a corner booth at the far end of the bar near the pass-through, she whipped out a cloth and wiped off the table, then motioned her friends to the table.

Bruce and Angie brought glasses of wine with them as they slid into the booth. Tristian and Hannah set icy mugs of stout on the table, then slipped into the booth. Empty-handed, Gale and Dillon grabbed a couple of chairs and pulled them up to the table. Shortly after everyone was seated, Tiarnan and Erin pushed through the door. A surprised silence greeted them.

"Thought 'twas a party being held here," Tiarnan's voice boomed. The noise level rebounded in the pub.

Erin shook her head surveying the room. Gale stood and waved them over. She scooched into the booth next to Hannah and pulled Dillon down beside her, offering the chairs to her aunt and uncle.

Leaning over to Gale, Erin whispered, "Trouble is sound asleep in her crate in the flat above Pixie Magic. Tiarnan and pup walked the cliffs before coming to the pub. Poor little lass was completely tuckered out. Left food and water in her crate."

"Thank you." Gale gave her aunt a quick squeeze.

From the other end of the booth, Bruce stood and slapped Tiarnan on the back. "Should have heard the ruckus when Gale and Dillon walked in." He laughed. "Good to see you." He held the chair for Erin. "How have you been?"

"Good. And you two?" Erin smiled up at the overlord. "Looks like marriage agrees with you."

"True enough." Bruce glanced over at Angie, with a beguiling smile.

Synn waited for them to be seated. "Whatcha drinking?"

After taking the orders, Synn flounced back to the bar.

"Bridget tells us your wedding is back on." Angie sipped her wine and studied Gale's ring. "Set a date yet?"

"Geesh, word travels fast." Gale glanced at her ring, a smile spreading across her face.

Synn sashayed over with three mugs and a glass of wine. She set the mugs in front of Gale, Dillon, and Tiarnan. Slid the glass of wine in front of Erin.

"The sooner, the better." Dillon grinned.

Synn leaned over and hugged Gale. "So glad to see that radiant smile of yours back where it belongs."

"Aye, me too. Business good?"

"Oh aye. Keeping us hopping. Glad Ma and Da are

back to help for a bit." She winked at Gavin across the room at the bar. "Life is good."

Bruce raised a glass. "To Synn. A far cry from the warrior she was to the woman she is. You do your ancient guardians proud! S*láinte.*"

"*Sláinte,*" echoed around the table as glasses and mugs were raised. Gavin raised a mug from behind the bar.

A blush crept up Synn's neck, across her cheeks, and to the points of her ears. She eyed Bruce with what appeared to be misty eyes. " 'Tis nothing. Friends, family, and home make all the difference to this lass."

Gavin sneaked up behind her and circled an arm around her waist, planting a gentle kiss on her cheek. "A lass that better get back to work before the boss docks her pay." He gave her arse an affectionate slap out of the view of patrons.

Synn whirled on him with hands on hips. "Look 'tis calling the kettle black. Got a line at the bar six people deep. Ma and Da are working their fingers to the bone while their boyo stands over here kissing me." With a quick kiss, a smile, and a wink, she danced away with the music to the next table.

Gale beamed. "She lived up to all her promises. Mastered that dark magic and lives with it nary a problem. Although Gavin might disagree. A couple of times he's been on the wrong side of the wife." She chortled.

Gavin shook his finger at her as he sprinted across the floor and bolted over the pass-through quick as you please. He landed on his feet pulling pints as if he never left.

Synn grinned and shook her head, going table to

table taking orders.

With a confused expression on his face, Gavin shot a look at the demon. "What's this all about Synn?" After toasting her without hesitation, he gulped. His stout gaze locked on Gale.

"Tale for another time, when we don't have to yell at each other to be heard."

"It is pretty lively tonight. All in your honor." Hannah spread her arms wide. "Good news travels fast. The not-so-good news about Dillon's family won't travel at all, since you aren't considered theirs…Yet. Won't be long. Will it, Tristian?"

"Unfortunately not. They don't even bat an eye when we breeze into town anymore. Enforcer or not. I'm theirs." He grimaced heaving a heavy sigh. "I enjoyed being the warlock that put fear into the hearts of magic folk."

Gale slung an arm around Tristian's neck. "You still do. Remember the reaction of the staff at the Dunlop firm?"

Tristian closed his eyes and pretended to bask in those words. "True music to my ears." He looked up as a bottle of ale flew across the room in front of him. He discreetly raised a hand and diverted the bottle to a nearby table. The bottle spun on its bottom, toppled over, and spilled the remaining contents on the table. Eyes narrowed, he surveyed the pub for the culprit.

Gavin already had the guilty party by the arm and was escorting him out of the door. When Gavin returned, he turned a stern eye to two other patrons. They nodded and meekly exited the establishment. The publican brushed his hands together and playfully jabbed Tristian in the ribs. "Didn't mean to disrupt your fun, but Shaughnessy's doesn't tolerate misbehavior that could harm our customers or the entertainers."

"Excellent job. In case you didn't know it, I'm on holiday with my beautiful bride."

"I'd heard rumor of that but had to see it for meself." Gavin roared with laughter.

As the crowd thinned out, Cori finished her set with Quinn's band and sauntered over to the booth. "Looks like we have royalty in the pub tonight."

Bruce sipped on his wine, his arm around his wife, Angie. "Nope, not tonight. Visiting family and friends on holiday. Celebrating Gale's re-engagement and hoping to attend the wedding before we leave. Isn't that right, King and Erin?"

Tiarnan and Erin grinned at each other and nodded.

Cori's eyes rounded. "So the wedding is back on, cousin. I hadn't heard." She flung her arms around Gale. "Couldn't happen to a better lass." She narrowed her eyes at Dillon. "Any more shenanigans from you, boyo, and they'll never find the body." With a smirk, Cori glanced around at all the magic power players seated at the table.

After the long evening of celebrating, Gavin closed and locked the door behind the last customers to leave. "Wow, what a night."

Hands raised in surrender, Dillon leaned back against the booth. "No problem here. The sooner we set the date, the happier I'll be." He slid a glance at Gale hoping for approval.

"If that be the case, I've a proposal. With the bride's permission, I'd like to offer my family's castle on the cliffs as a venue for your wedding and reception. That way Gavin, Synn, Mary, and Tim could attend the wedding and reception without worrying about customers seeing things they shouldn't. Not to mention enjoy a night of fun and frivolity." Bruce paused a couple beats took another sip of wine. "Just a thought."

"Would this be the beautiful castle that hosted the infamous Halloween party last year?" Gale raised an eyebrow.

"It would be one and the same." Bruce grinned. "Minus the expectation of the appearance of bad actors to ruin the night."

"We could have the venue ready within hours," Angie suggested, switching her gaze from Gale to Dillon.

"Sounds perfect. My family and friends are all here." Gale glanced at Erin and Tiarnan, who both nodded in agreement. "But what about your family and the tangle they are trying to mitigate?" She put a hand on Dillon's arm.

Dillon mulled over the situation for a few minutes. "Well, I have promises of my family's attendance provided they can get away. Rebuilding will be time-consuming. Ian, my driver, could be here in a flash. Patrice would be the first I'd expect, and she'll just port over, glad for the diversion. It's going to be a long while before the firm's back to what it was before the scandal. Make no mistake, I have faith Mother, Patrice, and Aiden will prevail, but it's going to take time. I'm ready to start the new chapter of my life with our wedding. Put all that drama behind me."

Angie clapped her hands together. "The winter solstice is but a week away. Plenty of time to get everything ready. Perfect wedding date. I love weddings."

"She loves to plan them too. Don't let her run roughshod over what you want," Bruce warned.

Appearing aghast, Angie waved away her husband's remark. "I've planned a few weddings, and they've gone off without a hitch. Thank you very much." She shot Bruce a scathing look. "Our own double wedding included, need I remind you."

"Enough already." Gale held up her hand palm out. "The wedding will be on the Winter Solstice. Angie, let me know what you need from me. The only thing I request is that you include Trouble, my pup, in the ceremony. I'll ask Cori, Synn, Bridget, and Erin to be my bridesmaids or matrons.

"The wedding will be immediate family only. Reception open to all friends that want to come." She turned to Tiarnan. "I'd like you to walk me down the aisle." Switching her attention to Bruce, she said, "I'd like it if you'd perform the ceremony." A quick glance at Dillon. "Is this all right with you?"

"Aye. I'll advise my friends, Ian and Cork, as well as the family they're invited." Dillon's face lit up like a Christmas tree.

Gale glanced at Angie. "If you could work your magic for my wedding, I'd be grateful."

Angie squealed, clapping her hands together. "I'd love to."

Chapter 24

A Wedding Surprise!

The morning dawned bright with sunshine over lightly falling snow. Gale rolled over to the other side of her empty bed. Dillon had reluctantly agreed to spend the night in Gavin and Synn's guest room. The women insisted that he not see the bride until she walked down the aisle.

Butterflies flitted in her stomach as she considered the upcoming nuptials. She was more than ready, but wrapping her head around how quickly everything had come together was awe-inspiring. Angie checked with her every step of the way, but the woman was a wedding genius. Seemed Angie knew what Gale wanted before she was able to verbalize it.

She and Dillon had toured the castle yesterday with Angie. It appeared no less than a magical wonderland of flowers, candles, and seating in an intimate setting for the ceremony. Quinn's band and Cori were excited to provide the entertainment for the reception set up in the great hall of the castle. The stage was set up with colored light blocks and professional sound system.

With the reception open to all at Gale's request, Angie wove a spell so they would see only what mortals were allowed to see and nothing more.

So what do I have to be nervous about? Still, the

butterflies continued their swooping and diving around the knot in her stomach that kept tightening. Trouble whimpered at the foot of her bed. "Coming girl." Gale climbed out of bed, slipped her feet into boots, wrapped a parka around her nightgown, and followed Trouble to the back door.

She released the lock and let her pup scamper down the stairs leaving little paw prints in the snow on the stairs. She waited on the little porch for the pup to do her business, then called her back. The pup still had her moments, but as a rule, obeyed pretty well given her young age. Trouble rushed inside the kitchen and shook. Snow flew everywhere.

The pup looked up at her with innocent, chocolate brown eyes and her heart melted. "Yep, you've wound me right around your little paw." Tearing off several sheets of paper towel, she bent down to wipe up the puddles on the floor when her cell played the tune for Dillon. "Good morning."

"Good morn, *mo ghràidh*. Soon to be my wife. I love the sound of that. How are you and Trouble on this glorious morn?"

"Just woke up and let the pup outside. It's cold out there, but Trouble seems to love it. She tunneled all over under the snow, then raced into the kitchen and flung the wet stuff all over the place."

He laughed. "Heard from Patrice. She'll be at the wedding. Sis'll be staying at the B&B down the block from the pub."

"Great. At least you'll have family. How about Ian and Cork?" She tossed the wet paper towel in the trash and walked into the bedroom.

"They arrived last night. Cork has friends here who

offered to have Ian and her stay with them."

She paused and almost in a whisper said, "You don't think Cork and Ian are an item. Do you?"

"No…Well…I'm not sure. Ian doesn't seem Cork's type, but—Aw, hell, who knows. More power to them if that's the case. Ian is a straight-up, good guy. But she did mention a guy in Wales, though she alluded to it being over. Cork deserves to find someone who understands her and has her back. She's been on her own way too long." He blew out a breath. "Something to consider."

"Just wondering. The guy in Wales probably disappeared as soon as he discovered what dating Cork could be like in the real…maybe not-so-real world to most." She paused pursing her lips. "Ah well, we can tell more when we see them together at the wedding." She snickered. "As if we won't have enough demanding our attention."

"All I care is that we get to the I do's and cement our new life together. Seems like a long struggle to get to this point."

She giggled. "The struggle is almost over. Speaking of new life, have you given any thought to a building to set up your business?"

"Not yet. Figured we'd wait until the wedding and honeymoon are over. I have plenty of money in reserve and investments to keep us afloat for the time being."

"Excuse me." She bristled. "I have my own income. Pixie Magic is a thriving business and could easily support us both."

"Whoa! Just meant that we won't have any money worries if I choose to remain unemployed for a while. Has nothing to do with you or Pixie Magic. I'm well aware you are an independent woman. That's one of the many things I love about you."

Someone pounded on the door. Trouble began barking and growling then raced to the door. "Hang on. I need to find out who's banging my door down and upsetting Trouble."

"It's time to get ready." Synn's cheerful voice came through the door.

"Dillon, I gotta go, Synn's here and I'm sure the rest of the girls will be right behind her. I love you. See you soon."

"Right back at ya." He disconnected the call.

Before opening the door, she took a deep breath, looked over at her wedding dress hanging on the closet door, and let out a long sigh. *It was finally going to happen.* She wrapped one arm around her middle in hopes of settling the butterflies as she opened the door to Synn, Bridget, and Cori.

"What are you doing still in your robe?" Synn squealed. "It's only two hours to the wedding. We have a bit of a drive to the castle."

"Simmer down, Synn." Bridget put her arm on her friend. "They won't start the wedding without the bride."

"Not good etiquette to be late to your own wedding." Synn shook her petite finger at Gale.

Cori snorted. "Says the woman who made everyone wait at her wedding, while she stepped outside to converse with ghosts, before walking down the aisle."

The other women burst out laughing.

Red patches bloomed on Synn's cheeks. "That was different." Hands on hips, she narrowed her eyes.

"Doesn't matter, ladies. It will only take me a moment to shower, do my hair and makeup." She glanced again at her wedding dress. Soft cream material of some kind, with Irish lace sleeves that V'd at the back of her hand. Little pearls were sewn into the bodice for accent with the back of the dress bared in a V to her waist. Her veil was only a crown of colorful flowers with multi-colored ribbons flowing down the back. She touched the dress hesitantly with her fingertips. "And put this beautiful gown on. By the way, thanks to all of you for supporting me through this fiasco."

"It's what friends do," Synn declared. The other women nodded.

****

One hour and fifty-five minutes later, the women piled into Bridget's car, following the winding road to what previously had looked like a crumbling castle on the cliffs. It had been transformed into a holiday/wedding extravaganza. Multi-colored lights twinkled around every window. Twinkle lights woven in pine garland adorned the wooden entrance door where a huge, festively decorated wreath of fresh pine boughs and holly hung.

Quinn dressed in his holiday best greeted them warmly at the door. "Lasses, follow me." He led them to a smaller room to the left of the main ballroom. "Your places are right around that column so no one can see you until it's time for your walk down the aisle." He leaned over and whispered in Gale's ear. "The woman playing the harp is fantastic." He gave her a thumbs up. "Good choice."

Gale chuckled. "I couldn't get your band to play

the wedding march, so I had to settle for Estella."

"Hey, no fair, we'd have done it, but I couldn't do the other duties assigned to me for the wedding too." Quinn grimaced and looked to Bridget for support.

"Not going there, boyo." Bridget waved him away. "Your band will play the reception, so it's all good. Cori is joining you too. Right?"

"Aye. You should see all the delicious food set up for the celebration. Mary, Tim, and Gavin outdid themselves."

"Oh, I think they had a little magical help from Angie and Matiah, Bruce's ma."

"Could be. I only know that my stomach has been growling since I arrived. And you're late."

Bridget laughed. "The bride is never late."

"I gotta go and get this party started. Time to signal Estella."

Gale stood out of sight in the little alcove outside the room Bruce and Angie had set up as the chapel inside the castle. Tiarnan stood at her side, smiling wide. The small intimate setting was perfect. Chairs were arranged in two rows with bouquets of cream and red roses at each end, a break in the center where she and Tiarnan would walk. A huge candelabra with twenty-four lit candles occupied the front of the room where Bruce patiently waited in front of the candles.

Dillon shifted from foot to foot, alternating between gazing backward where she would start her walk down the aisle or talking with Ian and Aiden. He was so handsome in his black pinstriped tux and tails, her heart fluttered in anticipation.

She was glad that Dillon had asked his brother, Aiden, to be his best man. The gesture went a long way toward family unity. His mother, Iris, sat next to Patrice in the front row.

She sucked in a breath as the first notes from the harp echoed through the room. *Here we go.* She gripped Tiarnan's arm tight and suddenly a calm washed over her. A calm only a faerie king could conjure given the circumstances. She was thankful and squeezed his arm in acknowledgment.

Tiarnan put his arm around her shoulder and squeezed. "Relax and enjoy your wedding day." His blue eyes sparkled as he glanced at her. "Seems only yesterday you were a little witch in pigtails taunting the heck out of all the lads near and far. Now, look at you all grown up and starting on your own journey." He kissed the top of her head as the strains of the wedding march signaled their walk down the aisle to begin behind Synn, Bridget, and Cori.

Everything seemed like in slow motion. *Are my feet really touching the ground?* Strolling down the aisle, she felt the love and excitement of each smiling face turned toward her. *I'm the luckiest woman on the planet. All the angst to get here—was well worth it.* The path in front of her was covered in red and cream rose petals sprinkled by Katie's youngest daughter, Kimberly. She inhaled deeply enjoying the fresh rose scent that filled the towering room.

When her gaze touched on Dillon, her heart thundered in her chest. His high sculpted cheekbones beneath the startling blue eyes that held such warmth as he gazed at her. *What was going on behind those eyes.* A radiant smile graced his full sexy lips as he mouthed, "I love you." He was the whole package, and he was all hers. A little sigh escaped her lips. Her meandering gaze found Trouble at Erin's feet in the front row gnawing quietly on a chewy.

Arriving at the altar, Tiarnan moved her hand from his arm to Dillon's, then raised an eyebrow and whispered, "I give you our precious Gale, but remember I'll always be watching, boyo." He glided to where Erin sat with Trouble who was now whining to get to Gale. Easing into the seat beside his wife, he picked up the pup and quieted her.

The ceremony commenced with Trouble waiting not too patiently at the altar, the vows recited, and after the rings were exchanged, Bruce said, "I pronounce you man and wife. Dillon, you may kiss your bride." The world ceased to exist from the moment he enveloped her in his loving embrace and she wound her arms around his neck. He touched his lips to hers and deepened the kiss. The passion of the kiss sent her stomach into a wild swirl of desire. His lips lingered on hers until the overlord cleared his throat and broke the spell, announcing with a hardy laugh, "It's time to party! Celebrate this union. Food and drink are set up in the main ballroom. Help yourselves."

When he raised his lips from hers, he gazed into her eyes. *"Tha gaol agam ort gu brath,"* he said in a low seductive rumble. Her brows knit together for a moment. The meaning of the old Gaelic words slowly penetrating her brain. Her eyes still locked on his, and she whispered, "I love you forever too."

She rested her head on his chest for a minute more, searing that precious moment in her mind before acknowledging the frivolity going on around them. He took her hand and glided into the ballroom where banners of "Congratulations Gale and Dillon" hung from the wall behind the long oak table set for the wedding party.

In the center of the table were two crystal wine glasses with Bride Gale, and Groom Dillon etched in gold on them. She giggled, dancing a jig around to the table. Sparkling double crystal wedding bells hung from each corner of the ballroom with red and cream streamers stretching to the polished stone floor.

Quinn's band was already set up and playing lively tunes as what looked like to Gale the entire town flooded into the reception. Dillon took her hand and swept her out on the dance floor for their first dance together as a married couple. She snuggled into him as he glided her around the dance floor to a slow waltz.

Tiarnan cut in toward the end of the song. "I believe it's my turn." No sooner than he'd spun her around the dance floor a couple of times, the music changed to an up-tempo Irish tune with a grinning Cori on the fiddle. After a couple of dueling quick steps with his niece, Tiarnan good-naturedly danced her over to Dillon.

After the jig, they joined the wedding party table. Tiarnan slipped an envelope into her hand. "Our wedding gift to you and Dillon. Open it tonight when you two are alone."

She stared at the envelope, kissed Tiarnan on the cheek, and hugged Erin. Gale handed it to Dillon who tucked it into his inside suit pocket.

Aiden raised his glass in a toast to his brother. "May joy and peace surround you. Contentment latch your door. And happiness be with you now and bless you ever more. *Sláinte!*"

Glasses all over the room raised. "*Sláinte!*"

To everyone's surprise, Tristian stood, his chair legs scraping the stone floor, and his glass raised. "May the best you've ever seen, be the worst you'll ever see. *Sláinte!*"

Ian got to his feet glass raised in a toast. "May you always keep hale and hearty till you're old enough to die. *Sláinte!*" He plopped back in his chair.

The room erupted in gales of laughter. There were a couple more toasts to health and happiness from Bruce and Tiarnan. Then everyone filled their plates and settled down to eat.

"So where's the honeymoon?" Tristian wanted to know.

"We'll probably stay here at the castle since Bruce has offered it to us for as long as we want."

"Oh, I can—" He glanced over at Hannah. "—we can do better than that. We've arranged for you two to stay at our beach cottage in Hawaii for two or three weeks, all services included. Bruce's private jet is fueled and awaiting your instructions. After the reception of course."

Gale's mouth dropped open just before she squealed, jumped up, and hugged Tristian, then Hannah. "Thank you both so much." She glanced at Dillon for a beat, then declared, "We accept."

Dillon sucked in a breath and blew it out. "I don't know what to say?"

"Just say thank you," Hannah teased.

Gale sobered. "Do you allow dogs in your cottage? Since we've been gone so much, Dillon and I decided to take Trouble with us on the honeymoon."

Tristian's eyebrow winged up. "Of course, Trouble is allowed." He shook his head. "That didn't come out like I meant it. But you get my drift. Right?"

In the wee hours of the morning, Dillon, Gale, and Trouble boarded the plane. After making sure Trouble was settled in her crate, Gale eased into a buttery soft navy and maroon leather seat next to Dillon. With fingertips, she gently touched the red and cream roses in one of the crystal vases attached to the wall of the plane nearest to her. She sniffed the wonderful fragrance of the flowers.

He brushed his lips over hers then pulled out the envelope Tiarnan had given them. "Do you want to see what's inside?" He offered the gift to her.

"Aye." She took the envelope from him and turned it over in her hand. Carefully, she slid a shimmering red nail under the flap and popped the blue wax seal open. Removing two sheets of paper, she read the first one. "Dearest Gale and Dillon. Along with our blessings, enclosed is the deed to a cottage near our Sidhe. It's been vacant since Gale grew up and opened Pixie Magic. Once filled with love and laughter of a family, it feels lonely and ready to be filled with your love and when the time comes, family. All our love, Tiarnan and Erin."

Her eyes misted over with unshed tears until one teardrop spilled over and trailed down her cheek. Dillon wiped it away with his thumb. "Tears of happiness, I assume," he whispered.

The second sheet of paper was the deed to the house. Holding out the deed, she nodded. "That cottage holds many wonderful memories. I hope you'll agree to make it our home. It's not huge or fancy like your properties in Scotland, but…"

"Of course, we'll make the cottage our home.

Happiness will surround us there. The one thing I've learned after all the events of recent months, is love and happiness are the most important things in life." He paused for a moment. "Power and money are way overrated. Now, I'm not saying I want to be poor, or without magic, I'm just saying making those your life's goal is a BIG mistake."

"I wholeheartedly agree. By the way, just how many buildings and land do you own in Scotland?"

He raised an eyebrow and grinned. "More than enough. What can I say, I'm a wise investor."

Several hours later, the plane landed smoothly at Daniel K. Inouye International Airport in Honolulu. When they stepped off the plane, a limo was waiting to whisk them off to Tristian's beach cottage. After finding a place to let Trouble do her business and run around a bit, they loaded the pup back in her crate with food and water, then lifted the crate into the vehicle situating it near Gale.

Inside the limo, she took out her phone and touched a preprogrammed number on the screen.

Erin answered on the first ring. "Hi, Gale. Everything all right?"

"More than all right. We wanted to let you know, we've arrived in Hawaii. And thank you so much for the unbelievable wedding gift. We love it and plan to make the cottage our home as soon as we return."

"I'm so glad the cottage will be filled with family, love, and happiness once again. Now go and enjoy your honeymoon."

"We will. Give everyone our love." She ended the call and glanced at Dillon. "What a wonderful way to start our life together." She sighed. Reaching through

301

the crate, she caressed the pup's paw, then brushed her lips over Dillon's and rested her head on his shoulder.

"I couldn't agree more." He wrapped his arm around her shoulder and sealed his thoughts with a searing kiss.

A word about the author…

Tena Stetler is a best-selling author of paranormal romance. She has an over-active imagination, which led to writing her first vampire romance as a tween to the chagrin of her mother and delight of her friends. After many years as a paralegal, then an IT Manager, she decided to live out her dream of pursuing a publishing career.

With the Rocky Mountains outside her window, she sits at her computer surrounded by a wide array of witches, shapeshifters, demons, faeries, and gryphons, with a Navy SEAL or two mixed in telling their tales. Her books tell stories of magical kick-ass women and mystical alpha males that dare to love them. Well, okay, there are a few companion animals to round out the tales.

Colorado is home, shared with her husband of many moons, a brilliant Chow Chow, a spoiled parrot, and a forty-five-year-old box turtle. When she's not writing, her time is spent kayaking, camping, hiking, biking, or just relaxing in the great Colorado outdoors. During the winter, you can find her curled up in front of a crackling fire with a good book, a mug of hot chocolate, and a big bowl of popcorn.

http://www.tenastetler.com